Magenta

VALVERDE MACLEAN

Magenta is the follow up novel to *The Disappearance of Merry*

Visit www.valverdemaclean.com

Cover: The King George River, Kimberley region, Western Australia.
Image courtesy of Kimberley Quest Cruises
www.kimberleyquest.com.au
Photo credit Lloyd-Smith Photography ©

DEDICATION

To M

A new Challenge,

Another journey,

And the best companion one could have.

CONTENTS

ACKNOWLEDGMENTS

Thank you to those readers whose interest in my first novel encouraged me to continue writing. I hope this story answers some of your questions.

Special thanks to Tristen Lindner. Our discussions when I was considering various ideas for the plot were most enjoyable and helpful.

I would like to thank Heidi Hauf for her comments on Darwin. It was great to hear another's viewpoint. Thanks also to Neville Muggeridge on his feedback on that part of the story based in the Northern Territory. The many years he has spent in the Territory made sure the story was grounded in reality.

My thanks to Marion and Charles Bull, Jenny and David Ross, and Malcolm and Ann Ferguson. Our conversations were of benefit to me in making sure my memory and my descriptions of places and sights in the Kimberley were accurate. Similarly thank you to Annette Howie for her comments on the south of Western Australia.

Readers should also be grateful to Esme Taylor and Peter and June Rogers for their comments on early drafts. Their suggestions have made the book a much better read.

Another thank you to Nahum Szumer for his advice and his skill with graphics in developing the cover design.

Once again special thanks to Stacey Pettersson for her diligence in editing and proof-reading the penultimate draft. Her patience and understanding, along with her comments and wise suggestions, are very much appreciated. Any errors remaining are mine alone.

Finally a thank you to my wife for her patience, understanding and advice. It is greatly valued.

1 The Blue Door

Suzie

The house was not as I expected.

Peter had told me how his home was set in a garden full of grevilleas, callistemons and other natives, and he had mentioned the timber steps leading up to the blue front door. He had spoken of airy rooms with views overlooking Pittwater, and the shimmer of the late afternoon sun on the calm waters. However stepping out of the car there was no view of water and the front door of which he had spoken was shut. The house looked empty. Dead leaves lay scattered across the pathway which appeared as if it had been neglected for weeks. The leaves could have been untouched from the time he had left me in Melbourne to return to his home. It was possible the leaves had been there even longer. Perhaps even from the time he had flown down to me— before our troubles had started—and now the taxi that had brought me from the train station had driven away.

The thoughts that had been with me on my flight from Melbourne to Sydney returned. What was I doing here? Worse, at the front door there was a posy of bright red roses and a note. The flowers were fresh. Obviously he was not here or they would not be sitting at the door. Did that mean he was expected soon? Who were the flowers from? Was there a woman in his life? A man would hardly leave a bunch of flowers so it must be a woman. He had not spoken to me of anyone special in his life, apart from me, and his wife. He had spoken very lovingly of her but she had died years earlier. I was sure there would have been women interested in him since his wife had died but he had never mentioned any particular person. Given our relationship I had assumed it was only me. Perhaps I was mistaken. All my doubts came back to me.

Yet I had to come. It seemed so unlike him not to return my phone calls or answer my emails. Even if he had decided our friendship, well it had been more than a friendship, was finished I was sure his politeness would make him answer. His disappearance seemed so out of character.

"Hello. What are you doing here?"

The sound of his voice caught me by surprise. I had been so deep in my thoughts I hadn't registered the sound of a car stopping in the street. I turned and there he was. Just the same as usual.

"Hello Peter. I'm so pleased to see you."

"You make it sound as if you didn't expect to find me."

I wasn't sure myself what I expected to find when I had arrived at the house. I just thought he had disappeared. Had Alexander Mayne or his associates taken revenge? Had he gone off somewhere? Did he want to avoid me? From the sound of his voice he was pleased to see me. Should I admit that I had been worried about him? It had all seemed so straightforward in Melbourne, but now, here, I wasn't so sure. I guess I had never been very good at subtlety so I would have to explain.

"When I didn't get a reply to my messages I was concerned. I decided I would have to come and check you out."

"Well I'm certainly pleased to see you but I don't know about any messages. I've been away visiting friends. You remember Ernie Young? I spoke about him once. He and his wife live overlooking the Jamison Valley. When I got back from Melbourne I had an invitation to visit them, so I went up to Leura. I have just come back. I suppose your messages will be on my message bank."

"Peter, I also left a message on your mobile and some emails."

"Well I didn't take my laptop and my mobile has died. I need a new one. I'm sorry I caused you concern. Come on in. These flowers look beautiful. Jenny must have left them."

I wondered, who was Jenny? Once through the blue door I discovered what Peter had said about the view. Far below, beyond the trees, yachts swung gently on their moorings. The sun was setting low in the sky and its reflection on the water sparkled like thousands of tiny diamonds with each small ripple stirred by the breeze. The room we entered was spacious and airy. On the wall facing the water four large glass doors opened onto a patio framed on two sides by serried rows of pink, purple, ruby and red boronias.

"Let me put my bags away and I will find us a drink or something. What would you like, tea or coffee, or a glass of wine? Are you hungry? When did you leave Melbourne?"

Peter dropped his luggage in a bedroom and carried mine through the door leaving them at a little alcove near the hallway. Then he poured a glass of white for me, a whisky for himself and found a bowl of nuts.

"I'm sorry. I will have to go shopping. Being away I don't have much in the house. Will you stay the night? We can go up the road to the local RSL club for dinner and I can go shopping in the morning. I don't even have any milk."

Peter's invitation to stay the night suddenly made me realise that I had given no consideration to what I would do when I found him. After the times we had spent together before I had turned down his invitation to live with him, did he think my appearance meant that I had changed my mind? Did that mean we would again share a bed? Why had he left my bags in the hallway and not in his bedroom? What did that mean? What did I think? What did I want? I really hadn't given any thought to what would happen when I found him. Yet he hadn't been missing, or in danger at all, simply visiting old friends. All my worries were pointless! I realised how relieved I was to find him. I wanted to reach out and touch him—but I hesitated.

As we sat in the restaurant of the local RSL club, Peter with a steak and a glass of shiraz, and me with a chardonnay and a plate of fresh leafy salad topped with prawns, salmon and oysters, he told me of his invitation to visit his friends in the Blue Mountains. The plan had been to spend a few days with them, but once there his old mining friend had asked him if he would like to revisit the site where he had once worked many years earlier. His friend had some consultancy work to do at the mine. It was the same copper mine where Peter had his first job after finishing university and before his trip to London where we had met all those years ago. Having nothing planned, Peter had accepted the invitation and they had gone off to the copper mine in the far west of New South Wales.

The work had taken longer than expected, but as he had no commitments that had not been a concern, and he had only returned yesterday to Ernie's home in the mountains. Then, today, he had caught a train, a bus, and a taxi to his home and walked in on me while I was standing looking troubled at the blue door. Still he had not mentioned the flowers or Jenny.

"Actually I have booked to go away on a trip. I have always wanted to see more of the north of Australia, especially the Top End and the Kimberley. I particularly want to see the Gwion Gwion art in situ, and flying back from Melbourne I decided I would do it. I am flying to Darwin and picking up a car. I will also visit a friend on a cattle station south of Broome and then go down to see my son in Karratha. Since I will be on the opposite side of the continent I thought I might as well make a trip of it and go down and check out the wineries in the south west. I will probably be away for six weeks, perhaps more. I've booked my flight. I leave in five days' time."

Peter's news shocked me. I had flown to Sydney to see him. Unexpectedly, admittedly, and he had already made plans to leave. Whatever my plans had been, they were now awry.

"Would you like to come with me? It will only require an extra airline ticket and that should be possible. I can organise it in the morning."

"Give me a bit of time to think about it. It is so unexpected I'm not sure what to do." I had flown to Sydney fearful for his wellbeing only to find he was well and happy, returned from one holiday break and now had major travel plans. He seemed to have moved on from a life with me, but then he did ask me if I would join him.

"Well I'm not planning to leave until Wednesday, so you have a few days. I hope you will come. It should be interesting. Have you ever been to that part of Australia before?"

Unlike Peter, whose work as a mining engineer had taken him to many parts of Australia and Africa and South America, my travels had been Europe and the eastern coast of Australia. I had never visited the Top End or the Kimberley although I had drunk wines from the Margaret River region. The thought of the adventure certainly held appeal, as did the thought of once again spending time with Peter.

"If you decide not to come I would still love to show you around this part of the world."

As we walked back to his house I made my decision. I would go with him. My son and daughter really didn't need me, and the rebuilding work on my house that had been damaged in the firebomb attack wouldn't start for at least another six weeks. Why not! I would just have to let my son and daughter know of my new plans. That decision answered the next question on my mind. If we were to be travelling together for a month then it could be one bed tonight. That thought was very pleasant. I hoped Peter would put my bags in his room.

In the morning Peter booked a seat for me on his flight to

Darwin, although it meant we would have to sit apart in different rows. Hopefully we would be able to change that at check in. Then it was the problem of clothing. I had packed for a few days in a big city, not for weeks in the remote tropics of the North. I would need some clothes but what sort? Peter was no help, although he patiently guided me around local shops so I could buy suitable clothes appropriate to our planned travels. That was not always so easy when the fashions now in the shops were for winter and our destination would be hot and dry, at least until we reached Perth. Even worse those shops which did sell clothing for holiday makers flying north for winter always wanted a premium price for their stock. Others, on hearing where we were going, wanted to fit me out as if I was leaving for some expedition to remotest Africa. Peter, with his experience working on mine sites suggested simple tees and shorts. That was still a concern. A young person could look good in tees and shorts but they did not look quite the same on an aging grandmother.

Then Peter needed a replacement phone. His problem was solved in minutes.

Over breakfast on my third day Peter told me he had organised a special occasion. It was something he had once done, and would love to do it again with me. He was very secretive saying that he had been lucky to be able to arrange it. Apparently a large group had cancelled as the business deal they were to celebrate had fallen over at the last moment, and he had been able to get a reservation. We would go out to lunch, but it would be a long lunch, and since we had to drive we would stay away overnight. He would give no more information but suggested it would be different.

We drove away from his home around eleven and an hour later we parked near a small wharf. A launch came to pick us up. Soon we were sitting at a table overlooking the water watching more diners arrive by the same launch as it shuttled to and fro between dock and wharf. A float plane landed on the river and slowly taxied up to the restaurant's dock and discharged a small group who had flown in to dine.

As Peter had promised it was a long lunch with a multitude of tiny courses and matched wines. I now understood his desire to spend the night nearby. The lunch had been beautiful, and I sensed Peter was trying to impress me. Yet there was something more. We talked about our first meeting, and our parting, all those years ago in London. We talked about our adventures, or misadventures, after we had met by chance in the art gallery in Melbourne, and we talked about our lives between those two periods. As he spoke about his wife I discovered the reason for our visit to the restaurant. He had first brought Claire here not long after they had married. It was their first luxurious treat when he had received a promotion. It held so many memories. He didn't say it, but I knew he was sharing his special place with me and how important it was to him.

Since my arrival, and being with him again, the days had taken on a strange feeling. It was as if time was in a bubble. Somehow the outside world had ceased to exist. There was only us, our memories, and the time we had together. I thought back to when I had first met the man I would eventually marry, and divorce, yet that had not really felt the same. Then there was the first time I had met Peter all those years ago in London. Even that had been different. Then I had run away, so strong were my feelings and the knowledge that to stay with him would change my life in a way I did not want. Even the time we had spent together in Melbourne and Ballarat solving the disappearance of my best friend had been different. Not even the romantic days we had together on Hayman Island had gone close to the pleasure of being together that I now felt. In the Whitsundays we still had to face the threat waiting for us on our return to Melbourne. Now I had a sense of relaxation, perhaps even relief. We could just be with each other without any worries.

Returning home the following morning Peter suggested we stop off at the Ku-Ring-Gai Chase National Park. It wasn't far out of our way and I would see more of the region where he lived. Sometimes, as we walked along the tracks among the scribbly gums and grevilleas, we talked, but at other times we just stood in companionable silence enjoying the view.

Peter was keen to show me more of the local area before we flew to Darwin. Did that mean he was trying to tell me how pleasant it would be to live here with him? I had already learnt that with him, it was often what he did that held significance. He rarely put his deepest thoughts in words. We drove to the Barrenjoey Lighthouse and slowly worked our way south through Palm Beach to a lovely spot overlooking the surf at Whale Beach. Sitting together on the grass with our picnic lunch we spent some leisurely hours watching the parade of afternoon walkers, either with or without dogs, the mothers with their young children playing on the sand, and in the cold water a few brave surfers practising their skills. Peter brought out a wet suit from his car and joined the swimmers in the water. I waited on the beach and soaked up the last of the afternoon sun while he surfed. Being a country girl from my youth, the beach and the view held more attraction than the cool water. I did decide I must go shopping for a swimsuit. I might need that in the north.

The days before our departure had passed quickly. That evening we packed our suitcases and prepared for our adventure together.

Waiting in the lounge for our flight to Darwin I reflected on what was happening. I had come to Sydney to find a man I thought was missing. Now I had agreed to visit the far reaches of Australia with him. It was something I had never considered. I was confused. I had been concerned about him, I knew I missed him, but this was the last thing I had planned. I had imagined, if I had imagined anything, that I would spend a few days with him, maybe a week, and then return to my family in Melbourne. I think I had kept the thought of living with him permanently buried deep in my mind. It was still a decision I wasn't prepared to face. After all I had my children and my gorgeous grandchild back in Melbourne. Travelling to the extreme ends of Australia with him might be interesting, and I was sure I would enjoy my time with him, but would it resolve what our future might be? Perhaps by the end of our trip I would know. I had seen friends set out on travels together but only to part acrimoniously mid journey. And there was still one unanswered question on my mind: Who was Jenny?

2 Arafura Sunset

Peter

As we landed at Darwin airport I remembered my first visit
to the town. Then, as now, it was the capital of the Northern
Territory, but in those days it had seemed like a frontier
town. Even today it still retained some of that same feel. My
first visit to Darwin had been before Cyclone Tracy blew
much of it away on Christmas Eve, 1974, leaving most of the
population homeless. That time I had arrived late in the
evening. Walking down the steps from the aeroplane into a
large corrugated iron building that was the airport terminal I
had immediately felt the heat of the night.

My next trip, years later, was towards the end of the year.
My second arrival was in the early evening and it was the
Build-up season: the time of oppressive heat and wild
electrical storms. By then a new modern terminal had been
built on the opposite side of the airport replacing the old tin
shed that had blown away. Now you left the plane by an air
bridge into the terminal. However I still remember the solid
wall of heat and humidity that moved through the cabin as a
rear door of the aircraft was opened to allow ground crew
access to the plane. The jagged and vivid display of
lightning, the thunder, and the torrential rain that followed
the lightning were a show that I had never seen before. It
made me appreciate the covered air bridge.

This time our arrival was in May. Our five hour flight had left Sydney in the morning and we arrived mid-afternoon to a cloudless blue sky. It was the Dry season; every sky would be cloudless, every sky would be blue. For months to come every day would be without rain, and the days would always be warm.

We found the desk of the car hire company and picked up our vehicle, a white four-wheel drive that was to be our home for five weeks. I had planned this trip ever since I had parted from Suzie in Melbourne. At last I would visit the rock art sites that I had long dreamt of seeing. Travelling on my own the thought of a four-wheel drive and a small tent had not been an issue. When I had asked Suzie to join me it had seemed like an adventure. Now, looking at the vehicle, it didn't seem such a good idea. What were we? Two middle-aged people pretending we were young and carefree backpackers exploring the world. Suzie had been that once. I had never really fitted that image. But here we were. We probably couldn't even climb up into the pop up tent on the roof of the vehicle.

The drive from the airport to our city hotel on the Esplanade was easy and quick. The capital of the Northern Territory may be home to half the population of the Territory, but even that meant there were only around one hundred and forty thousand residents, and traffic was never a problem, especially to someone used to big crowded cities. Peak hour rush would only last a few minutes!

As I drove into the city I saw the changes that had taken place since my last visit. The city had grown in height. Now high rise apartments and hotels had become common where once they had been rare. While not yet really a city it had certainly changed from the large country town it had once been, however it still had a feeling that was different to the rest of Australia. In the centre of the town the streets seemed to be full of young people of many nationalities: tanned backpackers in their uniform of tees and shorts and sandals. At the bigger hotels tour buses were dropping off or picking up tourists with larger travel budgets, usually older tourists or families on their adventure holidays. After some confusion with hotel names we found the correct hotel and settled into our room with a view overlooking a park and the bay beyond.

Later as we sat on the small balcony we watched a few people disappear into the tall grass beyond the park. I told Suzie these were 'long grassers': homeless people that set up camp in hidden places in the tall grass. With the dry warm climate at this time of year they had no need of blankets or shelter from the rain. Later in the year when the storms arrived, and then the monsoons, it would be a different story.

"Isn't there somewhere they can go?"

"Often they are not wanted in their communities because they cause trouble," I explained to Suzie. "Most are Aboriginal people, although not exclusively, and usually there is a problem with alcohol or drugs."

"Peter, surely there must be centres that will look after them."

Again I explained to Suzie that often they choose to avoid the restrictions that government treatment centres would impose upon them, preferring the freedom of life on their own terms. In big cities such people were often hidden away in areas most people never visited. Here the problem was obvious although the solution just as intractable.

"How do they live? What do they do for food?"

"Usually their problems mean they are unlikely to get or keep jobs. Like all citizens they are entitled to social security and health benefits. Unfortunately the money they get in benefits is spent on booze and drugs rather than food and shelter. Sometimes they have come from remote communities out bush and are unable to return, even if they wanted to. Perhaps they have been expelled from their communities because of the problems they cause. Here they are a problem for the local police who have to deal with them. I think we had better decide on our plans for tomorrow. What would you like to do?"

"I have heard about the Mindil Beach Market, I would like to see that, and I've heard so much about crocodiles in the Territory. Is there somewhere we can see them? I know it's very touristy but we *are* tourists. Then there is Kakadu. I have heard so much about it."

"We could go there but it is 250 kilometres away. If we want to be back for the market we would not have enough time to do it justice. It really needs a few days at least. It would only be ticking a box. There are various places where we can see crocodiles but we could go out to the Adelaide River and take a cruise. Then we could go to Fogg Dam and Beatrice Hill to see the wetlands and the birdlife. That's often very interesting."

Our drive out to the Arnhem Highway and on to the Adelaide River Crossing took us through the outskirts of the city to Humpty Doo. Once a rural area it was now almost a suburb of Darwin. Humpty Doo had been the site of an early rice growing venture. Like many Territory ventures over the years it had proved unsuccessful. The problem was birdlife. The rice fields were a magnet for Magpie Geese which had devastated the crop. After many unsuccessful efforts to control the bird damage the venture ceased. The geese had won. Or lost, as their new source of food also vanished.

"The Territory seems to have a history of failed ventures."

"Many things have been tried and people are still looking for some way of utilising all the land and water that is available. Rice, sugarcane, vegetables, bananas, cotton and dairying have all been tried. The soils are often poor due to leaching caused by the high rainfall in the northern parts and in the south the rainfall is low and variable. As well the problem is markets. The big markets are a long way away and freight is expensive. It is difficult to develop sufficient scale to make the industry economic. All the same the cattle industry has gone well exporting live cattle to markets in Asia. Although even that industry has had some tough years. There is also a big gas industry developing. Horticulture is also far larger than people realise, especially mangoes and melons. Do you like mangoes?"

We arrived at the Adelaide River Crossing amid a crush of tour buses and caravans. As we entered the carpark Suzie pointed out a small van. On its side was a colourful painting of Elvis Presley. Graffiti was scrawled across the rear door. Joining the other tourists we bought our ticket for the popular cruise. The boat we chose was a small craft sitting low in the water. Suzie had wanted to see crocodiles. She would be very close to them. It would be unwise to put a hand in the water. The boat moved off from the dock and soon we were with the reptiles. Sitting in the trees beside the river were a host of birds, almost as if they were waiting for the show to commence. In the tall grass on the river bank we could see the occasional water buffalo, an import from Asia that had gone feral. Tracks and wallows showed signs of the activity of feral pigs, another imported pest to the floodplains.

The boat slowed and stopped. Our guide hung a dead chook from a rod and dangled it over the water. Suddenly the quiet river erupted as a four metre crocodile rose vertically from the stream. The animal must have reached almost two metres above the river to catch its meal. The splash as it fell back into the river sprayed water over us. Suddenly the atmosphere on the boat changed. In the water below us there were lurking monsters. Monsters that could kill us. Again the guide held out more morsels for the reptiles. Again and again the crocodiles leapt higher and higher from the water. Each one seemed to come closer and closer to us. From the look on her face I think Suzie had decided that the best crocodile was a handbag.

Off to the right side of the road to Darwin, perched on the top of a hill, were the upswept roofs of the Beatrice Hill Visitors Centre. From the top storey we looked out across the floodplains. Already the floodwaters which covered the area in the Wet were receding. The moist land left by the retreating waters was now rapidly drying and baking in the hot sun. Like the receding floodwaters the birds we had come to see had also retreated and found shelter during the heat of the day. At least we were fortunate to see two brolgas and a jabiru. The large black-necked stork was a bird I had never seen before. Display boards at the centre answered many of the questions we had asked each other during our boat trip. Now we could put names to the birds and plants we were seeing. Even more fortunate was to hear a ranger talk about the local environment, its plants and animals.

Returning to the car we headed back along the highway to find another viewpoint of the floodplain and its birdlife.

After the drama and excitement of the jumping crocodiles, the Fogg Dam was a quiet, gentle experience. However our plan to walk out across the dam wall was changed when Suzie saw the warning sign about crocodile attacks. With our experience earlier in the day it was one warning she was not going to ignore. Instead we took a path through the forest fringing the floodplain until we reached a boardwalk that led us out into the wetlands proper with its waterlilies and lotuses and birdlife. From a platform we could see the mass of waterbirds—mostly Magpie Geese that had ruined the attempts at rice growing.

By now the day was at its hottest, and it was pleasant to be in the air-conditioned car as we drove back to Darwin. Coming from the south where it was approaching winter the warmth of the northern day felt like a very hot summer's day. Even with a short walk I would begin to sweat. I was sure I couldn't cope having to work outside in the heat all day. How the locals did it during the Build-up season had amazed me on my earlier visit. It had been so many years since I had last worked outside in the heat. I had become soft from my days in offices and rarely venturing out to do fieldwork. Fortunately we would have time for a quiet break before our visit to the Mindil Beach Market.

The heat of earlier in the day had vanished, and the evening air was warm and balmy. We decided to walk to the Market. Walking along we chatted about our day's sightseeing and our plans for tomorrow. As we passed the entrance to the Casino the first of the night's customers were already arriving: optimistic dreamers hopeful that tonight would be their big night. With us we had a pack with a bottle of bubbles bought earlier and two glasses from our hotel room. Our plan was to find food from some of the many stalls selling a huge variety from so many nations, sit on the beach, drink our wine and watch the sun sink over the Arafura Sea. Like Suzie, I had heard of the Mindil Beach Market and it was on my 'to do' list. I had planned my trip so I could visit on a Thursday night—reputedly the best night. When I was making my original plans I had not thought I would have Suzie by my side. I had always enjoyed being with her, but I felt she was still hesitant. The next few weeks would resolve that in one way or another.

The colours, the smells and activity of the market hit our senses as soon as we entered. The aromatic scents of Asian spices mixed with the aroma of barbequing meats, and the smell of frying chicken jostled with the odour of seafood. Thai, Chinese, Spanish, Middle Eastern, Brazilian, Italian, Greek; the choice would be ours. Even exotic local meats of crocodiles, camels, and buffalo were available. We made our selection of oysters for starters, a platter of barbequed seafood and a plate of spicy Sri Lankan chicken and started our way down to the beach.

Then across the alleyway of food stalls I saw her. A striking young woman with long, bright, magenta-coloured hair. She was wrapped in a colourful Asian-looking sarong which swept down to her ankles. On a bare brown shoulder was a tattoo of a small green frog. Even in the colourful crowd of tourists and locals she stood out. While not particularly tall she had a presence that attracted attention, not just men but women also kept glancing at her. Then she turned away, and I saw the magenta hair was completely shaved on one side on her head. It was as if you were looking at a different person. One seemed open and free, breezing through life, the other closed and remote—a life hidden and untouchable. I pointed her out to Suzie.

"What do you make of that girl?"

"She certainly has an individual style. That hairstyle makes a statement, although what it is apart from 'I am different' I don't know."

While we were looking at her the girl turned again. Now we were back with the young elegant woman with long magenta hair. Then she vanished into the crowd.

In the early evening with the warmth, the sun setting over the Arafura Sea, music drifting down from the market place, life seemed beautiful. Even our strange mix of food and wine seemed to work together. Perhaps it was the company. I hoped the next five weeks would be as good as tonight. Off the beach only the eyes of a crocodile were visible as it cruised up and down the shoreline. Perhaps it remembered the days of plenty when the meatworks disposed of its offal into the sea at Vesty's Beach. Perhaps it was avoiding the rangers who sought to keep the waters safe for those silly enough to enter them.

Next morning our first call was to the supermarket to stock our four-wheel drive with food and necessities. We found the shopping complex and while Suzie went into the supermarket I stayed with the vehicle and read the manual to try and figure out how the camping gear worked. My main concern was how the tiny tent on the roof would unfold, but I was even more concerned about how to repack it back into its container. As I was contemplating the problem I looked across the carpark and there was the girl from the previous evening. Today, Magenta as I had christened her, was in a bright crop top and short shorts. Her hair was still striking but even more so were the two entwined snakes tattooed on her left leg. They reached from her ankle to her thigh. Last night they had been hidden by the long sarong she had worn. She was transferring her purchases from the shopping trolley to the small minivan with the image of Elvis Presley that we had seen at Adelaide River Crossing. Inside the van I could see half a dozen cartons of beer stacked neatly behind the seats. It looked as if she was planning a party. Having finished loading the van she drove off.

When Suzie returned she had a trolley load of supplies. We packed them away in various nooks and crannies of the vehicle, hoping we would remember where we had put them and be able to access them without too much trouble when we needed them.

"I saw your friend in the supermarket."

"My friend?"

"Yes, the girl with magenta hair."

"I would hardly call her my friend. I saw her as well. She was parked just over there. It looked like she had been shopping."

"Yes, she was buying food. She seemed to be doing the same thing as me, buying similar items. I thought she might be a tourist. I smiled at her and asked her if she was a local or a tourist. She said she was hoping to meet some friends. She seemed quite nice but didn't say very much."

"Did you see the tattoo?"

"I saw something on her leg but I was too close to make it out? What was it?"

"Two snakes, wrapped around each other. It was very unusual. The thought makes me feel uncomfortable."

"I think she might be a very unusual girl. Your son isn't married. How do you think she would go?"

"Matthew is an engineer. I don't think the personalities and lifestyles would meld very well."

Then we were away. Our road trip had begun. As we left Darwin behind my concerns grew. Weeks of being together in the bush, at night sleeping perched in a tiny tent on top of a four-wheel drive, was an unusual way to start a life with a new partner. I wondered how Suzie was feeling. What were her concerns? Where we were going there would be vast spaces with few towns or villages. Any residents would be few and far between, often out of sight of the road. Perhaps all we would see would be a sign pointing to some cattle station fifty or a hundred kilometres down a dirt road. Suzie had spent most of her life in big cities or in London. How would she cope with the isolation of the Top End and the Kimberley? I knew she had grown up on the Riverina Plains so perhaps she would feel a link, although the country was very different. I was unsure. If she wished she could always leave at Katherine and return home. After that it would be more difficult. Then there was Magenta, the girl with the purple hair and partly shaved head. She kept returning to my mind. I could see no reason why I should keep thinking of her, and yet, somehow, I felt she would have an effect on all our lives.

3 Katherine

Suzie

"Do you know about the cemetery?"

Peter's question roused me from my thoughts.

"Cemetery?"

We were heading south along the Stuart Highway. Peter was driving and my mind had wandered off. What was I doing here? I had flown to Sydney to find him thinking he had gone missing, only to find he had been away with a friend. Then all of a sudden here I was, somewhere in the Northern Territory, on a road trip to the far side of the country. Not only that, I was going to live in a tiny tent on top of a car. That was certainly not my style, and from the look on Peter's face when I had returned from the supermarket I wasn't sure that he had worked out how to erect it. He may have been a mining engineer but it didn't look as if his training included tents!

"We are coming into Adelaide River. It's a small settlement with a roadhouse, however its main claim to fame is the War Cemetery where the victims from the bombing of Darwin in 1942 were buried."

Like many Australians, I knew that Darwin had been bombed at the commencement of World War Two in the

Pacific, two months after the bombing of Pearl Harbour on December 7, 1941, but like most Australians, I knew few details. Peter suggested we stop and see it. He had visited there on a previous trip and had found it very moving. It had also broadened his understanding of Australian history.

Walking through the entrance of the War Cemetery I was immediately moved by a sense of quietness and peace. While small compared to the huge war cemeteries scattered across Europe, the little green oasis in the surrounding dry countryside brought to mind the loss that families must have felt. A mixture of sadness and gratitude came over me as I walked amongst the headstones and memorials of soldiers, sailors, airmen and civilians. It was an unexpected feeling.

The first wave of bombings of Darwin on the 19th of February, 1942 had destroyed twenty-three aircraft and sunk eight ships. The death toll was two hundred and forty-three people. While tiny compared to the losses in battles in Europe and the Middle East it was the first time the Australian mainland had been attacked, and it sent shockwaves through the country. That day was the first of the sixty-four times Darwin was bombed. Japanese air attacks had reached as far south as Katherine, our next stop, and also caused heavy losses of aircraft in Broome. One poignant grave site was of the sixty-four people killed in the bomb blast that destroyed the Darwin Post Office. By the time I walked back out the gateway of the cemetery I realised how poor my knowledge of that period had been.

As we left the cemetery Peter suggested we find a shady spot for our lunch. After spreading a blanket on the grass we rummaged through our nooks and crannies to locate a kettle to boil water for coffee, and plates for the cold meat and salads I had purchased. As we sat and ate we talked of our feelings at the cemetery. So many events of that time had been hidden for fear of panic, and subsequently overlooked by history. To most Australians the Battle of the Coral Sea, a major turning point in World War Two, was a remote sea battle far from Australia. In fact the epic battle was in the sea bordered by the north Queensland coast, the northern section of the Great Barrier Reef, New Guinea and the Solomon Islands. The battle was much closer to Cairns than Cairns was to Sydney, or even as Brisbane was to Cairns.

The multitude of different greens we could see on our drive south amazed me. The variety of textures of the plants and leaves, and the many shades of green in the tall grasses, the trees and the shrubs were incredible. I had never realised there could be so many greens. My thoughts of the Northern Territory were based on the Red Centre, but as Peter pointed out that was another thirteen hundred kilometres south from where we were. I knew Darwin was in the tropics but somehow that thought had never really changed my image of the Territory as a dry arid desert.

Peter explained that while much of the Territory was best described as arid tropics, Darwin actually had a high rainfall which decreased as we drove south. Further south it would become dryer and dryer, although even Alice Springs could have occasional heavy falls of rain. Unfortunately it was infrequent and the long dry spells could last for years.

Approaching Katherine I asked Peter if he knew the town.

"I once did some consulting work for a gold mining company that had a mine not far from here. About five kilometres up ahead on the left. I had to visit a few times."

"How did it work out?"

"There was a lot of gold but it was spread out in many tonnes of very hard rock. The cost of crushing the rock to get to the few grams of gold per tonne was very expensive. A fall in the gold price and the mine became uneconomic. They eventually ran up big losses and went broke."

"That must have been sad for the workers."

"Another business bought the company cheaply and reopened the mine. They ran it at a loss for about two years until the parent company which was very profitable could legally use all the tax losses. Then they shut it down again. That saved the parent company a lot of tax and made the deal worthwhile."

"So the workers were sacked for a second time?"

"Yes. Katherine was a boom bust town in those days. At least they got two more years of work."

As we drove into the township Peter asked if I had any plans of what I would like to see. He suggested I might be interested in the School of the Air and see the classes in operation. The other big attraction was the Gorge, but first we should find somewhere to spend the night.

"Have you worked out how to set up the tent?" I asked.

"I will only know when I have to do it."

His reply suggested we may have an interesting session when we stopped for our first camp. From his earlier visits he knew of a lovely resort on the edge of town. They had motel rooms, cabins, a camping ground, a restaurant and bar, plus a pool. It was also green and shady which made it very pleasant especially later in the year when everywhere else was hot and dry and dusty.

As we drove into the resort I made a decision. We could book into a motel room. That would be more comfortable and I would pay. No need yet for the tent! Peter almost looked relieved as he went into the booking office. He quickly came back.

"All the rooms are booked. It is a busy weekend. A lot of cattlemen and their families are in town. All I could get is a cabin. That will have to do."

The cabin was very comfortable with all the facilities of a motel room plus a tiny kitchen for preparing meals. Unlike our tent it also had air-conditioning. Having not yet acclimatised from the early winter cold of Melbourne to the warmth of the Territory, the coolness from the air-conditioning would be a plus if the night was hot.

After settling in to the cabin we decided to visit reception and see what arrangements we could make for tomorrow. My wish to see the School of the Air would not be fulfilled as the school did not operate over the weekend, however some of the children around the pool were students, and the receptionist was sure their parents would be happy to talk with us. Our wish to visit the Gorge was easier. The resort was beside the road leading to the park, and another twenty-five kilometres would bring us to the park entrance. There we could arrange a boat cruise to see either two or three gorges. Peter suggested we head for the bar, buy a drink, check out the locals and discuss our plans.

Sitting overlooking the noisy children playing and splashing with their friends in the resort pool we discovered two types of fellow residents. One group of men and women were wearing shorts and singlets or shirts, or light shifts. The other group of men were very tanned and mostly wearing jeans with big belt buckles and colourful shirts, sometimes with sleeves rolled up, other times buttoned at the wrist. They were all wearing boots and often a big hat. The women with them, obviously the mothers of the playing children, seemed to be more stylishly dressed. While formal would be an overstatement, they were certainly dressed as if on a special outing: quite different to the tourists. Not being school holidays few tourists had children with them.

As Peter went to the bar to buy a second drink for us, I spoke to a woman sitting at the next table watching two young girls play in the pool. Her children were both on School of the Air although the eldest would finish this year and would have to go away to Toowoomba in Queensland for her high school education. I asked how she felt about that. She would miss not having her eldest daughter around, but it was the best option. The School of the Air, or School of Distance Education as it was now called, was very good but it was too difficult to give an older child a good education with home schooling in the bush. Besides, having interaction with a broader group of children was a big advantage. The other options were to have her board in Katherine or go to school in Darwin. In some families the wife actually moved into town so the children could have an education. This could place strains on the family but then so did boarding school fees. At least in Toowoomba or Brisbane she would get a broader experience and would still know kids from School of the Air who were in the same situation.

"How often will she come home?"

"Usually for the main holidays. She will have to take a bus

from the school down to Brisbane airport, then fly to Darwin where we, or other parents with kids on the plane, will meet her and bring her back part of the way. A group of us will arrange to pick up our kids either here, or somewhere on the road depending on who is the pick-up. Then we have the drive home. Occasionally in the wet we have to use a helicopter to get them home or back to school."

"How far do you live from town?"

"We are out down the Buntine Highway. It's a bit over six hundred kilometres from here."

"Are there towns closer?"

"No. You would hardly call Top Springs or Kalkarindji towns. This is our service centre."

"What about neighbours?"

"Apart from the crew on the station our nearest neighbour is ninety kilometres away. Fortunately we are able to talk to neighbours and friends easily these days. The satellite Internet and phone has made such a difference—provided they are working."

Her husband came over and joined her, and when Peter finished chatting with some men at the bar and returned with our drinks, they invited us to join them.

Keith's family had been in the Territory for many years. He had grown up with the cattle industry and its changes. Bev had come to the Territory looking for adventure and had found not only that but also a husband and the father of her children. The industry had changed greatly with the opening up of live export of cattle to Asia. The improved prices meant more money was available to improve breeding stock and facilities. As well the program to eradicate TB in the cattle had meant a huge change in management of the herd. This was a big plus, although some of the old hands had not been able to cope with the change. These days there is more TB in people than in the cattle.

Peter asked how the ban on live exports had affected them.

"It is a disaster. Suddenly none of us could sell cattle. It was not just us but all the service people, trucks, vets, feed companies, banks, wharfies. How would you feel if someone just said you won't have an income but you have to keep spending money to run the business? We were all relying on early season cattle sales to pay our bills. Some people will never recover. Others will struggle through but it will take years to recover even though the markets have re-opened. It also upset the overseas buyers who no longer trust us, and the sudden increase in stock numbers because we couldn't sell put pressure on the environment."

"Why don't you process the cattle in Australia?"

"The problem has been the meatworks. The labour costs are so high. By the time we pay the costs it is uneconomic. The meatworks that existed have closed down over the years. They haven't been able to make a go of it. As well if we want to sell beef in a box we have to compete with Brazil. Their costs are so much lower that we would have trouble competing. Also the Asian countries want to buy live cattle. It is a foolish person how refuses to acknowledge the buyer's wishes."

"Who owns all the cattle stations?"

"It is a mix. Some, like ours, are family owned. Others are

owned by big companies or even investment funds. Some are owned by overseas interests. It always changes. Companies come and go. A few years ago the Sultan of Brunei was a big landowner. Before him there were owners from the States and the Vestey family from the UK. The industry has its ups and downs. There is a rush of money when people think it will boom, and some unhappy people leave when it busts, but for us it is our home and hopefully our kids' future. That is why we have to look after the land and our cattle. They are our livelihood and our future. We harm them at our peril."

Back in our cabin we finalised our plans for the next day as I put together a meal. Peter thought we should make an early start and take a cruise up the Gorge. Then we could head towards Kununurra and stop overnight at one of the wayside camping spots like the ones we had seen driving from Darwin. I had another idea. When I was at school I had read Jeanie Gunn's book *We of the Never Never* about the early years on Elsey Station. Then the story and location had seemed so far away and exotic. Now that it was only a hundred and thirty kilometres away, I would love to visit the site. If we were to go to Mataranka then we could visit the site of the old station and the cemetery where Jeanie Gunn's husband, 'the Maluka', was buried, then we could head to the Thermal Springs for a swim. Peter pointed out that time and distance meant we would have to stay in either Mataranka or Katherine for another night. Decisions made, Peter went off to arrange another night in our cabin and book places on a cruise up the Gorge. I was also relieved that we would have another night in a room and not in a tent on the roof of a car. At least when the time came for Peter to erect our tent we would probably be where we would have helpful, experienced campers around us. Meanwhile, I was having my doubts about being able to produce a variety of meals with the one small gas ring I had available in our camper. Peter would be easy: sausages, steak, bacon and eggs. I suspected his daily needs were basic.

At the dock we joined our boat group for a trip up the first three gorges. After our experience a few days earlier I was beginning to feel like a typical tourist. Again there were crocodiles but these were much smaller and had a different snout: longer and finer. They looked much less ferocious than the crocs on the Adelaide River. Our guide explained these were freshwater crocodiles, or crocodylus johnsoni, unlike the saltwater crocodiles, crocodylus porosus. These were harmless; the salties were the killers. However, he also warned saltwater crocs live in freshwater so take extreme care! Fortunately this area was monitored and it was safe to swim in this section of the river. His advice was to take care near the water's edge or else. Each year people were taken by crocodiles and often they were tourists. I decided I would keep my swimming to hotel pools!

As we looked at the high escarpments on either side of the river we gained an insight into the deep cut the river had made over the millennium. When our guide described the high and intense rainfall which fell in the catchment during the wet, and showed us the flood levels of the river, we could appreciate the combined power of so many small drops of rain.

Returning from our cruise Peter asked me if I would like a helicopter flight over the Gorge. He had noticed advertisements for flights and thought it would be a great way of seeing how the gorges related to the surrounding countryside, rather than just seeing the river and the gorge walls from the boat. I could see he was really interested and agreed, besides, the thought of a flight in one of the beautiful little helicopters I had seen buzzing overhead was quite exciting. There were a range of options available and Peter decided the flight over the thirteen gorges would give us the best appreciation of the country.

From the air the river was in a deep narrow scar cutting through the flat scrub-covered land. To the north we could see the rough broken land our guide on the boat had referred to as 'Stone Country'. In the distance plumes of smoke showed where early season fires were burning. Our guide on the boat had spoken of these burns being done as a precaution to protect country from the more destructive fires caused by lightning strikes later in the year. He also told us they helped manage the vegetation. Our friends of the previous evening had also spoken of the importance of fire management and the effect it could have, for good or bad, on pastures and vegetation. They had also spoken of the importance of managing the massive amounts of grass which could feed huge fires with fronts of sixty to one hundred kilometres. Fires that could only be controlled by restricting their movement until they burnt out or rains came to extinguish them. When I asked why they didn't put them out, my cattleman explained that sometimes the country was inaccessible, and you would have to wait for the fire to reach country where you could fight it. Usually you would need to fight fire with fire and grade firebreaks and back burn from them to enclose the wild fire with burnt country. Besides, there were so few people available in the area. Neighbours would work together but even then you might only have ten people for a fire covering thousands of square kilometres.

From him I also detected a strong feeling that not all fires were as 'managed' as our guide had claimed and were sometimes lit without any thought of the effect. Keith had rather cryptically referred to two sorts of lightning. It was obviously a local reference that I did not understand.

The highway south to Mataranka was an easy drive. Already a few campers were finding their evening stops beside the highway and setting up their chairs, a beer or glass of wine at hand, to watch the passing traffic. Soon that would be us! Twelve kilometres south of Mataranka we turned left and took the track to the Elsey cemetery. I wondered about our trip, four days, and already I was visiting my second cemetery.

The old Elsey cemetery was tiny. The sadness of the story I remembered reading at school became more vivid as I looked at the grave of the author's husband. He and his wife had come to what was an incredibly remote and lonely cattle station only months after their marriage in faraway Melbourne in December 1901. By March 1903, Jeanie, a minister's daughter, was a widow, her husband, Aeneas, dead from Blackwater Fever. Then she made the sad return voyage to Melbourne, never again to see the Territory. The cemetery was close to the site of the original station homestead, a new station complex had long since been built at a better site. In the cemetery were graves and memorials to the real life characters that filled her books, including little Bet Bet of *The Little Black Princess*.

After our day spent sightseeing and driving the stopover at the Thermal Springs was a relaxing tonic. Parking near a replica of the original Elsey homestead that had been made for a movie of the book, we walked down through the palms, the paperbarks, and the pandanus into a clear flowing pool. Bathing in the thirty-four degrees spring-fed waters was like luxuriating in a giant bath whose temperature never changed. Below us gentle currents rose from the floor of the pool as more water seeped up from the sandy base and flowed over the pool wall to make its way into the Waterhouse River and eventually the Roper River. Finally, relaxed and wrinkled, we made our way back to Katherine.

The atmosphere around the resort bar was different when we returned from our day's sightseeing. Last night it had been noisy and full of tanned cattlemen and their wives, but they had returned to their homes far away from Katherine. Tonight the room was almost empty with only a group of American tourists sitting together discussing their day's travels. Like us they had been to the Gorge, some had done a cruise and others had actually paddled the Gorges in canoes. They invited Peter and me to join them, keen to meet locals. On that score we had to disappoint them. We were tourists just like them. Nevertheless we passed a few enjoyable hours as we learnt their thoughts on Sydney and The Great Barrier Reef, and we found out about life in Wisconsin and Florida. It seemed most of the group preferred to avoid northern winters. We left them with their plans to return to Darwin and take a flight to Alice Springs to see Ayers Rock (Uluru). Little did they seem to realise that the Rock was five hours drive away from Alice Springs. As we left our newfound friends I realised I was not the only one who didn't know the Territory was twice the size of Texas.

I went to bed thinking of tomorrow. Five hundred kilometres away to the west, Kununurra, and pink diamonds.

4 Wyndham

Peter

Talking with the Americans at the bar last night, Suzie had been very excited at the thought of seeing pink diamonds. I didn't share her excitement. Jewellery was not a great interest of mine. I knew of the Argyle diamond mine near Kununurra as a friend had once worked there. His stories of giant dump trucks moving tonnes of rock to the crusher had not matched the romantic image of sparkling gemstones. While rare rough gems were hidden in the huge quantity of rock mined, most of the diamonds were tiny particles destined for industrial use. Nevertheless, I was certain when we reached Kununurra Suzie would want to visit a shop selling the local specialty.

The highway heading west was easy driving. Already caravanners were on the road, appearing out of wayside stops where they had camped for the night. One day when I was more confident about camping I hoped we would join them in the layoffs. But first I needed to be sure that I could erect and dismantle the tent on top of the vehicle. Tonight I would have to face that challenge. I suspected Suzie would prefer the comfort of a room, even if it was a small cabin.

The road trains amazed me. The trucks were huge with

three trailers each. Some were carting cattle, probably heading for the Port of Darwin, and were two levels high. Our newly-met friends of our first night in Katherine had talked of 'decks' as a standard unit of trade in the cattle industry. One road train would be six 'decks' and carry one hundred and fifty head of cattle bound for Indonesia or other parts of Asia. Sometimes we would be passed by convoys of four or five of these massive trucks. Other road trains were carting fuel or general freight. Still others were bringing up cars or food from factories in the south, or returning empty, or sometimes carrying loads of fruit and vegetables to southern markets. To overtake one of these goliaths required a long straight stretch of road with good visibility.

Suzie pointed out the Buntine Highway turnoff. Five hundred kilometres down that road, ninety kilometres from the neighbouring station, lived two small girls and their parents.

Occasionally there would be groups of cattle standing near a water trough or dam. Sometimes we would see a string of cattle, nose to tail, walking a fence line and soon we would come upon another watering point. Only rarely did we see a station homestead.

"Where do all the people live?"

I answered Suzie's question as best I could. "Keith was telling me the other night that there are not that many people living in this region and often their homes are out of sight. With the trees you have no idea what might be a kilometre away. There could be homestead complexes, cattle yards, airstrips, all sorts of infrastructure. The land is not as empty and unused as it looks. Apparently even the land types can change dramatically behind some tree lines. There are some very large rural businesses in the bush. We just don't see them from the road."

Once we crossed the Victoria River the countryside changed. The road now ran between a beautiful escarpment on our left and the river, sometimes hidden behind scrub, on our right. Every now and again a road sign showed the distance to cattle stations down gravel, or more often, dirt roads.

We stopped for a break and a coffee at Timber Creek. There Suzie took over the driving until we eventually decided on a shady spot to stop for a picnic lunch. Once again we changed drivers. I was behind the wheel when we crossed the border and reached the quarantine checkpoint. The fruit Suzie had bought the previous day had to be surrendered, as well as my small pot of honey that I had wanted for my breakfast time toast. Being unaware of the regulations we had not realised the seriousness of disease and pests entering a region that was free of fruit fly. The inspector who searched our car certainly knew the damage that disease could do to the livelihood of his fellow residents of the Ord irrigation area—as we saw when some tourists pretended not to be carrying fruit. Half an hour later we were at the outskirts of Kununurra. Plenty of time to find a caravan park for our evening stay. No motels tonight.

After checking in to the campground we realised we had gained time, or rather Western Australian clocks were an hour and a half behind the Northern Territory. We would have time to visit the diversion dam and then drive out to the lake itself. Lake Argyle, backed by the red of the Carr Boyd Range, was huge. It was there that we found the old Argyle Downs homestead. The original home of the pioneering Durack family, the homestead had once stood in the valley now flooded by the lake. It had been dismantled stone by stone and rebuilt as a memorial to early pastoralists on a site above the waters. Today the lake provided water for the irrigated fields of fruit trees, vegetables, crops and the improved pastures we had seen on our drive. Many crops and ventures had been trialled in the Ord. Many had been unsuccessful, but not all. Today the area was home to the world's largest sandalwood plantation, as well as producing melons and other vegetables. The dream of developing the north still existed with new plans constantly being made.

Sitting on a rock, looking at the old homestead, I thought of those early pioneers and their families. I had lived in small exploration camps and mine sites, but there I had company and ready access to civilisation. Those early pioneers to this country were far from any support. What was today a simple health issue could be fatal. The nearest help a long horse ride to a town that may not have anyone who could assist anyway. I thought of those women giving birth. Perhaps their only female company an experienced native woman. Then I thought of Suzie. How would she have coped? She had grown up on the Riverina Plains but had spent most of her time in Melbourne or London. She was a city girl, yet I sensed a toughness that would have enabled her to cope if that was what she had chosen to do.

Back in the campsite I tackled the tent. Catches released, a few tugs and the tent popped up, the annexe dropped down and we were set for the night. What had been my concern? All we had to do was climb the ladder to our bed on the roof, and not roll out during the night. Perhaps it would be safer to put the mattress on the floor of the annexe? Hopefully we would not have nocturnal visits from snakes. Suzie decided upstairs would be better after all.

I had always wanted to see Wyndham. There was really no reason why I had that wish but the place had always been lodged in my mind since I was a child. I think it was some vague memory of reading a story about the town, the wild frontier and the remoteness. To a child it seemed so different to my life in a big city. Now when it was less than an hour away I had to go there. I would probably never have another opportunity. It was something I just wanted to do. One thing I was not going to do was go near the water. A story circulating amongst the campers was of a local woman who had been sitting beside the water when a croc attacked her. Apparently she had lost part of her arm but escaped with her life.

The town had long ago had its heyday when it was the port for the gold field at Hall's Creek. The meatworks, that were once important to the region, had been closed for many years. Even its resurgence as a port to service the development of the new town of Kununurra had faded as highways improved. It had long since been surpassed by Kununurra.

We visited the small port area and the site of the closed meatworks then drove up the increasingly steep and winding road to reach the lookout, The Bastion, high above the small town. From there we had a panoramic view of the town and the five rivers that entered the Cambridge Gulf. The Ord we had already seen, but here were also the Pentecost, the King, the Forrest and the Durack. The last two were names familiar to many Australians; especially Western Australians.

We were the only customers of the Wyndham Town Hotel and the barmaid was obviously not busy. We chatted, and eventually she decided to sit down and join us. Soon we were learning the history and gossip of the town.

At present things were very busy. Looking around the pub it seemed unlikely.

"We've got the police and customs and all sorts of other government people here. Most of them are down in the caravan park. There are only a few of the bosses staying here."

"Where are they now?" I asked, looking around at the empty street and pub.

"They come and go. All of a sudden they will rush off somewhere, and then a few hours later they'll be back. They have some sort of command centre in a big truck down in the park."

"What are they doing?"

The barmaid shrugged. "They don't talk about it much. Just say it is an exercise. I suppose it must be about drugs, or illegal immigrants, or guns."

"Guns?"

"I don't know. You hear stories. Sometimes it's smuggling drugs in and guns out. The next time it's guns in and people out."

"Do you ever see strange people around here?"

"We did the other day. She was strange, weird."

"Why?"

"The way she looked, and the way she shot through. We see a few odd people here but she stood out."

"What do you mean?"

"She came in this little camper with Elvis Presley painted on the side. You know the sort of camper that some of the backpackers use. Booked into the caravan park for a week and paid. Then next day she'd gone."

"Did she have long magenta hair on one side of her head with the other side shaved?"

"That's her. You're not her father? You're not trying to find her?"

"No, no. I don't know her, but I saw her a couple of times in Darwin. She sure makes an impact."

"She made an impact in the bar. There were some ringers in from the local cattle stations having a piss up. Half the boys looked scared to even talk to her. The girls spoke to her briefly and then avoided her. A couple of the boys tried to chat her up and buy her a beer but she wiped them. Told them she wasn't drinking beer, she only drank vodka. Then Django really tried it on the chick. There was some music playing and he decided to dance with her and smooze up to her. She told him where to go, but he tried again and was all over her. The next thing he was hopping around in agony. She'd kneed him in the balls. After that she was left alone at one end of the bar with her vodka and everyone else stayed at the other end. It didn't make for a happy night. Next morning she just drove out of town. That was the last we saw of her."

Back in Kununurra Suzie had identified two possible shops to see pink diamonds. We entered the one she thought most promising. A sales assistant immediately took us in hand. My hesitation about gemstones was quickly replaced by curiosity about diamonds, and the saleswoman was very informative. Soon I was engrossed learning about carats as a measurement of size, clarity and inclusions, the various cuts and their ability to reflect light, and finally colour. With gems from the Argyle mine the deeper the pink the rarer the stone, and the dearer the price. It soon became obvious that Suzie had a definite desire to buy a ring. From the prices on the stones I saw it looked as if it would be an expensive purchase. The saleslady also showed us some white diamonds. The price differential between white and pink was huge. The jewellery workshop could make any style Suzie desired and it would be sent to her address. It would be insured against any loss in transit. On the saleswoman's suggestion Suzie decided on a setting with a beautiful dark pink diamond surrounded by a cluster of small white diamonds. At that stage I left Suzie to conduct her negotiations and finalise the making of the ring. I was sure it would not be cheap. It bought home to me how little I still really knew about this lady.

As we were leaving I asked the saleswoman who were her best customers.

"There are all sorts. You can never judge who will buy. Some people come in and look very affluent and just look at everything and leave buying nothing. Another person will come in wearing shorts and a singlet and buy a very expensive ring for his wife as a reward for letting him go on a fishing trip with the boys. I remember a time when a

Northern Territory cattleman came and bought a beautiful ring for his wife. He said she had always admired pink diamonds, and he wanted to give it to her to say thank you for the times she had been beside him as they struggled on the station. Only the other morning we had a young woman come in. She looked like a hippy but she knew her gemstones. She didn't spend long, bought two very good unset pink stones, top of the range, paid with a credit card and left. The price didn't seem to be an issue. I don't know what she was going to do with them. She didn't look like the type who would wear diamond rings. Perhaps she would have them made into ear studs. She certainly stood out from the crowd."

"What was she like?"

"Different. Striking purple hair and a very unusual cut."

Suzie looked at me. "Magenta?"

5 Derby

Suzie

Sitting beside our camper eating our breakfast we planned the day.

Peter asked me if I wanted to join a tour which would fly over the Bungle Bungles and then land at the Argyle Mine and see where my pink diamond had come from. Alternately we could drive out and stay overnight at the campsite near the entrance to the Bungle Bungles. A third option was to just do a flight over the striated rock formations. The first option would mean two more nights in the camping ground as the day's flights had already left, and we would have to wait until tomorrow for a flight. To drive out would mean a night at the campground at the entrance to the park and a night back in Kununurra on our return. The flight over the Bungles might be possible in the afternoon, but it was likely that a flight in a light plane would become rougher and more uncomfortable as the day became hotter. Neither Peter nor I had great enthusiasm for any of the options. I had my diamond and I didn't need to see where it had come from. Besides I was a little concerned about Peter's view of my purchase. I had decided I wanted the ring and I was paying for it, so it was really nothing to do with him. Yet I felt he thought I was being extravagant. We had never discussed money in our relationship. He knew my home, he had stayed there before it had been burnt down, and I knew his house.

So we both had some idea of our possible financial situations, but neither of us knew exactly what they really were. I had paid for my airfare to Darwin, but Peter had already booked the four-wheel drive and the hotel room in Darwin and said it would be no more expensive for two than if he was travelling alone. I had paid for the cabin in Katherine so we didn't need to erect the tent. If we were to ever live together then we would have to come to some understanding. Perhaps it was still a little too soon.

After we had washed and cleared away our breakfast mugs and bowls we decided to move on. We still had a long trip ahead of us, and there were sure to be many other tours we could do. Peter tried several times to fold up the tent but somehow it never managed fit back into its container. Eventually another traveller in the campground came over to help. A few quick flicks and the tent was stowed and the cover fastened. Peter may be a mining engineer but he does have some gaps in his skills.

Driving into Halls Creek I was struck by the change in the population. I had always thought of Darwin as being a multicultural town with its European, Aboriginal, Chinese and other South East Asian peoples. However, with the changes in modern Australia, the ethnic mix was now much more obvious in central Melbourne or Sydney than in Darwin. In Katherine I had seen more Aboriginal people, but the town appeared predominately European. Here in Halls Creek the local population was definitely Aboriginal. The gold rush of 1885 which had created the settlement had only lasted three years, and then the town had become a ghost town. Today life for many looked to be a struggle to survive on government benefits. Yet once men had walked all the way from Queensland, lured by gold and the thought of possible fortunes. I couldn't imagine today's generations making such a trek to what was then an even more remote and wild place.

After refuelling the vehicle we drove out of town and found a quiet shady spot for a sandwich and coffee. I took over the driving to give Peter a break. As someone who had spent most of my life in England or Melbourne the distances between the towns—hours apart—had really brought home the size of the country. Compared to where we were now, Darwin seemed huge; Katherine a big city. Fitzroy Crossing where we were heading was almost three hundred kilometres away, and there was nothing in between. It was important to know how far your fuel tank would take you. Out here there was nowhere to get more fuel if you made a mistake—and it would be a long way to walk!

We found the information centre in Fitzroy Crossing and considered the possibilities. I had always thought of Peter as organised, 'in control', for him the future was 'planned'. That was probably what frightened me when I had first met him in London. I considered myself and my life much more open to change. Yet here Peter seemed to have no immediate plans. Plans made over breakfast could be changed by lunchtime. I wondered whether I had misunderstood him all those years ago, or whether he was trying to change to suit me. I knew women who claimed to have changed men. It usually ended in sorrow for everybody.

We made our decision to spend the night at Fitzroy Crossing. The information centre had told us the roads to Windjana Gorge and Tunnel Creek were open and, while it would take longer to reach Derby, it would make for an interesting side trip. We drove back out of town to a park beside the river that we had seen earlier and Peter set up our camp.

Sitting beside our camper, as the daylight slowly dimmed and the campground lights began to throw pools of pale yellow light over the riverside park, we watched the more adventurous kangaroos creep in from the bush to graze on the green grasses of the campground.

In the soft light and gentle warmth of the evening we discussed our day. Our drive had taken us through some very beautiful country and I had enjoyed the scenery around Halls Creek, but I had been depressed by what I had seen in town. Sitting here overlooking the river I was in a pleasant oasis that I doubted reflected the life of many of the locals. I knew from television the problems of some Aboriginal communities, but here in Halls Creek and Fitzroy Crossing it was right in front of you.

"How do you think the lives of the locals could be improved?"

Peter thought for a moment before replying. "There has been a fortune spent on education and health and housing, but it seems to have had little effect out here. Land rights and native title don't appear to have made a difference either. Aboriginal groups and organisations own the greater part of the Kimberley region including many cattle stations. I suspect the only answer will be when people stop seeing themselves as victims. If you are a victim then your problems are caused by somebody else, and they should change. You don't need to do anything about it yourself. It's not exclusively an Aboriginal problem. People have to take charge of their lives and make decisions, not expect others to solve their problems. That can be very hard. There is a whole industry and many careers based on Aboriginal disadvantage. Once a tribe had to work together, hunting and gathering, in the bush in order to survive. It was a hard life, and each member had to contribute or the group would suffer. That was a strength, but now that culture has become a disadvantage in the modern world. With government providing housing and an income there is no incentive to work. If someone does get a job the rest of the family want to share the rewards without doing any work to help earn it. The workers decide it's not worth their effort."

"That's if there are jobs."

"There is certainly work to be done. Unfortunately it is often done by workers brought in from outside. The locals either don't acquire the skills necessary, or don't do the work. Also people want to stay in their home country. I had to travel to find my jobs. Many people do. There are jobs in the cattle industry and mining. The horticulture industry has to employ international backpackers even though there may be a community right alongside the farm with unemployed young people."

"Do you see an answer?"

"I think it needs a far wiser man than me. I once met an old man who was very concerned about the young people in his community. He wanted them to get an education, but to do that they had to go to Darwin. Then once they were educated they didn't want to come back to their home community. If they did, they sometimes no longer respected the old ways he valued. It was a sad situation for him to be in."

"But they lack money."

"There's always money for alcohol and tobacco, and for gambling. That's a big problem too. Drugs are an even bigger problem now. Marijuana, kava, ice. There's money for that. That feeds the violence and neglect. For some, food and kids come last. You and I have to supply and maintain our homes, even if the cost is built into the rent. Here it is expected that the government will provide everything and you don't need to care for it. You make demands, but you don't try to provide for yourself."

We walked down beside the quiet river trying to imagine it in flood during a big wet season. I thought of Peter's answers. It was an old way of life that wanted the trappings of the modern world, yet was often not prepared or ready to accept the demands of this new world surrounding them. The kids would watch videos of rappers in the States and try to emulate them, dreaming of instant riches and the latest fashions. Yet they were trapped in a life on the edge of the desert and in the reality that surrounded them—ignoring the changes that were necessary.

"OK Mr Know-it-all, why is this place called Fitzroy Crossing?"

"Because it's where you cross the Fitzroy River."

"OK, why is it called the Fitzroy river?"

"Because that is what Stokes called it. He was the surveyor on the Beagle on its third voyage. This time surveying parts of Australia. He named it after his earlier commander."

"The Beagle. Wasn't that the boat that Darwin went to the Galapagos on?"

"Yes. Fitzroy had taken command partway through the first voyage after the previous captain had committed suicide. He was in command on the second voyage with Darwin that made the boat famous. They sailed down the east coast of South America, through the Straits of Magellan, up the west coast and out to the Galapagos. Eventually it returned to England via Tahiti, New Zealand, Tasmania, Mauritius and South Africa. The history of the Beagle, with its three big voyages and its eventual fate, is fascinating."

"How do you know?"

"I read the book!"

It was time to go to bed.

We started early in the morning. Today we were going bush. Soon we left the asphalt of the highway and the road to Tunnel Creek National Park turned to dirt. It was already corrugated from the tourist traffic and our progress was slowed. The one hundred and fifteen kilometres trip took us around two hours. We had been warned and made sure we had our torches with good batteries. We had been told we would need them. The other piece of advice given at the campground was to be prepared to wade through water. Fortunately both Peter and I had packed rubber shoes for walking on rocky beaches.

A short path led us to the tunnel. The walls of the Napier Range towered over us as we squeezed through large boulders to reach the entrance. Once inside we found ourselves in a big hall. The tunnel itself was dark but roomy, and in places the beams of our torches lit up small waterfalls tumbling over ledges, and the little stalactites hanging from the ceiling. Part way through the tunnel the ceiling had collapsed and let in some light. Above us we could see the tree roots exposed by the fall. Continuing the walk we re-entered the murky water and darkness until we reached the far side of the range. It was nice to leave the dank blackness and be back in the sunlight and a gentle breeze, and to hear the calls of the birds and the murmur of the creek.

Back in the car we headed for Windjana Gorge. The gorge was so different to the tunnel. Here the river running through the gorge had retreated to a series of ponds fringed by trees and shrubs. The trees and the water were a haven for the noisy corellas, a colony of smelly squabbling bats and numerous water birds. By the pool at Bandingan Rock fresh water crocodiles were sunning themselves. I knew they were not the man-eating 'salties', but I still decided against going for a swim.

As we sat looking at the limestone walls of the range it was hard to imagine that once they would have been under the ocean. Peter had been hoping he might see some Aboriginal rock art. Wandjina was a sacred spirit and a particular style of art. He reached into his pack and pulled out a book and showed me images of the Wandjina and the large spaceman like characters that were a theme of the art. However he would have to wait until we went on our tour before we would see the images in real life.

When we turned onto the Gibb River Road I asked Peter if he had thought about doing that trip. I had heard people speak of the adventure. For some of the campers we had met it was to be their big challenge.

"Yes. I did think of it. Much of the Aboriginal rock art

that I want to see is up in that region. However you still need to find the actual sites, and it is hard country to move around in if you don't know it, especially if you aren't used to driving in those remote areas. I decided that I would be better with a guide. The Gibb River Road and the Canning Stock route are the great dream of some people who really want to go bush, but I had other things that were more important to me. I'm not interested in just ticking the box and getting kudos from fellow travellers."

It was late afternoon as we drove into Derby. Just as we reached the intersection of the Gibb River Road and the highway I glimpsed a small van with Elvis Presley on the side driving out along the highway. Whether it was heading to Broome or someplace else was impossible to tell, but it seemed as if our paths were continuing to cross.

The boab trees lining the main street of Derby were amazing. I had already seen boabs in other places but here, used as street trees, they were far more numerous. A friend had once described them as inverted trees with their roots in the air. It was a very apt description: their bare branches were just like roots. Peter found the campground and erected our tent. I set up our tiny kitchen and prepared a casserole. We were becoming very proficient campers.

That night I had a dream. Around me swirled white ghost like figures with huge eyes and no mouths. They crowded in on me, and would then dissolve. A van with Elvis Presley on the side would spin across my head only to be replaced by an image of Magenta. The snakes tattooed on her leg untwined and struck out towards me. Again the ghostly shapes would reappear dancing around her, the snakes and then me. The dream repeated itself again and again. None of it made sense. The figures in Peter's book had nothing to do with the van or Magenta; indeed Magenta had nothing to do with us. She was only a person we had seen and heard about. The dream made no sense, and I decided not to mention it to Peter.

Chatting with fellow campers we discovered that Derby was home to the Kimberley School of the Air and we could visit this morning. We headed there after breakfast.

Once upon a time the school had operated through radio. Today the students connected with their teachers via the Internet, and now the teachers and students could see each other on a screen. I watched the varied students report in to their class and answer their teacher, 'Yes Miss' or 'Yes Mr Noble', just like any other school. Even more interesting were the reports of the previous day's activities, or their plans for later that day. Several were to go with their father to muster cattle. Some were already excited about the prospect of meeting their friends at the Fitzroy Crossing Rodeo. However this only covered a small part of their education. It still required a great deal of effort by mothers or governesses to complete the lessons that were sent out to the students. The video contact was only a small but valuable part of the system. Then when the children had finished primary school there was the next problem: high school. For that they would have to leave their isolated homes. A map on the wall showed where the students lived. Scattered across four hundred thousand square kilometres they may only see their teachers and fellow students at school camps or on a rare visit to their home by a teacher. I bought a cookbook and Peter bought a stubby holder as a memento of our visit and as support for the students and their parents.

Our next stop was the information centre to find out more about the town. Like Darwin, Katherine and Wyndham, Derby had also been bombed during the Second World War. Derby's other claim to fame was its huge tides and the mudflats and mangroves that seemed to go on forever. Derby was famous for its tides in the King Sound. The long jetty running out into the harbour was designed to cope with the twice daily tides of almost twelve metres. That certainly made access to the jetty interesting for yachts and boats.

We were told we had timed our visit too early. We should have come for the big event of the year: the Boab Festival. July was the time to come. The locals were already preparing for the festival and it was the main conversation around town.

Then we took a drive around the town. On the jetty some fishermen were already sitting with their lines dangling hopefully in the water. Like jetties everywhere there didn't seem to be any fish caught as we walked its length. Out on the mudflats a few boats were sitting waiting for the tide to return and float them off the mud. We bought a pie at the jetty café and walked back to our car to drive to Broome. I decided that in Broome we would find a motel or hotel. Camping was OK, but I preferred a room with a wider bed and a solid base, a private bathroom, and no risk of falling off the roof.

Not far out of town we stopped beside an immense boab tree. The tree was reputedly fifteen hundred years old and had once been used as a staging point for walking Aboriginal prisoners to Derby. Nearby, a bath house had stood beside the bore and the trough that had served to water the cattle that were the economic lifeblood of the region. Standing with Peter, looking at the trough, I thought of the days a hundred or more years earlier when drovers moved large mobs of cattle across the land. Then, there were no asphalt highways and road trains, only bush tracks between small remote settlements, or between water holes or bores like this one. The cattle industry had brought big changes to the region, and especially to the lives of the indigenous people. Their lives had been unchanged for thousands of years. Change, and challenges that were still unresolved. The tree and the bore were powerful relics of those earlier times.

Then we drove on. A few hours later Broome appeared in front of us.

6 Broome

Suzie

I felt a frisson of excitement as I drove our car into Broome. I knew of the town and Cable Beach. Indeed some of my friends had once visited for a holiday, but I had never really thought of coming here. My idea of a beach holiday was in Queensland, and became even more so after my visit to the Whitsundays with Peter. Now I was here. In my mind it had always been some exotic, remote part of Australia: an outpost with pearl luggers and Japanese divers. Thinking back, my memories were probably influenced by a book I had read at school about the pearl divers of Broome written by Ion L Idriess and set in the 1930s. As much as I tried to remember the name of the book it would not return. Just a partial image of the cover and the word 'fathoms'. I was probably twelve or thirteen when I had read it. That had been so long ago.

What had stayed in my mind was the remote location and the exotic range of people who lived there: the Japanese divers, the Manilamen, the Koepangers from Indonesia—then called the Dutch East Indies—the Timorese, the men from Hong Kong and from the Caribbean. All attracted to the possibility of making their fortunes with pearls and pearl shell. It was so different to the very Anglo-Saxon community I was growing up in. There even the Greek and Italian migrants from Europe were a different culture. Old Broome of which Idriess wrote was populated by far more exotic species: yet it was still part of Australia.

My teachers had been intrigued by my interest in the book. They thought of it as a 'boys' book. It was a tale of far-off adventure and danger. Girls read Jane Austin or the Brontë sisters. Times were different then. I told Peter of my thoughts.

"How did you like school?"

I thought before I answered Peter's question. "I enjoyed school. I liked being with the other girls. Where I lived with my parents there were no young people my age. I liked the teachers as well. Most were really great women. I think having that community around me, especially people my own age, was something I really enjoyed and didn't have in my life in the bush where our closest neighbours were miles away over roads that were sometimes impassable when we had heavy rain. Later when I became older the jackaroos on the station were an exciting find for a teenage girl, but when I first started boarding school they had seemed so much older and mature. It was only in my later teens that their attractiveness appeared, but by then my father had given strict orders about how they should behave. It was probably the sense of community that drew me to teaching, and then later in England into promotion and PR work. I also liked learning. What about you?"

"I never really thought about it much. You went to school and did your work. I wasn't the smartest kid but I was an OK student. It was really only when I got to university that the light came on for me. Then I discovered the pleasure of finding solutions to problems. I enjoyed that."

"What about sport?"

"No. I was hopeless. Couldn't hit a ball. Couldn't catch a ball. Slow but steady when it came to running. The only thing I could do was long distance running. I outlasted all the sprinters because I just kept going. Too silly to know when I should give up. I did, still do, enjoy reading."

The town now was so different to the book I had read. Modern shops had replaced the scraggly street described in the book. The Japanese divers and the timber-hulled luggers had gone, apart from some restored and displayed in the town as a memorial to those past days. Glimpses still remained of the early days in names and the occasional building, but much had changed with the Second World War when the Japanese forces had bombed the Dutch and Australian seaplanes operating from Roebuck Bay. Where once divers sought pearl beds for shell, now pearl farms along the coast were serviced by large steel workboats. Some of these looked like luxury yachts and could easily be confused with the boats servicing the wealthy tourists wanting to get away to the remote islands and inlets to the north of Broome. The old wooden luggers were just an historic curiosity. The great days of the pearl shell industry with markets for pearl shell buttons and ornaments had gone: the pearl shell replaced by synthetics. Where once a few traders sold the rare pearls found in nature to international dealers visiting the outpost of the country, now bright, smart shops sought to draw in the cashed up tourists from Australia and the rest of the world. Still, the town did retain a little of its past.

Peter decided it might be best if we stayed in a campground. "It's the start of the peak season for tourists and hotels will be very expensive. They are probably booked out anyway." My thought of a wide, comfortable bed and private bathroom vanished. After finding a campsite for the evening we headed out to Cable Beach. Our camp receptionist had given us definite instructions on what to do: we should leave immediately, take a bottle of wine or some beers, drive down onto the beach and park looking out to the west. Any delay would mean we would miss a good place to view the sight. For Easterners with few, if any, beaches facing west it would be a rare experience to see the sun set over the ocean. After the previous four nights Peter had decided he had mastered the tent and could erect it in the dark. There would be no problems popping it up when we returned.

Our receptionist was right. The beach was lined with cars and vans of all sorts. A long line of tourists with their chairs and tables sat half way up the beach waiting for the sun to sink over the ocean. With the breeze off the water, the sound of the waves rolling in and the feel of sand under our feet, it felt like a good end to a day. As we sat watching the sun gently falling towards the ocean two strings of camels plodded along near the water's edge and slowly crossed in front of us. Beyond them a yacht with its sails fully rigged was highlighted by the golden yellow of the sinking sun in a cloudless sky. It was a magic scene that I thought only existed in tourist brochures.

With the sun down and darkness falling quickly, leaving the beach was like a city traffic jam as we all attempted to drive away at the same time. The traffic slowed by the camels we had seen on the beach. As they slowly padded their way back to their overnight yard little red lights flashed on their tails to warn impatient drivers of their presence.

Back in the campground Peter released a few catches and our home popped into place. I was sure I heard an audible sound of relief. There was a different sound as he tripped over a tent peg.

"Forty Fathoms Deep'. That was the name of the book I read." The name had come to me as we woke in the morning. "How much is a fathom?" I was sure Peter would know the answer.

"Six feet, one point eight metres in metric. Forty fathoms would be about two hundred and forty feet. Seventy-two metres. Why?"

"That was the name of a book I read at school about the pearl industry in Broome. I never thought I would be here."

Peter's booking for the Aboriginal art tour had been made before we left Sydney. In fact he had made it before I had even arrived to try to find him. The tour commenced on Monday. That gave us two days to enjoy Broome. Today was to be an easy day, no driving, well not much, a chance to catch up on some washing, a walk in the town, and maybe some time on the beach: an Indian Ocean beach. I had thought his travel arrangements had been very flexible. An extra day here, a day less somewhere else; it wasn't important. It had all seemed so unplanned, yet I now realised that it was all geared to being in Broome, ready on Monday morning to see the Aboriginal art that he had so long wanted to see in real life and not just in books.

We drove into the old part of town, parked, and commenced our exploration on foot. It was fascinating to see pearl luggers, like the ones mentioned in *Forty Fathoms Deep*, now preserved and on display. The stories told in the book came flooding back. We walked to Streeter's Jetty, the jetty that had once serviced the pearl luggers in the early days, and from there walked back through Chinatown. In Johnny Chi Lane the many signboards displayed the history of Broome. In my mind I tried to envisage the streets as they would have been in the 1930s, when the life of the town depended on men from many parts of the world facing risks and possible death as they sought their fortunes. Today there were people from many parts of the world, but they were tourists.

Now the streets of the old Chinatown had become the new retail hub aimed at tourists. The windows of upmarket boutiques were full of beautiful jewellery, strings of pearls of all sizes, necklaces, chokers, bracelets and rings. Inside were even more beautiful pieces. As a keen sales woman in one of these galleries was showing her jewellery I glanced across at Peter. He was struggling between interest in the stories of how pearls are made and valued, and whether I would be a buyer, and if I was a buyer would I expect him to pay. I leant over and put him out of his misery. I had no plans to buy. We really would have to sort the financial arrangements out if we were to stay together.

We found a museum and spent hours browsing the collection of pearling equipment and memorabilia. We saw a different part of Broome history at the Heritage Centre. In what had once been a convent, the photos, multimedia displays and storyboards showed the hundred-year history of the Sisters of St John of God and the Aboriginal women and girls of the Kimberley.

"Let's go to the pictures tonight. It's Saturday night. Saturday was always movie night when I was young." Peter turned and looked at me but made no comment. "I remember going to an open air picture theatre when I was on a school holiday. It was fun to sit in the open in deck chairs watching the latest Hollywood flick. It won't rain tonight."

We had been walking along the street and had come to the old weathered, corrugated iron building that was the home to Sun Pictures. It must have been the last operating open air movie theatre in Australia. Sure there were now festivals running that showed movies in the open, but this was an original. We made enquiries and bought our tickets for the eight-thirty session.

In the evening we joined the crowd in the foyer of the open air picture theatre and made our way through to the garden. It was full of rows of deck chairs, all facing a large screen. These days the seating arrangements had changed from earlier years when there had been segregation based on race and community importance. In those days crews from the working luggers had to use a different entrance and were segregated from the European and non-Europeans by a low fence and sat on benches rather than have the luxury of a deck chair. Today everybody had a deck chair. I wondered if most of the patrons were like us: tourists reliving, or perhaps experiencing, a memory they had known from their youth. After all, the picture theatre was approaching its centenary and claimed to be the oldest operating garden cinema in the world. Fortunately these days a levy bank prevented the tide from lapping around the movie goers' ankles during the screening. There were stories of patrons in the old days catching fish during the movie. I suspected the locals probably favoured the new air-conditioned twin screen cinema behind McDonalds. Nor was their attention to the movie affected by the roar and flashing lights of a passenger jet, seemingly within touching distance, as it made its final approach to Broome airport.

Sunday, like every other day, began with a warm sun and a cloudless blue sky. It would only get hotter as the day progressed. The wet season and the rain was still months away. We decided to spend the morning on the beach, have lunch at one of the restaurants at Cable Beach, and in the evening find a spot on the Town Beach to see the 'Staircase to the Moon' as the moon rose over Roebuck Bay. Peter also wanted to visit the site of the dinosaur prints at Gantheaume Point. That would be only possible at low tide. I guess for a mining engineer specialising in rocks it would be interesting.

Like so many beaches in the north of Australia, Cable Beach could be affected by the seasonal invasion of marine stingers. Being early June, the risk of attack by the jellyfish should have passed. Peter asked a local on the beach if the water was safe.

"Yeah mate, the stingers have gone, and the sharks shouldn't be a problem."

I hoped his confidence was well placed!

The white sandy beach stretched away into the far distance. At the edge of the sand lay the turquoise waters and white surf breaks of the Indian Ocean. They, in turn, gave way to the lighter blue cloudless sky. The blues and the whites were framed by the red of the Pindan, with its red cliffs and soils of ironstone, and the green of the eucalypts, wattles and grevilleas that fringed the coastline.

We laid side by side on towels, we splashed in the water, Peter tried to catch a few waves, and we read our books and talked, or just lay silent. Eventually we were driven from the beach by the sun and found a café for a meal. We talked some more until the tide had receded. It was time for Peter to go dinosaur hunting.

It was only a short drive from Cable Beach to Gantheaume Point. We took the well-worn track past the replica casts of footprints surrounded by curious children, and after reading the signs at the interpretive centre clambered down the slippery cliff to the sandstone exposed by the retreating tide. There, embedded in the sandstone, were the prints Peter had come to see. To me they looked like small rock pools or undulations in the sandstone. Peter pointed out the shapes and their significance. As he talked his excitement was infectious.

"I still find it difficult to comprehend that these tracks were made by an animal, or animals—for there are different tracks—one hundred and thirty million years ago. This would be the cretaceous period, and back then this area would have been very different: probably a river delta and had dinosaurs walking all over it. Apparently there were sauropods and ornithopods and theropods. I am in awe of nature. The timescale, the changes that the planet has undergone. The species that thrived and then disappeared to be replaced by something else. When I look at rock formations and see hard rock that has been pushed up from the depths of the ocean into mountains then twisted on its side or curved and bent, I have trouble comprehending the force that must have been at work. And that's only this planet. Who knows what lies beyond our galaxy. Maybe our kids will know more.

That evening we drove down to the Town Beach in Broome. We worked our way through the stalls selling food and tourist tat, bought some plates of Chinese and some drinks and found a place to sit on the grass and watch the local monthly event of the moon rising over Roebuck Bay and its mudflats. I looked around, I half expected to see Magenta appear from the crowd, but she was nowhere to be seen.

We had been lucky. Without any planning we had arrived on a full moon. A few days either side and there would be nothing, but tonight we would see the staircase to the moon. A clear night sky free of clouds was never a problem at this time of the year. On cue the full moon rose and lit up a narrow path of water, and in the moonlight the tiny strips of reflected light continued to rise up as the moon itself rose. It appeared, as if not perhaps a stairway to Heaven, at least there was a staircase to the moon.

"OK Mr Know-it-all. You read the book about The Beagle. What is a roebuck?"

"It is a male Roe deer. They are found all over Europe and the UK."

"Well why name a bay after a deer that isn't indigenous to Australia?"

"You should know. You were the school teacher."

"Peter, I know my history. Well, some of it. The Roebuck was a Royal Navy ship captained by William Dampier which carried out the first English scientific expedition to Australia in, I think, 1699. It was long before the time of Captain Cook and the discovery of the east coast of Australia about seventy years later.

"Did you read the book?"

I reached out and hit him on the shoulder as the staircase and the moon parted.

7 Gwion Gwion

Peter

Today was finally the day.

I had thought many times about this trip, but had never taken the final step of making a booking. When Suzie and I were viewing the early Australian and Aboriginal art at the National Gallery of Victoria, after our chance meeting, I had told her of my interest in the Bradshaw art of the Kimberley. On the flight home from Melbourne after her decision and our parting, I decided I should do it now, or I would never do it.

There had always seemed to be some reason not to take that final step. Time commitments. Family commitments. The expense. The wrong season. Maybe next year. No more excuses. I had booked my flight to Darwin and made my arrangements. I just hadn't expected to have Suzie sitting beside me for the flight from Broome to the Mitchell Plateau.

Organising the trip had not been as easy as I had expected. There were many tour companies with itineraries in the region. Some even advertised tours of rock art but appeared to include only a few sites and mostly visited the other popular tourist attractions in the area.

Finally I had been given a name and had made contact

with a man who could guide me to various sites and explain the different styles of art and the changes in each style over time. He would be waiting to meet Suzie and me at the airstrip on the Mitchell Plateau. He would have camping gear and supplies for the days and nights we would spend in the bush.

If Suzie preferred the comfort of a motel room to our tent on the vehicle, I wondered how she would cope with the next few nights in a swag on the ground and a mosquito net over her. Would she accept the lack of showers and bathrooms for days? Perhaps I had been remiss in not warning her earlier. I really should give her an option before it was too late. "I have to warn you. Our accommodation for the next few nights will be very basic."

"How basic?"

"Really basic. Just a swag and a mosquito net. No facilities. You can change your mind and back out now. If you decide you don't want to go you can wait here in Broome until I get back. Book into a resort. I'll pay."

"I guess it will be an adventure. I'll manage. I know how much this means to you, and I'll stick with you. It should be an interesting experience. Anyway, at last you will get to see in situ the art that you have read so much about."

"It was after talking about it with you that I finally decided that I had to go—and not just think about it."

"Peter, I'm sorry I caused you so much trouble when we parted, but I suppose the good thing is that you decided to act."

I noticed she used the word 'parted', not 'separated'. I suppose we had never really been close enough to have 'separated'.

The small Cessna was waiting for us when we arrived at the airport. Flying north we had passed to the east of Talbot Bay and in the distance we had seen two very expensive looking boats anchored in the bay. A helicopter was approaching one boat and preparing to land on it. Then we left the blue waters behind and continued our flight over the scrub-covered country and approached the plateau.

The airstrip was a cleared strip of graded red dirt. The terminal, if it could be called that, was a flimsy construction of wood covered with green shade cloth. Under its shelter stood a table with two attached benches plus a large oil drum with a hole in the top that served as a rubbish bin. A sign board proudly proclaimed 'Mitchell Plateau—Arrivals and Departures Lounge'. Light aircraft were busy shuttling in sightseeing tourists from Broome and Derby, all heading for the Mitchell Falls. A few were boarding a helicopter for a quick comfortable flight over the falls, others were getting into four-wheel drive wagons for the half hour transit to the Falls. Standing off to one side was a man I recognised as our guide from the email he had sent me. When our pilot cut his engine and the propeller had stopped spinning he came over to the plane. He was a slight man with a wispy grey beard and a grey ponytail. Like so many tourist guides in the area he was deeply tanned and wearing khaki trousers and a khaki shirt with an emblem on the pocket. I noticed Suzie looking at him intently. I asked her if she was concerned.

"I had expected a big man, someone more my image of the outback bushman, and our guide is small. Without the tan, his big hat, wrap around sunglass and in different clothes, I could see him in an inner city coffee shop of Melbourne. He could be a member of my daughter's environment group."

"Well here he is in the environment, and experiencing it every day not just talking about it." When I had met Suzie's daughter I had been a little irritated by her environmental causes that were fashionable but failed to look at the ramifications and their effect on the lives of people. I thought she needed to consider the issues a bit more fully and consider all views rather than just blindly follow the latest popular cause.

Alan introduced himself to Suzie and me. He suggested we spend our first night in the campground at the Falls. There were some nearby sites with both styles of art where we could compare the difference. They were on the walk to the Falls, and since we were here we might as well have a look at the Falls. The four tiers of the Falls were all different and well worth seeing. Then the next day he would take us bush to some other sites he knew. Some were much less visited, and we would have to do some walking. He hoped we had taken his advice and brought good walking boots or shoes. Tonight, and tomorrow night we would be in campgrounds, but for our final night we would camp in the bush. He had all the necessary gear on the four-wheel drive. He had also arranged permission to visit certain sites away from the usual tourist route. The area was either National Park, Aboriginal land of some form, or private cattle stations. I looked across at the Toyota with its roof rack of swags and three old fashioned folding wire beds. At least Suzie would be off the ground and above any snakes. Also strapped to the roof rack were some strips of heavy steel mesh and a high lift jack. The cargo compartment of the vehicle appeared full of boxes and equipment, and I noticed two tyres, an axe and a shovel on the back door. I decided that I had picked a guide who was prepared for the local conditions.

The drive to the campground took us thirty minutes and the country we drove through was different to the dry looking land we had flown over. Here the livistonia palms gave it a different appearance, not really rainforest or lush tropics, but certainly different to the straggly woodlands we had seen from the aircraft. When we reached the campground Alan produced a cake and some biscuits and made us a pot of tea. "We'll give the day-trippers time to get up ahead of us. That way we can have a better look. From speaking with you I take it you know the difference between Wandjina and Gwion Gwion styles?"

I answered. "Yes, the Wandjina are the big faces and the Gwion Gwion are the elegant action figures."

"Yes. That's a simple difference. Both styles have various other forms as well. For example, the Bradshaws, or the Gwion Gwions as they are also called, have Tassel, Sash, Elegant Action and Clothes Peg styles. You will see some of the differences in the next few days. The Wandjinas are usually the ones most people see. They are the ones connected with the present day Aboriginal culture. Big faces without a mouth and big black eyes and a beak like nose. The faces are often in white.

"In the photos in Peter's book some of them have lines radiating out from their heads. What does that signify?"

Alan turned to Suzie. "It supposedly depicts lightning. The Dreamtime stories are that they are beings or spirits who came down from the sky and created the earth and its people. Then they disappeared into the earth and live at the bottom of the water sources they control. When you are out here you can understand how important water is. Some also returned to the sky and can be seen as lights moving across the sky at night. According to the culture they control everything that happens on land, sea and sky, especially the wet season storms and rain. Upset them, by breaking the law, will bring punishment by floods, lightning and cyclones. Don't mess with the Wandjinas."

"How old are they?"

"The accepted view is about three to maybe four thousand years old."

"That would make them about the same age as the earliest Egyptian pyramids." Suzie had obviously paid more attention in history class at school than I had.

"Yes, but these are paintings and not structures. The Gwion Gwion are much older, and there are even earlier paintings of animals. Since the Wandjinas are connected to the present day indigenous culture they are sometimes difficult to date. Certain elders have tribal responsibility to refresh them so they keep their power. Only those people are allowed to paint them or else!"

"Are they all the same?"

"No, all the major styles have variations. Probably over time ideas, beliefs or fashions changed. Look at European art. Here, artists from the different periods used the same rock ledges and caves so you can have a range of styles and ages all on the same wall or ceiling."

"When do we see some?"

"From the campground we have to walk. It's about four

kilometres each way. You don't drive up and just walk across from a bus to see these paintings. It's walk, walk, walk. I'll have plenty of water because it can get hot walking in this country, but it is best if you each carry a bottle as well."

Alan was right. The day was becoming much hotter. The walk wasn't hard, and crossing the creek we soon reached our first gallery at Little Mertens Falls. Climbing down a small rock face we reached a path leading to a cave behind the falls. There on a cliff face were the paintings I had come to see.

"You have both styles here. These are the Wandjinas down low. This other style up here is the Gwion Gwion. As well there are some paintings of animals."

"What age are the animal paintings?"

"They are thought to predate the Gwion Gwion. There are sites where the animal paintings could go back forty thousand years. It would indicate human habitation in the area at that time.

"The styles really are all quite different."

"Yes, you will become familiar with the different styles of Gwion Gwion over the next couple of days. You will also see the other styles. As well there are some petroglyphs. They are cupules, incisions and grooves that mark the rock. They could be even older but possibly cover a wide range of epochs."

Suzie asked a question. "What is the difference between Gwion Gwion and Bradshaw?"

Alan answered. "They are the same. Joseph Bradshaw was the first European who saw them in 1891. Originally they were named after him. Then later it was decided that really they should have an Aboriginal name. Gwion Gwion refers to the bird, the sandstone shrike thrush, that was supposed to make them. Pecking at the rock with its long beak searching for insects it drew blood and made the images. Different tribes have different names for the bird in their own languages."

"Don't all Aborigines speak the same language?"

Again Alan answered Suzie's question. "No. Each tribal group has, or had, its own language. It's thought there would have been around two hundred and fifty languages and dialects when Europeans arrived. Some claim there were even more. Many have died out completely. Others have only a few speakers left. Nowadays there are thought to be perhaps one hundred and fifty languages still surviving, although many of them are endangered. Probably only twenty or so are commonly used."

"So how did the various tribes communicate?"

"Some languages are closely related, but others are quite different. Of course there were often some people who knew enough of another language to be able to communicate with the next tribe, but these days, across the north anyway, it is usually a form of English. It's called Kriol, a sort of pidgin English."

"I thought creole was a mix of French and African in the southern part of the USA. When you say creole I think of New Orleans, and the food and music."

Suzie and I had shared the same thought.

"That's true, but creole can also refer to a mix of languages. Here it is spelt k-r-i-o-l. It came out of a mix of

English and the local languages. A sort of pidgin English that developed at the Roper River Mission in the Northern Territory in the early twentieth century so the missionaries and the different groups in the area could communicate."

"So it isn't really a traditional language?"

"That's correct, Suzie. By the nineteen sixties it was being used for church services and had spread westward across the north into the Kimberley. It is now considered a language in its own right. Since then it has even developed local variations. However, because it uses some local indigenous words and concepts, communities only a few hundred kilometres apart may speak different versions. For example, Ngukurr and Beswick near Katherine. Some, like the Gurindji, even claim their form of Kriol, which mixes Kriol with their traditional language, as yet another separate language. However it does help tribal groups that otherwise could not talk together communicate in a common language. Like everything indigenous it becomes very tangled. There are questions whether the traditional language should be taught in preference to Kriol, or should standard English be taught. It can be a hot potato."

"When did the Gwion Gwion period happen?" I asked. Already I was getting a sense of the complexity and sensitivities of the culture around us.

"The Gwion Gwion are thought to be seventeen thousand years old, perhaps even as far back as twenty-five thousand years. The dating is difficult because they are made with ochre that has fused with the rock. There was no organic material used to create them so you cannot date them that way. They have got an age by dating mud wasps' nests built over the art. There's a lot of discussion about how old they are. I believe there are some new techniques of dating about to be tried. That may resolve some of the uncertainty. Of course some paintings are older than others, so everyone has an opinion about 'their' sites."

"So that makes them much older than the Wandjinas?"

"Much. In fact they are possibly the oldest art portraying humans in the world. That's what is so interesting about them, and the puzzle."

Again Suzie's history lessons came to the fore. "So they could be older than the Palaeolithic paintings in the Lascaux Caves in France which are around seventeen thousand three hundred years old. I've seen those paintings but they are of animals, not people."

"Yes. Some of the paintings here showing human forms could be older than even the recently discovered animal paintings in Spain."

"You spoke of a puzzle. So what happened between the two periods? The Wandjinas and the Bradshaws? There is at least fourteen thousand years unaccounted."

"This is where it gets interesting, Peter. Forty thousand years ago this region was thought to have been open tropical forest and woodland. Then the last ice age arrived eighteen to twenty thousand years ago, and this region became dry and arid. At this time the sea level dropped one hundred and forty metres and Australia was connected by land to New Guinea. What is now Indonesia was only ninety kilometres away across water. This dry period could have put pressure on the civilisation and it is thought the Kimberley may have been emptied of people. Then with the climate changing again, a new culture emerged."

We continued our walk. We passed through the shade of a patch of rainforest and off to our left came the sound of water running over rapids. Alan turned away from the path and led us down to the creek. There above us on a rock slab was more of the Bradshaw art.

Walking on we crossed the shallow water above the Big Mertens Falls with its sheer drop to a pool far below. Then, after passing across rocks and boulders and through spikey spinifex grass, in front of us was the Mitchell Falls proper with its four falls each tumbling into a pool before starting over the next fall to another pool. Alan led us on to the lookout. Around us, the rocks of the gorges carved out by the river showed a variety of colours: reds, yellows, various greys and browns. In the heat of the afternoon Suzie and I decided against taking the walking track to the base of the falls. We also decided against the ease of a waiting helicopter offering a quick flight to our campground. After resting a while, we turned on our tracks to head back towards our swags for the night.

Walking past the pool at Little Mertens Falls Suzie noticed some swimmers in the pool.

"Is it safe to swim there?"

Alan replied. "Yeah. The rangers check it. The crocs don't come up this far. You are safe here but I wouldn't go anywhere downstream. Especially down near the coast. The crocs are bad down there. If in doubt, don't!"

The water looked very tempting, but neither Suzie or I were dressed to plunge in. I didn't think my jocks would pass the test in the water. I could see Suzie was giving the idea some thought. We were both hot and sweaty, but even she was not ready to strip to bra and panties in public.

8 Bushed

Peter

Back at the campground Alan set up our beds and swags and covered them with a framework and a light tarpaulin. At this time of year he doubted we would need a mosquito net. Then, while Suzie and I tried to remove the day's dust in a small pan of water, he set about preparing a meal. By the time we had finished washing, a casserole was bubbling over a small fire, while beside it potatoes and vegetables simmered in a second pot. He offered us a choice of cold beers or a bottle of wine from the fridge in his vehicle.

"I can only offer you each two stubbies a night. My supply is limited by the space in the fridge and the food we need for our trip."

We accepted his offer of the beers and sat down on the chairs he had produced from the back of his vehicle. It was a lot more comfortable than sitting cross-legged in the dust of the campsite. Then we had his flavoursome casserole and chatted.

Alan was full of information. "The boat you saw with the helicopter would probably be the Kimberley Quest. It does cruises along the coast from Broome to Wyndham, or Wyndham to Broome. Sometimes it has a helicopter on board for sightseeing and ferrying people ashore. There has been another privately owned boat poking around the coast lately. Some rich foreigner owns it. My mate, he's another guide, was talking about it last night. There were some Chinese on it. He thinks they were from Singapore. Two couples. The men looked as if they would be happier on a golf course and weren't very interested in sightseeing. He didn't know why they were there. The women were real stunners. One of them was interested in what they were visiting, but the other was a real pain."

I was curious. "In what way?"

"Never happy. Turned up in shoes with big chunky soles and wedgy sort of heels. Tottered around everywhere. Always complaining and demanding. I think her boyfriend was getting very tired of her demands. I reckon she'll be bushed when he gets home."

"Bushed?" Suzie obviously didn't understand Alan's idiom.

I explained. "You know bush is country with shrubs and small trees as opposed to forests with big trees. It can also mean country away from big cities. To go bush means to go out into the countryside. To get bushed means to become lost. I've heard John Satto, who we will meet next week, use the term when talking about drafting in his cattle yards. He'd call 'bush' when he wanted an animal drafted into a yard with other animals that were being returned to their paddock. However, in this case Alan means the man will dump his girlfriend when he returns to Singapore. He's had enough of her. You understand bush now?"

Alan broke in. "I'm bushed if I know."

"So you don't think they were married?"

Alan answered Suzie's question. "From my mate's description I think the girls had found some rich boyfriends to indulge them, and vice-a-versa. You know what I mean. He reckons the wives were probably at home playing mahjong or something."

"I have a question for you, Alan." Suzie had obviously been thinking about something apart from two good time girls and their futures. "With the Wandjinas, they have white faces. Yet the artists are black, very black. What is the significance of the white faces?"

"Wandjinas are spirit beings, not real people. Most cultures make some distinction. Think of halos on saints, angels with wings. There are all sorts of religious and cultural imagery. It is generally considered as being the cultural way of depicting a spirit as opposed to a human being."

"When we were in Derby, Peter showed me a book with photos of Wandjinas. That night I had a dream. Well, more a nightmare. I was surrounded by Wandjinas and the image of a girl we had seen briefly in Darwin. Then I felt a sense of foreboding and death." Suzie looked across the dying embers of the fire to me. "I didn't tell you because it seemed so silly, but now having seen the images in reality I don't have that feeling anymore."

Suzie may have lost the sense of foreboding and death, but I suddenly felt a coldness settle over me, and a feeling that something was waiting for us. Out there, somewhere in our futures.

We woke with the sunrise and the raucous sound of black

cockatoos screeching in the bush. Around us campers were already packing their vehicles preparing to continue their treks. Today our plan was to move on to some more sites that Alan knew and then spend the night at the crossing of the King Edward River after visiting sites close to the river. Before we left, Suzie and I decided a quick swim in the waterhole at Little Mertens was necessary. This time we were dressed to plunge in, cool off and remove the dust.

With Alan behind the wheel we drove out of the campground and headed towards the intersection with the Kalumburu road. Before we reached the crossing at the King Edward River we stopped, left the car, and Alan led us along a walking track. At several small sites were more of the Wandjina and Bradshaw art I had come to see.

Returning to our vehicle we drove on until we were almost at the river crossing. Alan parked beside a straggly clump of trees and again we walked. Here in an area of sandstone boulders he pointed out a group of wonderful Wandjina figures.

Over a pot of tea and some sandwiches Alan had produced from his supplies we discussed the paintings we had seen. "After lunch I will take you to another site that has Bradshaws, and then to a site with work that is even older. It has paintings of plants and animals. That particular era is called the 'Naturalistic Animal Period'. It will be obvious when you see the paintings."

The collection of the Bradshaw stick figures that Alan took us to were so old the paint had vanished and only the stain of the artwork remained on the rock.

He explained the paintings. "Some Bradshaws look as if the parts of the body are disconnected, but it is because some colours have faded so much and have completely disappeared. That style is thought to be the youngest of the Gwion Gwions, or possibly even a later style. Another puzzle is that many of the Bradshaw styles have been damaged, apparently deliberately, and sometimes overpainted. Yet the elegant action style figures are not damaged. Nor do they appear to have had images superimposed on them."

"I've noticed a lot of stencil images of hands. Where do they fit in?"

"My understanding is that they are after the Gwion Gwion but before the Wandjina. Another difference between Wandjinas and Bradshaws are the location. Wandjinas are painted on ledges and the ceilings of larger rock shelters which could have been used as living quarters. Bradshaws are generally found painted on the sides of cliffs. They are usually less protected by rock overhands. They also have a much wider regional distribution."

The older paintings of plants and animals had intrigued me. I had known of the Wandjinas and Bradshaws. What I had not expected to see was so many paintings of different styles all together, sometimes even painted over an earlier painting. I had known nothing of the earliest naturalistic style.

Once again Alan led us on a walk. This time we followed the river downstream before turning away from the river and scrambling through the bush. In the distance a solitary dingo silently disappeared into the high grass. Soon our guide had led us to more small displays of artwork.

"How many sites of art are known? There must be a great number?"

Alan answered Suzie's question. "Graeme Walsh, who did a huge amount of work in this region, claimed to have recorded fifteen hundred sites and over one and a half million images. Certainly there are very many recorded and photographed. How many are still undiscovered or forgotten I wouldn't know."

As the afternoon shadows lengthened we returned to our campsite beside the river. By now we were experienced bush campers and helped Alan set up the beds, the swags and the fly sheets. Tonight he had promised us an Indonesian meal and very soon two courses of stir-fry and some rice appeared on the folding table. To conclude the meal he brought out some ice-creams from his freezer in the back of the car. It was strange to be sitting in a campground in a remote corner of the Kimberley eating an ice-cream; thousands of kilometres from where it had been made.

I thought now might be the time to find out more about our guide. "Have you always lived in the Kimberley?"

"No, my parents lived in Melbourne. My mum still does, the old dear. I grew up down there and went to school there. But after I got married my wife and I had a few issues and we split the blanket. I saved a few bob and bought a van and headed north. I picked up jobs here and there and eventually ended up in north Queensland. By then I'd decided I'd never make a surfie. I kept falling off, and I don't like sharks and stingers so I decided to head inland. Eventually I got to Katherine and tossed a coin to see if I'd go north or west. Headed west and got here. Well Kununurra, and decided this was the country for me. I loved the colours and the space. And the people."

"But you're not in Kununurra now, are you?"

"No. I came over to Broome for a visit and there were seasonal jobs available in the tourist industry so I got one. Then I met this woman. So I ended up staying."

"Is she still here?" This time Suzie asked the question.

"Yeah. This one worked out. I found a good woman. Someone that sticks with you when things get tough. We've been together twenty-one years now."

"Do you have any children?"

When it comes to relationships and families women always seem so much more upfront than men, and I had already discovered Suzie was no different in asking those sorts of questions.

"Two. A boy, he's working down in the iron ore mines, and Kate. She's finishing school at the end of the year. She wants to be a nurse."

"I suppose that means she will have to leave home?"

"Yeah. She'll probably go down to Perth. She'll find that a bit different to Broome."

I decided to bring the subject back to where we were. "Where did you pick up your knowledge about Aboriginal rock art?"

"Poking around, reading, talking to people. I had a job taking tour groups through the country. That took in a few sites. Then I got interested and started reading up on it. I got lucky. A group of researchers wanted someone to take them around, and I got the job so I learnt a lot from them. It just built up from there. I haven't got a piece of paper but I reckon I've seen more sites than most of the academics who study it."

"How do you find the academics? I believe there are a few controversies about the art?"

"There certainly are. Walsh was an amateur. He had no university degree or anything. Anyway, he had a few ideas about who did the painting. His theory didn't fit the current politics about Aboriginal culture. That's upset some people. There can be a lot of egos and status, and sometimes just plain bitchiness in some academic circles. And of course his theory upset the Ab politics."

"How?"

"Walsh reckoned the art was much older than the stuff the present indigenous people claim as theirs. He was right. He also reckoned it was much more sophisticated in its depiction of people and animals. I suppose sophistication is in the eye of the beholder, but it does seem more complex. Anyway, if the art is older than the Wandjina stuff, and more complex, what happened to the Gwion Gwion culture? Did it die out? Did a new group arrive and drive out the first group or did the early group move on and the land become vacant?"

"So what's the answer?" Alan's comments had certainly raised some interesting questions.

"There are various theories. There are later peg figure Bradshaws showing groups of figures as if preparing to fight—perhaps over scarce resources. Or perhaps the culture slowly changed and lost its sophistication. This affects present day politics. If new arrivals from Southeast Asia drove out the earlier group, then the present mob are not the original people. Makes it a bit hard to argue with the British.

If their culture went backwards, that doesn't look good either. It also brings into question how old the culture is. You can't claim to go back sixty thousand years if that culture is not really yours. So some want to claim the Gwion Gwion culture but early reports show the old fellas denying it was theirs. There can be a bit of rewriting of history at times!

"It certainly raises some interesting questions."

"When you live up here mate, you see the politics that goes on within the indigenous groups. Who gets what. Which families are on top. Who gets the plum positions in some of the organisations. Then you have the guilt business. Keep the southerners feeling guilty so the money keeps flowing."

"So what's your opinion?" I was interested in hearing Alan's thoughts.

"I don't know. You get one idea then another. It does seem that there was a culture here that did the Bradshaws or Gwion Gwion as they became known. You couldn't have an Aboriginal art named after a white man, could you? So that had to change. That culture appeared to have died out. Maybe it was an ice age that changed the environment. The dates could fit. Anyway, the culture weakened and faded or even died out completely. Perhaps a new wave of migrants moved in from Southeast Asia and was the base of what we have now. There needs to be a lot more work done to find answers, but of course some people don't really want to find out if it upsets their ideas."

"I can see a lot of contentious issues. Land rights, climate change, migrants and refugees, funding."

"Yeah, and jobs, respect, status. It's a rat's nest of issues.

I'll leave it to others to sort that out."

"What about people from outer space?"

"You've heard that one have you, Peter? There is an idea that spacemen came down, and the Wandjina figures show them in their spacesuits. Then they decided they had enough of the locals and shot through again. There are also theories that the culture was into hallucinogenics—that suits the hippy lot—or that the paintings show men taking the power away from women—that irritates the feminists. Pick your poison!"

I suspected Alan was like me and thought the spacemen theory was a bit farfetched. But the idea pops up all over the world. I remembered hearing that the Nazca Lines in southern Peru were a landing field for spaceships or something similar. These ideas had always intrigued me. "The spacemen always seem to look like the astronauts who landed on the moon. If, or when, someone lands on Earth from outer space, they will probably have much more developed technology, and God knows what they will look like. Probably be a cockroach or a bug of some type." I could see Suzie didn't like my choice of interstellar visitor.

Again the day began at sunrise. When you are away from electric lights and power at the click of a switch your life changes. Today Alan planned to take us towards Kalumburu and on the way see some more sites. Once again we would have to walk.

Over breakfast, as I listened to a cool gentle breeze moving through the surrounding trees, I thought of the thousand or more generations of families that would have passed over this land. How would they have resolved the personal tensions we can all have? How would they have associated with their neighbours? Faced the changes in weather patterns? Decide to propitiate their Gods or Spirits? How would I have lived in those earlier times?

Unlike the previous day, our visits today were on land that was not accessible to the normal run of tourists. Some were located on country controlled by Aboriginal groups and some on a privately owned cattle station. Here the landscape was different to that which we had seen on the plateau proper. Gone were the palm trees, and the land seemed much drier. Nevertheless, Alan told us that even here we would find rugged country with escarpments and shelters that held treasuries of art.

The camp for our third night was out in the bush in a clearing beside the track. Alan had selected the campsite well away from rivers or creeks and warned us to take care if near water. We were back in crocodile country.

The campsite was tidy but looked as if it was used only infrequently. Whoever had stayed before us had been very careful to remove any rubbish and to care for the area, unlike some campsites we had seen. Here there were no overflowing rubbish bins or litter. Alan raked away the leaves from the area that had previously been used for cooking and set up his small gas barbeque.

"I'm very careful about fire. It can so easily get away if you aren't super careful. Then there is no way to control it. You can burn out a lot of country from one small leaf or twig that isn't put out."

"How do you fight fires here?" The question had been on my mind for some time. As we had travelled across the north we had seen large plumes of smoke in the distance, often in the hottest part of the afternoon. I was sure Alan could answer my query.

"Unfortunately if a fire starts, say with lightning, or by accident, or deliberately, it can be a big problem. It can burn huge areas because there is no access to round it up. You've probably seen the smoke and some burnt areas in your travels. If you have a grader or dozer perhaps you can make a break around it and then burn a wider break to enclose the fire. A fire with the wind behind it can jump over a firebreak made by a grader, and fires make their own wind. Anyway, often the equipment isn't available in the area. It could be hundreds of miles away. Besides, there aren't many people available to actually fight the fire. Sometimes fires just burn until the rains start and put them out. Other times a fire will reach country that has already been burnt and stop. It also depends on the seasons. I have seen fires early in the wet season burn what appears to be green grass. The reason is that there is a lot of dry undergrowth which will carry the fire until the heat dries the green grass and then it burns."

"Don't the Aboriginal people use fire to manage the country?"

Alan answered Suzie's question.

"Yes. According to tradition they will burn a small area to encourage fresh re-growth so kangaroos and wallabies will come in and graze there and make hunting easier. In the old days that would be very important. Unfortunately, these fires can easily get out of control and become wildfires. These days I suspect the management is not quite so careful.

We hear about traditional practices but the reality can be different. Once a fire starts at this time of the year it can be very difficult to put out. You can't just burn a small patch: it won't stop unless it is very early in the dry season when it might go out overnight. The theory's great, but putting it into practise is another thing."

"The cattlemen must hate fire. It would burn all their grass." The thought of all the smoke we had seen was still fresh in my mind.

"The pastoralists also use fire to manage the country. Depending on the type of fire, the time of the year, and the vegetation coupled with grazing pressure from animals, the desirable plant species in the burnt area can be increased or harmed. It is a case of balancing the loss of feed quantity and improving the quality of the pasture."

"With the rock art scattered over such a huge area it must be a problem protecting it from fire?"

"Yes. Many have been damaged. Unfortunately fire is part of the environment out here. Lightning, lightning strikes, wildfires are part of nature. Protective burns are used to reduce the intensity of fire but it is still fire. It is impossible to protect every single rock ledge or gallery.

Sitting beside our small barbeque with a beer, a steak and some boiled vegetables, just the three of us in the wilderness, the immenseness and emptiness of the region came home to me. Even to get here had meant a long flight from the other side of the continent. Then days of driving if the roads were passable, or hours in a light aircraft, and then more driving. In Europe we would have crossed many countries. Cairo was closer to London than this camp was to my home in Sydney. Even then the number of people in the country for hundreds of kilometres around us could be measured in the hundreds, and most of them were tourists.

Nor had I expected the grandeur of the country. While often it could seem endlessly the same, over time you became aware of the subtle changes in the landscape. Then there were the gorges. The rock walls showed a palette of colours, and the power of nature and its rainfall over millenniums.

Today would be our final morning on the plateau. We had a commitment to be back at the Mitchell Falls airstrip for our return flight to Broome. Over breakfast I asked Alan about the local people.

"Like anywhere, there are good people and bad people. They just want to get on with their lives. They have lots of problems. Really they don't know what they want. Or more accurately, they know what they want but it doesn't fit into the modern world. They want their old way of life, their languages and culture, but they also want all the benefits of the modern world. Toyotas, cash, health services and schools. The kids want the latest fashions from the States that they see on TV. They have them but they don't value them because they don't have to work to get them. The kids don't see the benefit of going to school. I guess I didn't when I was their age either. The young don't want the discipline of the old ways, and the elders feel that they don't get respect."

"Where do they get the money?"

"Royalties from mines or gas fields, perhaps income from a cattle station they own, government benefits and business ventures set up for them. But often they don't have to work for it and they fritter it away."

I could see Suzie's growing concern. "Surely that must be changing?"

"Sometimes you think it is, then you see situations and you despair. Unfortunately, like the rest of us, they are also prone to the scourges of the modern world: drugs, gambling, and other social problems. They go seeking help for some program that will change their lives, but they aren't prepared to put in the sweat to make it work. I'd better be careful or I could talk myself out of a job. Tourists would love to do this trip with a full blood Aboriginal man or woman as a guide, but so few of them want to make the commitment that is needed to learn what to do and turn up for work every day. They do a training course and get a job but then go bush when it suits them. That doesn't work when somebody has paid thousands of dollars travelling across the country, or the world, to get here."

"Do you see a solution?"

"No. Not while they can go on TV, claim 'poor bugger me, it's your fault' and ask for more help. I guess change will only happen when they decide to pay the price of being in the real world. They will have to make that decision themselves. One day they will realise there are more new migrants in Australia than there are people claiming to be Aboriginal. The new comers won't have the same feeling of owing the Abs a living."

Our return flight once again took us over the edge of the waters of Talbot Bay. Again our timing was wrong. We were heading south, but the rapidly lowering sun to our west hindered our view, and we could see no sign of the rush of water that caused the Horizontal Waterfalls. It was late afternoon and becoming dark as we landed at Broome airport. After the days in the bush and the dust we both wanted a long hot shower to remove the sweat and the fine red dust that had crept into our every pore. Then we wanted a long cool drink. I had heard of just the place that would provide the drink and could be interesting.

9 The Roey

Suzie

When I told the receptionist at the resort that we thought we might go to the Roebuck Bay Hotel for a counter meal he had suggested that perhaps we might prefer the resort restaurant, or a restaurant at one of the bigger hotels. He also suggested several other possibilities for dining. "It's Thursday night" was his comment.

The beer garden of the hotel was alive. The noise from the band could be heard blocks away and the bar was packed with men. I did notice the house rules stipulated footwear—thongs would be adequate—but that seemed to be the only rule. Singlets and shorts were the fashionable style for both the men and the women. Singlets for the men appeared optional. I suddenly understood why the man in the office of the campground had given me a strange look and offered an alternative. We were certainly out of our scene. Of all the nights to pick we had chosen Thursday. Wet T-shirt Thursday night at the Roey.

"Did you know it was wet T-shirt night?"

"No. I'd just heard some tourists saying that it was an interesting place to see the locals. They reckoned there were some real characters."

"Well that's certainly looks like being true!"

As the T-shirts became wetter and briefer the noise from the crush of spectators egging them on further—or to less modesty and no T-shirts—increased. Then on the far side of the room I saw her. The girl with the purple hair was talking to two men. Both men were deeply tanned. One, with long unruly sun-bleached blond hair, was wearing a singlet, shorts and thongs, the other was well-groomed with a shaven head and wearing shorts and a polo shirt with some sort of logo on it that I could not make out. Looking at them across the room I thought of Django in Wyndham. Would they suffer the same fate? By the expression on her face Magenta was far from happy. Nor were the men looking pleased. There was tension between them, but from a distance it was impossible to know what it might be. The blond man went to the bar, bought drinks for the group, and returned to Magenta and his companion. Then, suddenly, Magenta left. As she walked away I saw her take her mobile phone from her shoulder bag and dial a number. The blond man was left holding three full glasses. I had no idea of how long they had been together. It was only when the crowd had moved that I had glimpsed them. By the time I attracted Peter's attention away from a rather brazen and buxom brunette in a very tight and wet T-shirt Magenta had vanished. Even I was left wondering if I had really seen her.

Peter and I kept watching the men as we finished our meal. There seemed to be some disagreement between them, but of course from the distance and with the noise we had no idea of what it could be. As the two men continued to refill their glasses their attitude to each other became more aggressive. While it had not become physical, the body language certainly suggested that violence could easily eventuate.

I was glad to escape from the bar with its noise and crowded revellers. Wet T-shirt competitions had been a fad when I was at teacher's college but I had never taken part. While I loved a party such exhibitionism was not part of my personality. Walking back to our resort I asked Peter what he thought of the evening's entertainment.

"I think the competition favours girls with big personalities, or big ... attributes. I suspect that may be their downfall in the future."

I looked at Peter. I wasn't sure whether he was serious or joking. "So what's your preference?"

"Personality. I've never understood girls who go in such competitions. Is it a need for attention? What drives them? You're a woman."

Thinking back to my youth, and the girls I had known who joined in such behaviour, it did seem to attract a certain type of personality. There was a mix of exhibitionism tinged with a need for attention. It also favoured girls with big bosoms. Perhaps that was why I was never interested. Where were those girls now? Where had life taken them? I had never kept in contact with them as our lives had taken different directions. "The boys may have liked wet T-shirt competitions, but there were also hairy chest competitions. Did you ever take part?"

"Oh, I was a prize winner. Twice."

I had a sudden flashback to the time when we had run away to Hayman Island and I had felt Peter's naked body beside mine. Then I had been shocked by the feel of his hairy chest and back, but now it was unimportant. It was the personality, sometimes serious, sometimes amusing, that I enjoyed being with. We fell into our large white bed and curled up together with the gentle swoosh of an overhead fan, and the smell of a tropical night wafting through the louvered screen doors, and I had a private bathroom!

I had decided to give Peter a present. Flying back from the Plateau he had been in conversation with our pilot about the Horizontal Falls. Peter had heard other tourists discussing how much they had enjoyed seeing them. He had also been curious about the Buccaneer Archipelago. The pilot had diverted his track to the west and flown over the Falls but the tide was not running. He had also told us you really had to be on the water to feel the full effect. The thought of the Falls had intrigued me, and I thought it would be great if we could see them. We would have to take a float plane to Talbot Bay and then be met by a fast boat which could take us up to and then through the Falls. On our flight we would fly over the mass of islands that made up the Archipelago named after the vocation of the English pirate who first charted the coast for his country in 1688. It all sounded rather exciting.

I made the arrangements. I had decided that rather than fly out and see the Falls we would make a day of it. It would be an early start. We would be picked up from our resort and travel by four-wheel drive to Beagle Bay and see the church built from pearl shell. I had a vague memory of once seeing pictures of the church. I couldn't remember if it was in a book or a documentary movie I had seen. Then we would travel on to Cape Leveque for breakfast. From there a float plane would pick us up and fly us across water and some more of the red and green Kimberley country to land on Talbot Bay. This flight would take us over the hundreds, or almost a thousand small islands, that make up the Buccaneer Archipelago. On landing at Talbot Bay we would be met by a fast boat that would be our ride into the Falls.

The road to Beagle Bay was bumpy. After the time spent searching out rock shelters I was becoming used to rough travel. I was also looking forward to the time when we would see some kinder, softer vegetation than the harsh dry grasses and bushes of the Kimberley.

Somewhere in my memory I had recalled the church at Beagle Bay with its altar of pearl shell, but I knew little about it. French Trappists had set up a Catholic mission and school in the late eighteen hundreds. Then German Pallottine missionaries had replaced them, and together with local workers, had built the little church in 1918. At that time the missionaries were themselves internees due to the Great War in Europe. Pearl shell and other shells decorated the altar and formed inlays in the floor giving the church a very special and unique feeling. Approaching its centenary, the building was still in use for masses and baptisms and had survived the ravages of cyclones and ants, the heat and damp, and age. It was pleasing to find that renovation work was planned to preserve the efforts of earlier generations.

I was relieved when we arrived at Cape Leveque and saw our float plane waiting. No more rough roads! As we came in to land on the calm waters of Talbot Bay I saw a large white boat lying at anchor. I wondered if it was the boat with the demanding girl that Alan had spoken of, or if it was a different cruise boat. The captain of our fast boat taking us to the Falls told me it was the Kimberley Quest, one of the luxury cruise boats that specialised in the region. The foreign boat had left two days earlier. He didn't get close enough to see its name but he had also seen it here about a year ago.

From the plane we had looked down on the hills and water, and the combination of cerulean water, white sand and the red hills had been spectacular. Down at water level we could see so much more variation in the hills. They weren't just red but had splashes of yellow and even white speckled or streaked across them. The green of the scattered vegetation formed tracery lines across the vivid colours. The patterns were beautiful, like some sort of colourful modern abstract painting.

Then we reached the Horizontal Falls themselves and the world changed. Surging through the narrow opening between two cliffs the power of the water immediately hit us. All the water from the huge tides that had pushed through the narrow opening was now rushing back out breaking and tumbling over itself creating waves and whirlpools that grabbed our boat and bounced it around as if it was a tiny toy. Finally, we were through into calmer water. I'm not an adrenalin junkie but even I was caught up in the excitement. I looked across at Peter and he was like a small boy with a big smile on his face. My gift had been enjoyed.

On our final night in Broome we decided to celebrate fulfilling Peter's ambition. We walked down to the bar and I decided on two gin-based Summer Mules. I thought we needed something different and unusual to mark the occasion. Sitting in the cool elegant surrounds of the resort, we were a world away from the red dusty shrubby country where we had spent days driving and walking as we searched out rock shelters and caves with the art he had come to see.

Looking across the room I saw two men. I pointed them out to Peter. Alan's mate was right; the girls with them were very attractive. With their grooming and clothes they would have stood out as beauties in any company. It was also obvious one girl was unhappy. She looked to be in a petulant mood with a sulky look on her face and took no part in the conversation between the other girl and the two men. Peter leant over and whispered in my ear. I knew what Alan's mate meant when he said the girl would be bushed when they returned to Singapore. The girl knew it already.

10 The Body

Suzie

Peter had often spoken of his friend John Satto. He had first met him during a visit to Perth and a friendship had developed. They had met on a number of occasions over the years, and John had several times visited Peter and his wife when in Sydney. Yet Peter had never had the opportunity to visit John at his home on the station about an hour's drive south of Broome.

We had arrived mid-morning, and after lunch John had taken us out for a drive around the station. At this time of the year they were very busy. One stock camp was drafting steers for sale to Indonesia and John was expecting a buyer to look at them in two days' time. Meanwhile the second camp was preparing to muster another mob of breeders and wean their calves. There was work to be done to make sure the yards that would be used were ready and in top repair, the road to the yards had to be graded and suitable for the station road-train so they could truck weaners back to the weaner yards, fresh horses had to be made ready for the stock camp, and fuel put in place for the helicopters that would do the mustering. For this paddock they were planning to use two machines. With one helicopter some cattle would break away when the helicopter was on the far side of the paddock and it would take time to round up the breakaways and bring them back into the mob. John explained that it worked out cheaper to use two machines and spend less time. Since you paid by the hour for the helicopter hire and fuel, time was important. It also meant less stress on the animals, and that was also important.

Driving around the huge paddocks I thought of my childhood in the Riverina. There the paddocks had been large but they were tiny compared to here. The pastures were different and the livestock were also different. I had grown up with Merino sheep and Hereford cattle. Here the cattle were mostly grey Brahmans with a few honey or red coloured ones in the mobs. John had decided to breed grey when he had introduced a change in the genetics of the herd. At that stage colour was important to buyers but that had all changed as the markets developed. Now the market wanted performance in feedlots, and it was a case of balancing feedlot efficiency with fertility and growth on the station's native pastures. In this country it was a difficult balancing act!

At night as we sat around the table enjoying a glass of red—Peter had warned me of John's love of red wine—the two men caught up on their recent experiences, including our adventures in Ballarat. Their stories became wilder and wilder as the night progressed. I left them to their tall tales and found my bed.

Next morning we were sitting at the homestead having breakfast when a Toyota tray back came racing up to the house leaving a trail of dust in its wake. The driver came running over to the table.

"Boss, there's a dead woman down on the beach. She's

locked in a car."

John settled the man down and we got the story. Jimmy had the day off from work so he decided to drive down to the beach to do some fishing. The station ran to the Indian Ocean and its boundary on the western side was the Eighty Mile beach. When he got to the parking spot there was another vehicle already there. That wasn't unusual. There were often fishermen or tourists parked there, sometimes camping overnight or even for a few days. The beach was famous for the shells that washed up on the shoreline. When he walked past the car he looked in and there was a girl slumped in the driver's seat. He reckoned she looked a bit strange. He looked closer. She was dead.

"Dead. Are you sure?"

"Yeah boss. She was dead. She had the look. At first I thought she was listening to music. She had those things in her ears, but when I got close I could see that something wasn't right. I tried to open the door to check but they were all locked. The windows were all up. I couldn't get in. Boss, she looks a weird chick. Funny hair. I decided to come back here and tell you. I'm sure she's dead. You had better ring the police."

"OK Jimmy, I'll do that. Then we had better get down there and wait for the police. Will you come with me Peter?"

"Can I come too?" I decided that I would rather be with Peter than sitting at the remote homestead.

As we drove up to the parking spot near the beach we could see the vehicle. It was a small van with a painting of Elvis Presley on the side, but it was empty. There was no young woman with magenta hair on one side of her head. There was no dead body.

11 Properly Dead

Peter

That evening Suzie and I were sitting around the table outside the staff quarters with John and the other station workers discussing the morning's finding. It was a warm night with a gentle cooling breeze, but around the table the feeling was one of confusion. Nobody doubted that Jimmy had seen the car with a body in it. The car was still there, but where was the body? Jimmy was not the sort of person who imagined such things, unlike a few people whose names were mentioned—they could imagine things when they were on a bender.

According to Jimmy the girl was dead and the car doors were locked. Perhaps she wasn't really dead.

"She was dead." Jimmy was definite.

"Are you sure?"

"Yeah boss, she was properly dead. I haven't seen a dead body before but I've seen plenty of dead cows and calves. I know the look. The eyes. She was dead!" There was no doubt in Jimmy's opinion.

"Yer missus reckons you've been smoking the gunja again Jimmy. You've been seein' things." The comment came from an older man who had been sitting at the far end of the table quietly nursing his beer.

"I give it up a long time ago Fred. She just doesn't believe me. I did see a body. She was properly dead I tell you."

"What do you mean 'properly dead'?" The question came from Suzie who had been following the conversation.

John Satto explained. "It's local lingo. Comes from the indigenous. To them 'dead' means sick. 'Properly dead' means you really are dead. But if she was dead where has she gone?" There was a touch of uncertainty in his voice as he asked the question. "Dead bodies don't sit up, unlock the door and walk away locking the door behind them. Someone must have taken her. But why? And who?"

"And how about the locked door?" I asked the question because it puzzled me. If there was a dead body in the car, and the door was locked, whoever removed her would need a key. Jimmy was quite adamant that the car was undamaged. He'd checked the driver's side and passenger side doors. They were locked. The sliding side door was locked, the windows up, and no broken windows. The keys were in the ignition. To get into the car somebody would need another key.

"Who else would have a key to the van? She was just a tourist checking out the beach." John's remarks made sense. Someone who just happened to turn up would hardly have a key, or the inclination to hide a body. That doesn't make sense.

"Were the keys still in the ignition?" It was Fred again. He'd just come back from the fridge with another beer.

"Yeah. I said I saw 'em there. I'm sure they were in the ignition. They had something hanging down from the ring."

Jimmy was confident he had seen the keys locked in the car.

"I saw the keys lying on the floor when I went down with the police. At that stage the doors were all locked and the windows up, no body, but the keys weren't in the ignition. They were lying on the floor." John Satto's information only compounded our puzzle. Were the keys inside the car when Jimmy found the body? Jimmy was quite sure they were in the ignition. But if they were, how did someone enter the car? Why remove the body, and why lock the doors leaving the keys inside? Maybe Jimmy was mistaken. Perhaps a door key was missing from the key ring when he had found the body. Someone else had it, removed the body when Jimmy left and then locked the keys in the car. That would be possible. But it still didn't make any sense.

"Jimmy, did you see anyone around, or any tracks, when you were down there this morning?"

I had always liked my friend's logical way of thinking. For John problems were there to be solved, and to him this was another problem. Perhaps it was because we thought in similar ways that I enjoyed his company.

"John, if we accept Jimmy's view that the girl was dead, and I see no reason to doubt him, and dead bodies don't get up and walk, then there must have been someone else there. Either Jimmy didn't see them, or they came and left between Jimmy finding the body and you and I going down to the beach. We were there until the police arrived, and we didn't see anyone come in or go out the track."

"Well Jimmy didn't see anyone on his way back to the homestead to find me and tell me about the body."

"Could someone have driven in after Jimmy reached the

highway and then taken the body and driven back to the highway before we drove over to the beach track?"

John's reply was that it was impossible. It would take around ten minutes driving from the homestead to the highway, then another twenty minutes down the track to the beach. Really that would only give a person twenty minutes plus the time that Jimmy took to give him the news, his phone call to the police and our departure for the beach. Maybe twenty-five, thirty minutes max. It would take too long to drive from the highway to the carpark, shift the body, and then return to the highway twenty minutes away. It would be possible if they had a car down on the beach, but then Jimmy would have seen it. There was only one place where you could leave a car. Besides we had seen no one and you would expect dust to still be hanging in the air if any vehicle had driven out.

"Did youse blokes check the bush for the body?" It was Fred again.

"Yes. Peter and I had a quick look when we arrived but we didn't want to upset the site for the police. The police did a very thorough search. They were all over the place this afternoon."

"Ignoring the key and the fact that a body disappeared, there must have been someone else around between the time Jimmy left and John and I arrived."

"Peter's right, but where was he—or maybe it was a she?" I was pleased John had supported my idea, but it only raised more questions.

It was Fred, on his third can of the night, who offered a solution. "Perhaps the car was unlocked, they found her, killed her and locked her in the car while they went to find out what to do with the body. Then they came back, shifted her and locked the car. I've seen things like that on the telly. Perhaps they didn't know Jimmy was coming. They killed her and locked her in the car until they had time to remove her. Jimmy just happened to arrive in between. It'll be drugs I reckon."

The theory was plausible. But if they killed her why lock her in the van? Sure, when they heard Jimmy coming they could have hidden, and when he left they came back, opened the door, removed Magenta and locked the door again. But why do that? Why bother locking an empty car? It was another unanswered question. Fred's theory was plausible but it still didn't say why someone would kill her, or who it was. Nor did it answer where the person or persons were and where they went. For some reason we had seemed to assume there must have been at least two people.

"But why do you lock a dead body in a car? It doesn't seem necessary to me." But then nothing was making sense to me. "Was there any beer in the van?" The whole group looked at me as if I was mad. Here was a poor girl dead, and her body missing, and I'm asking about beer. I explained. "When she was putting groceries in her car in Darwin I saw cartons of beer in the van. At Wyndham the bar maid said she was drinking vodka. Perhaps the beer was for someone else. If the beer was gone perhaps she had met whoever she was planning to meet. If it was still there she hadn't met her friend."

"Or she drank it herself. Maybe she didn't only drink vodka." It was another quiet comment from Fred.

"There was an empty bottle of something on the floor of

the van. I'll check with the police in the morning, but I doubt someone would kill for a few cartons of beer. Thieve yes, but hardly kill." John had assumed the role of the communicator with the police. He knew some of them from his local dealings. I suspected he may have had to bail out a few of his ringers who had overdone their weekends in town.

"Perhaps they came from the sea." It was Fred again from the far end of the table.

"What do you mean, and why do you keep saying 'they'?" I asked.

"Well, if they didn't drive in, there were no other cars in the carpark, they would hardly be walkin' around out there. It is obvious they came in on a boat. Don't know why I say 'they', just reckon there would be."

"It's possible," was John's reply. "The deep water is not far of the shoreline there. You could bring a small boat or a yacht in close enough to row ashore. We didn't look for that but then the tide would have removed any sign of a boat coming up onto the beach."

"But John, wouldn't we have seen a boat off that long empty beach? There are no headlands for it to hide behind."

"Peter, there was a boat, a long way off the coast, when we were down on the beach, but it was a big boat. You wouldn't row ashore from it. It was too far out."

"Could someone have come in on a zodiac?"

"Possibly, but unlikely. It looked like a big cruise ship. They sometimes do trips around the coast."

"John, what about her clothes and luggage?" It was Suzie

who asked the question.

"According to the police it looked like all her effects were untouched. There was a large case and a smaller bag, usual carry-on size. There was no indication that anything was missing. They took all her belongings back to town."

"What about her phone?"

"It wouldn't work out here, unless it was a satellite phone. We don't have any coverage here. We are way too far from town."

"John, just a thought, in the morning when you are checking about the beer for Peter, could you also ask the police about her purse and her phone. Women are very attached to their purses or bags, even hippies. It's part of our lives. Most women never move without their purse, and a young woman like Magenta would be sure to have a mobile phone. In fact, I saw her talking on it in Broome. There are also the diamonds."

Suzie was certainly adding a different dimension to the mystery than the rest of us males.

"In Kununurra she bought two very expensive diamonds. What has happened to them?"

12 Police Enquiries

Suzie

We were sitting outside our just erected tent in the red dirt campground at the Sandfire Roadhouse reviewing the day, and deciding whether we would take a bottle of red wine or a bottle of white wine when we took our chairs, glasses and drinks to join the other grey nomads in the campground. The group had already started drifting together for their evening session when Peter's phone rang. It was his friend John Satto from the station near Broome. I listened, but most of the talk was from John with only the occasional question from Peter, and I couldn't follow their conversation. After they had ended the call Peter gave me a run down.

John told Peter of a phone call to his friend in the Broome Police station. He had asked about the missing woman and if any information had been discovered. It seemed the local policeman was much more forthcoming in his communications than you would expect to get in a big city.

They had found the woman's wallet and identified her as Naomi Masters. She was an American.

They had contacted the car rental company, and then the police in Darwin who had managed to track down more information. They had checked airline arrivals and immigration records. She had come to Darwin from Bali in the middle of May and rented the van one week later. The Northern Territory police had made more enquires and found she had checked into an apartment in the Cullen Bay Marina area until she had left Darwin.

The van had been booked for three weeks and was to be returned to the company's Brisbane depot.

The police had made a thorough search of the van but had found no sign of her passport or mobile phone. The wallet had credit cards and over one thousand dollars in Australian currency plus some US dollars and a few rupiah from Indonesia. They had carried out another very careful search of the car for the diamonds but had found nothing.

They had found a small tablet on the floor of the van which they thought was possibly a drug or prescription medicine. They were still waiting on test results from the laboratory. There was an almost empty bottle of vodka but no beer, empty beer stubbies, or any sign of packaging for beer.

The police had made enquiries in Broome and had found video from a service station showing Magenta, or Naomi Masters as we now knew her to be, putting fuel in her van at eight thirty-nine the evening before Jimmy had found the body.

They had decided that if she had refuelled the car, and then driven straight to the beach parking lot, she must have died between ten pm and six the following morning when Jimmy had found her—but of course there was no body so it was not possible to confirm a time of death.

Police had also checked the vehicle and there were no signs of mechanical problems, and no problems with flat tyres or the car being bogged. It would appear she knew where she was going because there was a roadmap with the turn off to the beach marked in pencil. Several other points on the coast were also marked with crosses, but they were much further south.

Peter passed on the details of John's report to me, and concluded with "It is a strange sort of robbery, if that was what it was. Why would someone take a mobile phone and passport but leave a wallet with so much money in it?"

"Perhaps it was the diamonds. Perhaps they didn't look in the wallet."

Peter shook his head. "To me it seems more than a robbery. If I stole the diamonds the cash would be a bonus. Why not take the wallet? It's as if the murderer didn't think her identification was important. It didn't seem to worry whoever killed her. Yet the passport was missing. Why leave a wallet, with cards with her name on them, and the money, yet take the passport?"

"But Peter, do we really know that whoever killed her knew that she had been found? We assume that she was killed and someone was hiding in the scrub when Jimmy drove up. Perhaps they weren't there at all but returned after Jimmy left, or came and found her dead after Jimmy had found her."

Peter shook his head. I wasn't sure if it was in disagreement or puzzlement. "The car would have eventually attracted police attention although it may have taken weeks. The phone is strange. Perhaps it was important. They are so common these days as to be almost worthless as stolen goods. The phone is missing but cash is left. Perhaps there was something on the phone that the murderer didn't want people to see. A photo? But then why leave the credit cards, and where is the passport?"

"Maybe there was something in the passport that the person who took the body wanted to keep hidden."

"Like what?"

I didn't have an answer to Peter's question. I was just going to tell him that when the thought occurred to me. "Perhaps they wanted to hide where she had come from. If she had flown into Darwin from Denpasar, then where had she been before that? Fred might be right when he talked about drugs. Southeast Asia is a hot spot for sourcing drugs, and it looks as if she was using."

"So you think this is about drugs, and why do you say 'they'?"

"I don't know. The little white pill is suspicious, and I just don't see one person being involved. I have no reason, but I'm like Fred back at the station, I just have a mindset of two men."

"Not a man and a woman? Suzie, how sexist!"

"Peter! While we were waiting for the police to come out to check the van, I went for a walk down to the beach. Do you remember when I told you about reading a book at school? Well one of the chapters was about a very bad cyclone that hit Broome and the northern coastline. Many boats, both schooners and luggers, were lost or badly damaged. Many of the crews died. One lugger was fortunate and even washed ashore safely on the Eighty Mile Beach. That was the beach we were on. Many bodies were also washed ashore there, and the story tells how the manager of a nearby station rode out from the homestead with a team of men to look for survivors. They buried any bodies they found in the sand hills behind the beach. It was John's station, the station where we were staying."

"So you think that Magenta has been buried somewhere on the beach?"

"I don't know. None of us saw any sign of freshly dug earth. It was just the thought of the book I had read all those years ago, and then to be standing there knowing somewhere, along that beach, were the bones of dead sailors."

"Let's join the group."

I agreed with Peter's suggestion. The thought of that beach and its sad history was prickling the hairs on the back of my neck.

The conversation of our fellow campers sitting under the shady trees revolved around the usual subjects that had come up at previous gatherings we had attended. Tonight the antics of a strutting peacock and his disinterested harem were an additional cause of much comment and mirth amongst the group. The informal get-togethers were a great way to meet a range of people. Most, like us, were retired, but there was an occasional family travelling around Australia to see the country for themselves. Where had we been? Where we were going? What to see? What and where to avoid? I had quickly learnt at my first experience of such get-togethers that it would be unwise for tourist operators to upset campers or their businesses would vanish overnight. Get a good reputation and business could boom as favourable comment passed up and down the tourist tracks.

Your success could be affected by a remark in a caravan park thousands of kilometres away as travellers gossiped over a beer.

The mystery of the vanishing body had become a subject of speculation in campgrounds along the West Coast. Everyone had a theory. Some that were aired by the group sitting around us were very fanciful. It seemed the facts of the case had been greatly exaggerated by repeated telling. Finally it became too much for Peter. He explained that he had been there and told of what he had seen and what he had learnt earlier in the evening from John. He also told the group of Jimmy finding the body sitting slumped in the car with earpods in her ears. This led to more discussion and even more theories. The general opinion was that she had been murdered and taken away by some maniac killer. The north had a history of such madmen carrying out random shootings and kidnapping and killing tourists. A collective shudder passed through the group. For city dwellers immune to the daily reports of murder and violence on the evening news the rare event in a far corner of Australia seemed much more graphic.

From the talk there was an assumption that Magenta—we still thought of her as Magenta rather than Naomi—had been murdered. For some, Jimmy was the obvious murderer. The poor man was accused of probably bashing and raping her.

While I had only met him briefly, Jimmy hadn't seemed to be that type of person. Not that I suppose I had a great deal of experience with murderers. I had thought of him as being very genuine, and very shaken by his discovery. I felt my anger rising at the two vocal loudmouths making the accusations. "He was a stockman. He'd be familiar with guns and knives. They can be pretty wild. I reckon he's the one." I sensed Peter was feeling the same as me. He pointed out that Jimmy couldn't have done it. He had found the body that then disappeared. If he was guilty he could have just claimed to have found the empty van. Neither Jimmy nor the police had made mention of seeing anything to indicate violence. No indications of gunshot or knife wounds. No mention of blood. When we had seen the empty car we hadn't noticed anything that looked as if it could be blood. Nor had the police report made any mention of blood or gunshot residue in the car.

I was about to reach out and put my hand on Peter's to let him know I agreed with his feelings, but I hesitated. Perhaps he would think I was trying to restrain him from speaking out so forcefully.

"Perhaps she was strangled or poisoned?" The question came from one of the campers sitting in the circle with a beer in a stubbie-holder showing the image of a dog. I had noticed that seasoned campers often advertised their travels by either their stubbie-holders or stickers on the back of their van or trailer.

Peter shook his head. "If she was strangled you would expect signs of a struggle, or perhaps an injury. Jimmy didn't notice anything. The earpods were still in her ears."

"I still think he did it?" It was our traveller with the stubbie-holder again.

"I don't think Jimmy is a candidate. He was distressed when he came back to the homestead. Besides, the woman was locked in the car. He couldn't open the door."

"Perhaps the door was unlocked when he arrived. Then he killed her and locked the door." Stubbie-holder was certainly insistent, but it just seemed so unlikely. I wondered if the police would come to the same idea.

"What about poison?" Another camper threw an idea into the discussion. The general consensus was why?

"Suicide!" It was Stubbie-holder again. He had moved on. It was a possibility, but then so were many other theories. Without a body nothing could be discounted.

Peter brought up the map the police had found which had shown three crosses. The first was where the van had been parked. The other two were further south. While it was possible that the woman had taken her own life, the other marks indicated she was probably planning to keep driving south. The problem remained. Even if she had committed suicide, where was the body?

"The dingo took it." The comment came from the self-appointed camp comedian, although he was quickly let know it was in very bad taste.

"It was an accident." The quiet words came from a woman sitting beside a man at the back of the group. I had seen her earlier and noticed the sadness in her eyes. The man with her, I assumed her husband or partner, had a similar sadness and an almost protective attitude towards her.

"It was drugs. The white pill. The music. It was like my daughter. A 'bad batch' they said. She took a tablet but it was an overdose. They checked the other tablets and some of them had a very high dose. She was in her room playing music, and we didn't know that she was taking drugs and she was dead." The man beside her put his hand around her shoulder as silence settled over the group. Even Stubbie-holder and the camp comedian stayed silent.

I thought to myself. Maybe the lady with the sad eyes was right. Perhaps it was just a drug overdose. Magenta looked as if she would know about the drug scene, and she had been in Indonesia. But it still didn't answer the questions. Where was her body? Who took it? And why?

13 Life Matters

Suzie

We had left the campground at the Sandfire Roadhouse and had been driving south for some time. We were both quiet, both lost in our thoughts and not speaking much. It was another hot day: another clear blue sky without a single cloud. A fine red dust coated the landscape. Today we would reach Karratha. Peter had already arranged to meet his son who worked in the natural gas industry based in the town. This meeting and the trip to see the Gwion Gwion art were the reasons for Peter's visit to the West. Now I was with him, and I was to meet his son face-to-face. Till then, Matthew would only have had an image of me derived from his father's phone calls. I wondered if this was the reason for Peter's silence. My thoughts were on a meeting earlier in the day, just before we had left the campground.

"Do you think it was a drug overdose?"

Peter gave a shake of his head. Like yesterday it was a half move that could have meant either 'no' or 'I don't know'. I would have to get to know the man's moods and mannerisms better.

"I don't think we can know. Without a body there is no way that we can be sure of anything. Perhaps Jimmy was wrong and she wasn't dead. That still leaves the question of where did she go? I don't think Jimmy would make a mistake like that. If the body disappeared someone must know what happened, but a drug overdose? It's possible, but with no body we can't know. Even if the police had a body I don't know enough about drugs to know how much they could learn."

I decided to tell Peter of my earlier conversation in the camp ground. "When I was in the ablutions block I spoke to the lady who raised the question of drugs last night. She still had those sad haunted eyes. She and her husband had decided to travel around Australia to get away from the death of their daughter. One night they went to their daughter's bedroom to say goodnight and they found her dead. She had ear pods in her ears and had been listening to music on her phone. They didn't even know that she was taking any drugs, but one of her girlfriends had given her some pills and told her they were awesome. When the police did tests they found the drug levels in the tablets were far in excess of the usual levels. The poor girl never had a chance. The story last night brought it all back for them. They were trying to escape from all that."

"Suzie, I don't think we will ever find out what happened. I expect the police will make more enquiries, and maybe they will find something in Magenta's past that gives them a lead. It will probably just become an unsolved missing person. They can't even say death without a body. Perhaps one day we will see something in the news about the body of a missing woman being found in the Kimberley. Somewhere, someone must know something, but they probably don't want it known."

With that Peter went quiet again.

"Peter, I felt so sorry for them. Their daughter's death had shattered their lives. I'm just so glad I have never had to face that loss."

Even though he was wearing sunglasses and I couldn't see his eyes, I was sure they went misty. The rest of his face had taken on a sad expression.

"Yes, it would be so hard. It could break a marriage. I remember when Claire lost our first baby. Fortunately our marriage was strong, but Claire never forgot. Nor I suppose did I."

"I didn't know you had lost a child."

"Yes, we lost a baby girl. She was stillborn. It really hit both of us hard, especially Claire who had held her. Fortunately we then had Matthew two years later. The last days before he was born were stressful, but as it turned out there was no problem."

"I'm so sorry. I had no idea."

"Well that's life. We don't have any choices about some things."

"What happened?"

"I was away on a worksite. Claire was still three weeks from being due, and I had planned to get back for the birth. She went into early labour and lost the baby. I wasn't there for her. To make matters worse I didn't have enough money to buy a ticket to get home quickly. We had put everything we had into buying the house and getting ready for the baby. Wages were coming, but I didn't have enough cash just then, and the company charter wasn't due for a week. Some friends gave me the money."

"They must have been good friends."

"They were. When I went to repay Pat and Laurie they refused to take any money. Just said that one day someone else might need a hand. Give it to them. Their kindness has always remained with me. They were very special people."

I thought of my life. I had been so fortunate. My parents had died, but they had had a good life and a long life. A few illness and aches and pains but not enough to make them suffer. Even my marriage had not been too painful, apart from the emotional heartache of being deceived by a womanising man and the realisation of my stupidity. Tony had always been good to me and the children, and never violent or abusive as some men could be. He had provided well for the kids, and even for me until I had a job. The many things I could say about him were insignificant compared to the heartbreak of some people.

My children had caused no great problems. A broken bone in the schoolyard and an occasional drama with 'best friends'. No traumatic illnesses. Fortunately my son had not even had a bout of teenage angst like some boys. I think my separation from his father had given him a maturity in his life and his relationships, and he had found a great companion in Amelia. I adored Amelia. She was a great mate for Max and beautiful mother for Charlie. Even my daughter had not been the problem that mothers can have with their daughters. We had some strong disagreements but they had all been resolved. The drugs that are everywhere around us, even in school yards, were always a worry, and while I felt confident with Max I was more concerned with Emma. She had a much more outgoing and adventurous spirit. I suspect she may have tried some but fortunately had not progressed to any serious use. Really I'd had a charmed life. Few illnesses, nothing serious. Only the occasional financial worry and they had been worked through and survived. I was blest. The only great loss was my closest school friend, Merry, and even her death had been resolved: thanks to Peter's help.

We drove through the seemingly endless expanse of the red dirt of the Pilbara and reached Port Headland. Peter was interested in seeing the harbour area and the ships loading ore, so we left the Great Northern Highway and drove into the port. Leaving our vehicle we walked the Esplanade, reading the signs explaining the workings of the port, and watching the movements of giant ore carriers entering and leaving the port through the narrow channel. Massive loaders drew ore from the stockpiles as long trains replenished the supplies in readiness for the next boat already queuing and waiting its turn to berth. For the first time I really had a comprehension of the size of the industry in the West. The massive loaders, the trains, and the ships anchored offshore waiting to load was more than I had ever imagined. This port exported more tonnage than any other port in Australia, and it shipped more tonnage of bulk minerals than any other port in the world. As far back as 2005 the port had shipped one hundred million tonnes of ore to feed to growing needs of Asia: first Japan and now China. Today it was even more. This was now the source of Australia's wealth. Driving back to the highway we stopped and watched as a train almost three kilometres long passed beside us carrying iron ore from the mines four hundred kilometres or more inland from the port.

Leaving the town we took the coastal road south.

Approaching Karratha Peter was still not talkative and I wondered if he was thinking about the couple from the campground, or his late wife. Or was it about how his son would view me? Would his son think of me as replacing his mother? I knew Peter had already told Matthew about me, but then we had gone our separate ways, and now here I was coming to meet him.

As we drew to a stop in front of Matthew's unit Peter finally spoke. "I'm sorry I've been so quiet. It's all the talk of bodies and death, and the thought of seeing Matthew. It's brought back memories. Coming here I've been thinking of Claire. It wasn't planned, but in two days' time it will be the anniversary of her death. I hope my son likes you."

14 Matthew

Suzie

Matthew was just as Peter had described him. Tall, clean shaven, well-groomed and well spoken. I could see Peter in his son, but there was also something else, some characteristic that I could not place. I decided that perhaps it came from his mother.

He was excited to see his father whom he had not seen for several years. I gathered they often spoke by phone, and these days skyped each other, but the opportunity to actually meet face-to-face was more difficult and expensive to arrange as they lived on opposite sides of the continent.

Matthew was certainly not the wild, rough, hard drinking miner or gas worker that television reports sometimes portrayed. In fact, he looked more like an engineer from a city construction site, although much more deeply suntanned than those I saw on worksites around Melbourne.

Matthew explained that his work at the natural gas plant had been on a rotational basis. When he started with the company he would have two weeks in Karratha then one week off down south in Perth. Eventually he decided that he preferred to remain in Karratha and had moved to a company supplied apartment and had a more normal work timetable. He still did shifts on a gas platform but remained in Karratha on his time off or on the days when he worked from the company's office. Since he didn't have room for us in the apartment he had booked a room at a motel. The thought of an air-conditioned room with a large bed, my own shower and comfortable armchairs after the hours spent sitting in the car was very appealing. I just hoped Peter would not decide that a campground and the tent would be enough.

Once we had checked in to the motel Matthew took us for a short guided tour of the town and showed us the gas plant where he worked. He would take us to the visitor's centre tomorrow where we could see a display and learn more about the project. The plant was huge. I had heard about size of the gas and iron ore developments in the west of Australia, but nothing had prepared me for the size of the projects that we had encountered in Port Headland and now here in Karratha. After our tour we returned to his apartment.

Matthew was a good cook. I thought of my own son who was able to feed himself but restricted his cooking to basic meals. His wife was the cook with flair. Matthew had flair. He was obviously interested in food and its presentation. We were just finishing our main course when there was a quick knock on the door and a man walked in. Matthew introduced his friend Ben.

After our very enjoyable meal Matthew returned Peter and me to our motel room. Driving back, the blaze of lights from the gas plant lit up the night sky, making an even greater impression of its scale than our view of the plant had made in the daylight.

Next morning Matthew took us to the Woodside visitor's centre as planned. Watching videos of the project, looking at the displays, and then looking out over the massive construction of the plant with its network of pipes and processing units set amongst the red dirt of the Pilbara, brought home to me how little I knew of how the wealth of Australia is created. Yet this was only part of the project. Far out to sea were the platforms and wells that produced the gas that the plant turned to liquid natural gas to load on the special ships that carried it away to fuel Asia. I was amazed by a video of huge sections of the plant, some weighing over eighteen hundred tonnes, arrive by ship and travel slowly by road from the dock to the worksite to connect to another of the seventy-five large prefabricated sections; without allowance of even a millimetre of error.

We returned to Matthew's apartment and Ben joined us for the drive out to Dampier to show us the iron ore loading operation. Again I was amazed by the scale of the port and the facilities. The size of the trains and the huge boats. While Port Headland was a BHP port, Dampier was a port for Rio—the other large company with mines in the Pilbara. Karratha was different. Here the industry was natural gas, and Woodside was the company that operated the wells and pipelines and the plant to refrigerate and compress the gas ready to ship to Asia on special tankers.

During the morning I got the feeling that there was more to Matthew and Ben's friendship than just being friends. There was nothing obvious, just two good friends spending time with one of their fathers and his new partner, yet there was something that made me think that all was not as it seemed.

Back in the motel I raised my suspicions with Peter.

"Nonsense. Matthew is not gay. There has never been any mention of the subject. He would tell me if he was."

"I remember you asked me once if my daughter was a lesbian. You told me that Matthew was a great honorary uncle for his friend's kids. Were you a little suspicious?"

"No, never. He is not gay!"

I decided to let the subject drop.

Later that afternoon we went back to Matthew's apartment. Once again Ben was there. They were in deep discussion when Peter and I arrived. As I got out of the car I thought I heard Ben say "You must tell ..." His attitude and closeness to Matthew made me even more suspicious of their friendship. Peter, on the opposite side of the car, would have heard nothing.

That evening Matthew prepared another wonderful meal, but there was a tension between him and Ben. Both were polite but there was a strain around the table. Even Peter was a little subdued. Finally, Ben informed us that he was going out. Matthew accompanied him to the door and they stood talking outside for some time. It sounded as though they were having a disagreement, but doing so in low voices so we would not hear. When Matthew re-entered he was very quiet and unsettled. An uneasy mood fell over the three of us remaining in the room, and it wasn't long before I suggested, under the pretence of weariness, that Peter and I should return to our motel.

Back at the motel I again raised the possibility of Matthew

being a homosexual. Peter was indignant. "How would you know? He definitely is not! You have their friendship all wrong."

By this time I was sure that I had picked the relationship, but Peter would not even consider the possibility. I think my use of the word homosexual had made him even more opposed to the idea. Gay was bad enough but calling the relationship by its proper name was even worse. We went to bed that night with a quick kiss, then Peter rolled away from me. He wanted his privacy.

Next morning Peter's mobile phone rang. It was Matthew. Could his dad come around? He wanted to chat. Could he come alone? Peter left immediately. I sat and waited, watching some inane game show on the television. I had a feeling that Peter may need me when he returned.

"Let's find some lunch." From the way Peter spoke when he came back from Matthew it wasn't so much a request as a command. His appearance was grim. From the way he moved he even looked as if he had suddenly aged ten years. We sat and ate our meal at a nearby pub but there was no conversation. Then we returned to our motel room. Still no conversation. Peter remained uncommunicative.

"What is the matter?" I asked.

"Nothing. We will leave in the morning."

"Are you going to see Matthew before we leave?"

"No."

"Peter, what is wrong?"

"Nothing. I don't want to talk about it."

It was another troubled night for both of us as we lay together in the bed, each of us in our own little private world. I was sure Peter and Matthew had discussed Matthew's sexuality. It had obviously not gone well, and Peter was not prepared to discuss it. I was surprised at Peter. He had so often spoken of his son and was very fond of him. It was so unexpected to see this reaction to the news I was sure he'd received. I knew Peter was a conservative man in many ways, perhaps it was one of the things about him that appealed to me, but his behaviour had surprised me. This was going to the extreme. I was sad to see him feeling this way and responding in this manner. His behaviour was so unreasonable.

As we drove away from town in the morning I asked if he wanted to drop by his son and make his farewell.

"No."

As we headed south I was unsure when, or if, Peter would ever again talk with his son. It also troubled me to be with a man who could behave in this manner. Worse, I wasn't sure whether I still wanted to be with Peter.

15 Loss

Peter

Driving away from Karratha I felt an emptiness greater than I had ever known. When Claire had died she had left a gap that would never be filled, but I still had our son. He had developed into a fine young man that I was proud of. Now I had lost him, and any future as well. Until yesterday I had thought we were close, but I had been wrong. I had not known my son at all. Even worse, he had not felt that he could be honest with me about his life.

Gone was the dream of family and grandchildren. Gone was the thought of continuing the family line. I had never really thought about the family line until last night. We were hardly a famous family with a distinguished past, but only now when it was not going to happen because my son preferred men to women had I realised how important it was to me. A girl could continue my line. That would be better than nothing although it was not what I really wanted. Besides, I didn't have a daughter. Now there was nothing. It would be the end of the family. The end of my genes.

I was driving, but in my mind I was going over and over my thoughts and feelings. I was swamped by a range of emotions. Anger, with Matthew. Anger with myself for how I felt. Loss. Sadness. Gratitude that Claire would never know, and mixed emotions about Suzie. I didn't feel very proud of myself. I knew I should have been more understanding of Matthew, but in my heart I could not. I couldn't accept his choice. Suzie tried to explain that it was not a choice, but to me it was.

The more Suzie tried to reason with me the more entrenched I became in my feelings. I knew I was wrong but I couldn't change. The atmosphere between us became more and more difficult. Eventually silence settled on the car.

I knew I was being selfish. Suzie had certainly let me know she disapproved of my attitude. Our road trip together which had started with such promise had descended into a disaster. I had thought that we were coming to an understanding, a relationship that looked as though it would develop into something ongoing. Now that was all over. The best plan would be to get the vehicle to Perth as quickly as possible, call off the rest of the trip, make our farewells and fly back to our separate homes.

"I've come so far with you. If I am to fly home then I want to make one more stop before we part. I want to see the dolphins at Monkey Mia. I will probably never be in this part of the world again. It is on our way to Perth and we can stop off."

I thought I owed that to Suzie, and agreed we would stop and see them.

It was a long day's drive. The road seemed endless. After our initial talk we spoke little. We pulled off at several wayside stops for a break, a coffee and some food and then drove on. Carnarvon we drove through without stopping. We were still both not saying anything to the other and it was late in the afternoon when we reached the campground at Denham close by Monkey Mia. Far too late to spend time with the dolphins as Suzie had requested so I agreed we would wait and only leave after seeing the dolphins come into the beach next morning.

We spent one more night in close physical proximity in our tiny tent, but both of us were somewhere else.

Next morning the campground was full of talk. A fisherman had hauled in an unusual catch on his line. He was shocked to find that it was a human leg. There was no sign of the rest of the body. It was presumed by locals to have been eaten by sharks. Shark Bay had lived up to its name. All that remained was a leg. And the leg carried the tattoo of two entwined snakes.

16 The Police

Suzie

The news of the dismembered leg had spread quickly.

A man and his son fishing off the beach had dragged in the leg thinking they had caught a large tailor. The fisherman had driven from his beachside camp to the nearest roadhouse and called the police in Carnarvon.

Naturally they were incredulous. Their usual work was with drunks, speeding drivers, drug problems, and domestic violence cases. While shark attacks were not unknown, for someone to phone in a report of a dismembered body was very unusual. A search of the area was organised, although by the time a helicopter and boats could reach the distant site the tide had turned making it difficult to identify the most likely places to concentrate their efforts. So far the search had found another dismembered leg washed up on the beach but had failed to find any sign of the rest of the body. A number of Great White sharks had been seen from the helicopter.

The stories circulating amongst the locals all spoke of the leg having teeth marks around the thigh, and a shark was the obvious suspect. After all, the area was called Shark Bay and was known to be home to many sharks. It was hard to be sure of the facts as more and more fanciful stories began spreading. With each telling the probable size of the shark grew. Stories of earlier shark attacks were retold. Animated discussions were taking place about whether it would be a Great White or a Tiger shark. Both were common in the area. Some storytellers claimed it would have been a pack of sharks in a feeding frenzy. Others disputed the claim saying a single shark could take the entire body. Not one of the self-appointed experts had actually been on the remote beach at the time the legs had been found. However all stories remained constant about one fact: the leg the fisherman had found had a tattoo of two entwined snakes. Amongst the local gossips there was no linkage of the find to the disappearance of a body from a beach much further north near Broome. Neither the police nor the public appeared to link the two events.

Peter decided we should find a police station and let them know of our suspicions. That was harder to do than we expected. When we reported to the police station at Denham there was little interest. After all, the original report had been to the much larger station in Carnarvon who were handling the case. They knew nothing of the missing body from the beach at a cattle station near Broome and were not interested in a missing person from outside their region. People went missing all the time. Even Peter's description of the tattoo did nothing to change their attitude. If we wanted to make a report we would have to go back to Carnarvon. We left disappointed. Carnarvon was three hundred and thirty kilometres away in the opposite direction to our plans. It would mean a back track of three and a half hours, and an end to our plan to see the dolphins, drive straight to Perth and fly home as soon as possible.

Peter made the decision we would drive to Monkey Mia to see the dolphins as he had promised me, then we would leave for Perth. The tattooed leg was none of our concern.

It wasn't far from the police station to Monkey Mia. The tourists were already lining the beach watching the arrival of the first of the pod of bottlenose dolphins. A ranger was standing in the clear shallow water supervising a teenage girl feed one of the arrivals. Her excitement and the smile on her face as the dolphin took the food from her was enough to make my visit worthwhile. Next, a ranger led a young boy into the shallows as another dolphin approached seeking its daily titbit, but this time he stopped the boy from placing the dolphin's meal of a small fish in the water. He explained to the onlookers that to make sure the dolphins continued to hunt, and to teach their young the skill of hunting, feeding was limited to small quantities and a dolphin could only receive three fish each day. Then they had to find their own meals! This dolphin was greedy. Another arrived, the greedy one left and the newest arrival was fed.

Standing watching the small pod swim around in the deeper light blue water, and then occasionally venture into the clear colourless shallows over the white sand when they sought a feed was a joy. Around us the children were excited and happy. Their parents and the older tourists looked relaxed and untroubled. I noticed even Peter's irritable mood that he had worn since we had left Karratha had softened. Back in the car he was quiet but the anger of yesterday had gone and was replaced by a gentler look.

"Did the dolphins get to you?" I asked. "People say that they can communicate with humans."

"No. It was not that. As I was standing there watching the pod I was thinking of families ... and Magenta. I don't know what her life has been like. Maybe she had problems. Maybe she brought problems on herself. I don't know, but somewhere she must have a mother and father. Well at least she must know her mother. Fathers are a bit more of an unknown for some people these days. I was also thinking of Matthew. I really have been more concerned about me than him. I was very self-centred. You were right. I behaved badly."

"What are you going to do?"

"I can't go and see Matthew. He told me he would be out working on a gas platform this week. I will ring him and have a talk. Hopefully we can patch up our relationship. The other thing I want to do is get some attention to the disappearance of Magenta. I would hate to think a child of mine could end up like that and no one cared, or wanted to find out, what happened. There is no way a dead body can leave a car, walk into the ocean and have body parts turn up fifteen hundred kilometres away after being eaten by a shark. There is more to this than just an overdose."

The police in Carnarvon were no more interested in our story than the police in Denham. In fact they seemed to view Peter's interest as suspicious. What was his relationship with the girl? Was he a relative? Did he know her? When had he last seen her? Why was he interested?

Peter attempted to explain what we knew of the girl and suggested contacting the Broome police. He also passed on the news he had been given by John Satto. The van on the beach carpark south of Broome was the one we had seen the girl driving in Darwin. The missing body. It would have to be the same girl. The leg with the two entwined snakes would not be common. The police had already identified her from the van hire company. They may not have a body, but it had to be her legs.

I could see the police were not greatly interested. I had to admit the story did seem rather farfetched, but then who else would have a leg with that tattoo. It had to be her. The police took a statement and our names and contact details and showed us the door.

We found a motel for the night. It was too late to start our drive south to Perth, and we didn't want to stop on the roadside. I could see Peter was disappointed with the attitude of the police officer who interviewed him. Still there was nothing he could do. The matter was out of his hands.

"Well that was less than successful. Now for the next thing. I hope it goes better."

I had no idea what Peter's 'next thing' was.

17 An Urgent Invitation

Peter

I was still unable to contact my son. I wasn't sure if he was getting my calls, or deliberately avoiding answering when my number came up on his phone. The opportunity to talk with him would have to wait for another day. I hoped that when he returned from his shift on the gas platform we could try to repair the relationship that had been so badly damaged.

The next problem was Suzie. Our relationship had collapsed over my behaviour towards Matthew. When we had left Karratha I had agreed to take her to Perth and put her on a plane to return to Melbourne. I had also decided to cut short my trip. It no longer held the thought of pleasure that it had once promised. I would cancel our visit to the wineries of Margaret River and fly back to Sydney as soon as I could arrange a flight and return the vehicle.

At her request I had made the short side trip to Monkey Mia so she could see the dolphins. That had necessitated an overnight stay in Denham. Retracing our steps to see the police in Carnarvon had meant another overnight stay. This time I had taken two rooms at a motel. Our relationship had improved since seeing the dolphins but the uncomfortable feeling of the previous night was still fresh in my mind. While at first Suzie had been hesitant to interfere, and had not commented on my behaviour towards Matthew, her disapproval had soon become apparent. I had made the mistake of discussing my feelings about my son with her, and Suzie had quickly, and directly, informed me that she thought I had behaved badly. She had taken a quite opposite view of the situation to me. She had also made it very clear that it would be an issue between us.

Whether it was the result of our experience with the dolphins, or perhaps just time, the feeling between us that had been so tense when we had first driven out of Karratha had started to ease by the time we were leaving Carnarvon for the second time. At least we were talking more as we continued our drive south. If Suzie and I were to get our relationship back together I would have to change. I hoped Suzie would come to excuse my behaviour. While it was obvious that we were very different in our natures and our ideas I realised how important she had become to me. I felt she had similar feelings about me, although they had been rather tried over the last few days. Perhaps it could be possible for us to get back to our past relationship.

We had decided to drive straight through from Carnarvon to Perth. With a nine hundred kilometre drive ahead of us it would be a long day. The road was full of road trains, semitrailers, and works vehicles with yellow strips down their sides and orange warning lights on their roofs. Scattered amid all this traffic were the grey nomads in their caravans, heading south on their anticlockwise circumnavigation of the continent. We also had to frequently slow down and pull off to the side of the road to allow massive trailers carrying earthmoving equipment or large components of industrial plant bound for the iron ore mines and gas projects to pass by. Living in the east of Australia I had read, and watched television programs, about the changes taking place in the West. It was only being amidst the traffic on the road and seeing some of the projects that I really appreciated how massive those changes were. Neither Suzie nor I had an idea how big the boom in the West was.

As the kilometres passed I thought more about my behaviour to Matthew. Ten hours of driving gives you time to think. Eventually you need to talk to break the boredom and try to bring some sense to your thoughts. Why had I reacted so strongly to Matthew's news? I realised how self-centred I had been. I had really only thought of my feelings and not of my son. Claire would probably have sided with Suzie.

The discovery that Matthew and Ben were in a relationship was a complete shock to me. Matthew had never mentioned anyone by the name of Ben, and had never given me any indication of being gay. While he had never spoken of any special woman in his life I had always assumed that he just hadn't met the right person. As far as I knew he had lots of friends and they were both male and female. The thought of him being gay had never entered my head. Yet the relationship was almost twelve months old. How much longer had he been that way?

It wasn't just the shock of the discovery. I was swamped with a tidal wave of other emotions. Surprise, and then horror, that he had not told me earlier. I had thought we had a close relationship, and yet there were things, major things, that he had kept from me. My dreams of my son in a happy stable life with a wife and family had disappeared. Any thought of grandchildren had vanished.

It wasn't that I hadn't had contact with homosexual men.

I had worked in a mining company head office in Sydney, and there was always someone on staff talking about the Oxford street scene and their friends in the Gay Mardi Gras. The mining camps had a few gay men. Generally they were accepted. Accepted, or tolerated. Most people just wanted to get on with their lives, and provided they did their jobs and no fuss was made, just let it be. Occasionally someone would try to make trouble but soon found that the rest of the camp was not interested and they were told to cool it. Even when I had first met Suzie in London, I had shared a basement flat with a bunch of fellow Australians. One of my flatmates had been gay, although I had not noticed, and only found out years later from a mutual friend.

Matthew didn't seem like the stereotype of a gay man. Nor did Ben. They just looked like normal men. Perhaps a bit more smartly presented that some of the tradies around town, but then they were management staff and that was to be expected. Certainly not the caricatures of a gay man that was so often presented and that I had in my mind.

The greatest loss to me was continuation of family. My line would stop. We weren't aristocracy, we hadn't even traced our family beyond my great grandfather, yet now it would end. I hadn't expected that sense of loss. In a strange way it was like bereavement. A bereavement for something that had never, and would never, happen. The intensity of that feeling surprised me. I wasn't sure which was the stronger feeling: the fact I would never have a grandchild, or I would never be a grandfather. I told Suzie about my feeling.

"You might."

I looked at Suzie.

"These days there are same sex couples with children. The way the law and society are changing two men may be able to adopt. Women have other options, and who knows what science will bring. That is if they want to have children."

"Suzie, children need a mother and father. Same sex parents are not natural. Kids need a mum and dad in their life."

"There are lots of families where there is no father, sometimes by choice, sometimes through circumstance, and there are families where there is no mother. What is important is someone that loves and cares for the children, regardless of who the parents are. I suppose you are going to say the parents should be married?"

"Well, yes. Yes. I think it is preferable that couples are married when they have children. It is a sign of commitment."

"So what about same sex marriage?"

"No. Marriage is between a man and a woman. Besides, I don't know how ongoing some of the same sex relationships are."

"You mean like marriages between men and women. About half of them end up in separation. You really are very old-fashioned aren't you?"

"Yes. I suppose I am, but that's the way I feel."

"Can't two same sex people have a relationship?"

"Yes, they can, but to me it is not, and never can be, a marriage. Call it something else if you wish, but leave marriage between a man and a woman."

"What is the difference if they both care for each other?"

"It's about having children. Kids need a role model. A dad and a mum."

"Even if one, or both, of the parents are bad parents? I think the quality of the relationship and the parents' care for their kids is more important. How would you feel about our relationship? Do we have to be married? We aren't. Does that make it less important?"

"But homosexuality is unnatural!" As soon as I made the remark I realised how ridiculous my statement was. Homosexuality has existed as long as mankind. At times it has been horribly repressed, and at other times glorified. I remembered once learning about the Spartan army and how they deliberately matched male lovers as soldiers in the belief that they would fight better. "How would you feel if your daughter, Emma, came home and told you she was a lesbian?"

"I would hope she was happy. It would worry me, but then I worried about some of the male relationships she has had. I would just hope that she finds someone she loves and who loves her, and they have a good life. What do you want for your son?"

Her question brought my confused emotions to a stop. What did I want for my son? Surely I wanted him to have a happy life. A life shared with someone special, as I had had with his mother, and perhaps could be fortunate and have with Suzie. Really so many of my emotions were about me not my son. I needed to talk with Matthew.

By the time we reached the outskirts of Perth we had decided to continue with our original holiday plans. No longer would we fly back to our separate homes in different cities. This time, when we found a motel with a vacancy, we had agreed on one room, and a double bed.

The evening news was on the television as we freshened up to go out to find a nearby restaurant for a meal. The dismembered legs were still making news. Search parties had found no traces of other body parts. Stories were circulating of possible missing people. Other stories spoke of criminal activities and gang warfare. Reporters were interviewing locals at Denham about a possible backpacker's abduction. Police would only say that investigations were ongoing. Just as we were walking out the door my mobile rang. The text message was brief and to the point. It was from the police in Perth. Detective-Inspector Adamson would like to see me. He was in charge of the Naomi Masters' investigation. Could I come and see him. Urgently!

18 Questions

Suzie

Our relationship had improved after Peter had phoned Matthew and was starting to come to terms with his son's news. Still I was beginning to wonder if the romance in our life had already ended and we had quickly become an 'old married couple', even though we weren't. It would be so sad if that was to be our fate, and it was a fate I did not want. Our relationship had changed so quickly, and I had seen a side of Peter I had not expected. From the moment of our arrival in Darwin the relationship had started to change. We were beginning to know each other and I was unsure where it was leading us. I wondered if Peter felt the same. Until Karratha I was sure he was interested in me, although the pop up tent and the thought of rolling out of bed and crashing to the ground had limited our ardour. After Karratha his thoughts were far from me, or us. Now that he was back from where his son's news had taken him, and once again sharing with me, I had realised I did still enjoy being with him. We had made a decision to not return to our separate homes but continue together with the trip that he had originally planned.

But first we had to see a policeman. We decided it would be easier to take a bus into the city and find the police station. At least that way we would not have to drive around an unknown city trying to find an empty car park.

The police headquarters was a nondescript office building that could have been any office block. Only the signage and the police cars parked outside betrayed its purpose. Inside was a different story. Somehow an air of criminality and guilt pervaded the atmosphere as soon as you entered. 'All ye who enter here are guilty.' That, at least, was my feeling as we fronted the desk to ask for Detective-Inspector Adamson.

"Sit over there and wait." The duty officer had not been to a charm school in customer relations and it was still only the morning. I wondered how the druggies and drunks would be received at the end of a busy Saturday night.

At last our man arrived. He was smartly dressed, looking like some city businessman from one of the offices in the adjoining buildings. He was younger than I expected and gave the impression of a man on the rise. In the interview room we were joined by an older man dressed in a once smart but now less stylish grey suit and blue tie. He had the look of an old-fashioned policeman, rather like you would expect to see in a vintage black and white cop show on TV; someone who had done years trawling through bars and the seedy side of the city. I even expected to see him light up a cigarette with nicotine stained fingers, but of course that would now be a forbidden pleasure which could only be indulged in private, far away from the office.

It was obvious the younger man was on his way up. I wondered what the older man had done wrong, or who he had upset at some stage. His future was going nowhere, and it looked as if he would serve out the days to his retirement as the gopher for a rising star.

The policemen we had spoken with in Denham and Carnarvon had all been young men starting out their careers, but they had shown no great interest in our information, merely compiled a report to be passed on and filed in a drawer in some cabinet in some office. With the first question he asked I knew our young interrogator had obviously done some homework—but needed to do more.

"When did you see Naomi Masters after the time in the Roebuck hotel?"

Peter answered. "No, that was the last time we saw her. She was talking to two men and then left. She was there one minute. I just caught a glimpse of her. The next time I looked she had gone."

"What about you?" The Inspector was looking at me as he asked the question.

"The same. I saw her talking with the two men, looked away to see what the noise was about, tried to get Peter's attention, and when I looked back she was leaving."

"What was the noise?"

"A large cheer had gone up. One of the girls in the wet T-shirt competition had removed her shirt and the boys were cheering her on, not that there was anything left to take off under the T-shirt."

"What about when the ringer found the body?"

Peter answered. "We didn't see her. When we went down to the carpark at the beach the car—the van—was empty. There was no body there."

"The report says you waited at the van. Did you see anyone around the area?"

"No, nothing. We waited for the police because my friend John Satto had called them before we left the homestead. We thought it best to wait onsite."

"And you saw no one?"

"No one."

"Did you see Masters anywhere else in Broome?"

Again Peter answered. "No, that was the only time we saw her. At the hotel."

"When did you first see her?"

"In Darwin. At the markets."

"What about you?" The older policeman looked across the table to me.

"I saw her at the markets."

"She was with your husband?"

"No. I was with Peter when we saw her, and we are not married." I wasn't sure why I had added that last comment. These days the police force would have little interest in two people's marital state. Probably half the world was living together without the blessing of the church or even a civil celebrant.

"Who was she with?"

Again it was Peter who answered. "As far as I could see she was on her own. She spoke to a few people but she was just buying food. I think she spoke to someone when she was watching a group of musicians but it looked like a casual conversation. I didn't think they knew each other."

"You seemed very interested in her. Why?"

"I wasn't. It was just that she really stood out in the crowd. She was a very attractive woman—well she could have been without the tattoos and hair style and colour. In any case she certainly stood out in the crowd. She had a style and an attitude that drew your attention, whether you liked the style or not."

Again the older man turned his eyes towards me. "Would you agree?"

"I would have to agree. She certainly attracted attention. We weren't the only people who looked at her. Everywhere she went people turned and looked at her."

"When did you see her next?"

"That would be in the shopping centre the next day. I was buying groceries. I spoke with her."

"What did she say?'

"Nothing really. I just said hello and she replied to me. I can't remember exactly what she said, just acknowledged my greeting. There was no conversation."

"What did she sound like?"

"I couldn't really say. She must have only said a few words. I thought she was probably foreign, perhaps American but not a big accent. I don't know if she was American or had learnt American English as a second language. You know how sometimes people learn a language and pick up an accent doing it. Perhaps by learning from watching videos and movies."

"What about you?" This time the question was to Peter.

"I've never spoken to her. Never heard her speak."

"But you saw her on the Friday, the twenty-fifth, in Darwin?"

"Yes, but it was across the carpark at the shopping centre. She would have been forty or fifty metres away. I only saw her and the van."

"Yet you could see that there were some cartons of beer in the van?"

"Yes, the yellow colour of the cartons was quite obvious."

"Did you see her in Katherine?"

We both shook our heads.

"What about in Kununurra? You must have been on the road about the same time."

I answered. "Probably. I expect we all left Darwin about the same time. In the supermarket she was buying food like I was."

"So it's possible she may have left the same day as you did?"

"Possibly. We don't know because we never saw her again until the hotel in Broome."

"Yet the report you gave the police in Carnarvon says you saw her in Wyndham."

"I don't think Peter said that. I certainly didn't. Your

report is wrong. We didn't see her. We heard about her from the barmaid at the Wyndham hotel. She had made an impression there when she kneed an unwelcome suitor in the groin."

"So when was that?"

I could see Peter counting back the days in his head. "It must have been before the Monday. The twenty-eighth I think. That was the day we were there so it had to have been before that."

"So why did she leave?"

"I have no idea. The barmaid said she had booked in for a few days but suddenly decided to leave. I gather she had paid for a week in the campground. She did say something about there being too many people around."

"The barmaid or Masters?"

"The barmaid said Magenta had said she was looking for a quiet place. Wyndham was too busy."

"Wyndham, too busy? I went there once; it was dead." The younger man's impressions of Wyndham were far from favourable.

Peter added an explanation. "There was some sort of Government exercise going on at the time. Police and immigration and customs from what I could make out. You should be able to check."

"I don't think that will be necessary." It was the younger man again. It appeared he preferred to ask questions rather than take suggestions.

It was now the turn of the older officer. "Did you see

Masters in Kununurra?"

"No." Peter and I both answered at the same time.

"Did you see her anywhere else?"

I answered Adamson's question. "We did see her van leaving Derby just when we were driving into town late in the afternoon. I don't know where it was going. It could have been heading to Broome, or maybe someplace else. She may have planned to camp beside the road."

"What day was that?"

I looked at Peter. "It would have been the Wednesday wouldn't it?"

Peter nodded.

The older policeman looked at his diary. "The thirtieth?"

"The Wednesday, whatever it was." They had a calendar and I had never worried about the dates while we were travelling.

"In your report you made a big issue about diamonds. Why were you so interested in diamonds? How do you know so much about them?"

"I bought a pink diamond for myself when we were in Kununurra. It will be a great memento of the trip. I've been interested in them for years and finally decided to buy myself a ring. Consequently, I have an idea of how expensive they are. The saleswoman spoke about a young woman with a distinctive appearance who had made a big purchase of two unset stones. From her description it would have been Masters. Obviously the stones must have been expensive. I know what I paid and the saleswoman had been impressed with the size and quality of the diamonds the girl bought. I thought the fact that they had not been found could be significant."

"There were three places marked on the map found in the van. One was the beach where the car was found. The others were further south. One south of the Sandfire roadhouse, and the other north of Carnarvon. Did you go there?"

This time Peter answered. "I don't know. I saw some marks on the map but I didn't have a good look. I don't know exactly where they were."

It was Adamson, the younger officer, who replied. "Both are off the highway and are carparks near the coast. In fact, both are looking out to the sea."

"We drove from Sandfire direct to Karratha. And from Karratha we drove straight through to Denham. We didn't go to the sea, except at Karratha and Monkey Mia. Even when we backtracked to Carnarvon we were only in the town. Where were these marked sites?"

"That's not important. Can you prove you didn't go onto the coast?"

"I don't know how. We didn't go to the coast. Only where I told you."

I could tell Peter was beginning to get annoyed with the questioning. I felt the mood in the room was becoming stressful and I decided to try to ease the tension. "Have you found out what happened to that poor girl?"

"That's not important. What does CDRMR mean?"

Peter and I looked at each other in puzzlement.

"CDRMR?" The tone of Peter's voice showed he had no idea of what the letters could mean.

"Yes. Do the letters mean anything to you?"

"No."

"Are you sure?"

"Yes. What are they?"

"What about you?" It was the older officer addressing me.

"No idea. What do they mean?"

Adamson explained that they were found written on a scrap of paper crumpled on the floor of Masters' van.

"Do you know anyone whose initials they may be?"

Peter answered first. "No. I would have thought that they are unlikely to be initials. Normally most people just use two, JB, TR, three maybe, five is unlikely."

"I knew a Cee Dee at school, Cecelia Davidson, but that was a long time ago." I doubted my contribution would be of any assistance.

"Where is she now?"

"I have no idea. I haven't seen her for over forty years?"

I could see Peter's mind working. This was the type of puzzle he enjoyed.

"Could it be an abbreviation?" the older man asked.

"Well, CD is compact disc, DR is doctor, MR is motor registry. They are probably not the correct answer, but perhaps it is something like that. See doctor at motor registry fits but would hardly be likely. It doesn't look like an acronym. Perhaps it is an initialism."

"What's the difference?" I could see both officers were troubled by Peter's logic.

"An acronym is an abbreviation pronounced as a word. For example, NATO, but an initialism you pronounce each letter, say ABC or NRL.

Both police officers decided it was time to move on.

"Who is Jason?"

Again Peter and I looked at each other. Neither of us showed any sign of knowing a Jason.

Peter answered. "The only Jason I know was in 'The Argonauts'."

"Where did you meet him?"

It was obvious the younger man lacked knowledge of the time before television. Newman, the older man, supplied an answer. "My eldest sister used to talk about 'The Argonauts'. It was a program on the radio. Years ago. Long before TV."

"A radio show?"

I decided to enlighten the young man. "Once upon a time there was an afternoon program for children on ABC radio. It was based on old Greek myths about the search for the Golden Fleece. Children were given names according to the Greek ships that were in the fleet led by Jason. I was Polynices 39. We used to send in poems, or stories, or art to the radio station and sometimes they would be read out over the radio and we would get points and could win rewards. I never won enough points but I used to love the program."

"I doubt that will help me find Jason today! Why was your friend's number on Master's phone?"

I gathered Adamson must have been referring to Peter.

Peter shook his head. "I don't know how I would be on her phone. I didn't think you found her phone."

"We haven't. However when she booked the van in Darwin she gave a contact number. The report I received says Darwin police were able to trace the calls that she made through the service provider. Your number and a John Satto's number were on the list. Why?"

"I have no idea. I have never spoken to her. I wouldn't know what her phone number was and she has never called me. Perhaps if you check my phone provider you will see that. I doubt if you would find that John Satto has ever spoken with her either. He has never even seen her. The body was missing by the time we got to the beach."

"Are you quite sure you haven't spoken to her by phone?"

"Quite sure! If your report says my number was on a list I think you should check the report."

"Besides your phone number and your friend Satto being on the list it seems she made very few other calls. One call out and one call in. The number was a mobile phone in Djakarta. Do you know anything about that?"

"No. Can you track the phone in Indonesia and find who she called?"

"We are working on that. By the way, Forensics have reported on the leg that the fisherman caught. It seems it wasn't a shark. It appears it was surgically amputated, rather roughly, with a handsaw. They think the other leg found on the beach may be the same. We have no idea where the rest of the torso is. Do you know who would do that?"

I went faint at the thought of someone sawing through a person's legs. Peter answered the younger man's question for both of us. "No. We don't have friends who go around sawing off people's legs and throwing them in the sea. You should be looking elsewhere." I shuddered at the thought of someone cutting through the legs of another person, even if the person was already dead as I assumed she would have been. It all seemed so senseless.

"And you don't know any Jason, at least someone living in this century."

We both shook our heads. Neither of us could recall ever knowing any Jasons.

The younger officer made a brusque thank you and walked out of the interview room. The older officer, whom we now knew as Keith Newman, smiled and made his farewell with a final comment. "Whoever is behind this is someone you should avoid. They don't mess around and they could be very dangerous. If there is any progress I will let you know."

As we left the police station we both had the same feeling. For some unknown reason we were under suspicion, but we had no idea why, and certainly no idea where it would lead us.

19 Freo

Peter

After we left the police station I was uptight and confused. The session with the two police officers had left me with the feeling I was somehow a suspect, or at least involved in something. Yet I had no idea of what. Talking with Suzie as we walked away from the building I found she had the same feeling.

It was late morning and I felt I needed a drink, or at least a coffee. The thought of returning to our motel room didn't appeal. I wanted to get away, to do something. We found a small coffee shop that served snacks and made our plans for the afternoon over two strong coffees and some quiche, and then another two strong coffees.

Suzie had heard friends speak of King's Park so we decided to visit it. My interest was Fremantle and especially the Maritime Museum of which some of my friends had spoken favourably. We made the decision to walk to King's Park and be tourists for the day. Tomorrow we would spend the whole day in Fremantle.

It was pleasant to be out walking. At least I had the feeling I was doing something, not just waiting for whatever the police thought was ahead of us. The words of the older policeman had unsettled us both.

The park was large, and at Suzie's suggestion we decided to explore the various sections devoted to the different climatic regions of the state: the plants of the Wheatbelt, the Goldfields, the Mulga and the Kimberley. While we were already familiar with the plants of the Kimberley, it was interesting to see the range of the flora of the other regions. As we walked Suzie explained the variations in the Boronias and the Hakeas, the Waxes and the Kangaroo Paws. Her knowledge of plants far exceeded mine.

We found a seat and sat and looked down on the Swan River and the CBD of Perth with its high towers. Surrounded by nature and the bush our concerns had faded and we had both become more at ease.

"What are you smiling at?" Suzie's face had taken on a very gentle smile, but I could see no reason for it.

"I was just thinking of a neighbour of mine in Melbourne. She and her husband used to live in Perth and some Sundays they would come here for an outing with their two small children. Her husband would hide ten cent coins at the base of some trees and she would tell the kids that fairies had left them there but only good children could find them. The children would run from tree to tree looking for the coins. Eventually, when the children were tired the family would go to the kiosk and the kids would buy ice-creams with the money they had found. Then they would sit on the grass and enjoy the space and beauty around then. She has fond memories of those times even though her kids have grown up and she is now a grandmother."

In the evening, back at the motel, our unsettled feeling reappeared. We drove to a local pub recommended by the receptionist and had a meal. Then we returned to the motel. It was clear our interview at the police station was still in the back of our minds. The words of the older police officer remained in our thoughts. I don't think either of us slept well that night.

It was another warm clear blue day in Perth as we boarded a bus and made our way to the railway station to catch the Fremantle train. The short twenty-minute trip took us along the Swan River and out to the coast.

Fremantle, or Freo to the locals, had once been the main sea port for the city of Perth and the whole of Western Australia. It was still the port for Perth but other ports servicing the iron ore, the gas and the agricultural industries had grown much larger and taken trade away from Fremantle. While Freo had grown over the years it had also changed from a tough working town of seamen and wharfies to a place of restaurants, art galleries, bars and tourists. It had also become a home to trendy residents seeking a more intimate community than they could find in a big city.

We wandered the streets lined with converted warehouses, old pubs, and offices. Some of the older offices and warehouses now formed part of a university. Suzie browsed the shops full of the usual tourist knick-knacks looking for gifts for her family, especially her grandson. I spent my time looking for a nearby seat, offering an opinion only when asked. I have never understood the attraction of shopping for women. If you needed something you looked for it and bought it. Spending hours 'just browsing' was not my idea of pleasure.

Eventually we reached the harbour area. Once it would have been full of sailing ships traveling the world trade routes. Today it was home to yachts and the motor cruisers of prosperous mining entrepreneurs and businessmen. In the distance one beautiful white boat stood out. While not quite the largest, it gleamed with a shine that only love, or a hardworking crew, could provide. A blue flag with the union jack in the corner flew from the ensign staff at the stern of the boat. The flag carried some sort of shield on it, but what it was we could not make out from the distance.

"Stand there. I want to take a photo of you with the boats in the background. Move to the left! I want to get some more boats in the background."

"I thought you had realised by now I don't move to the left. I am a right leaning person!" All the same I obeyed Suzie's direction.

"Peter, I don't care what your politics are, move to the left. You had a mast coming out of the top of your head!"

Sometimes it's best to obey instructions.

From the harbour we found the sign to the Maritime museum.

We wandered the collection of boats: canoes, fishing boats, naval craft, even a river ferry. The displays showed maps of Indian Ocean trade routes, old navigation techniques, and goods that had passed through the port. But my favourite had to be 'Australia II'. The memory of the day the yacht won the Americas Cup was etched in the mind of every Australian of my generation.

Not far away was the Shipwreck Museum. I guess there is still something of the little boy in me who thinks of shipwrecks, adventure and Robert Louis Stevenson. I convinced Suzie I had to see it. The reality was far less pleasant. The coast of Western Australia had caused the death of many Dutch sailors bound for the riches of the East Indies and what is now Jakarta, or as it was then called Batavia.

Indeed, the captain of the famous 'Beagle' who had mapped so much of the western coastline of Australia thought he had discovered the wreckage of the Dutch East Indies ship of that name in 1840. In fact, the 'Beagle' had discovered the wreck of the 'Zeewyk'. The 'Batavia' had been shipwrecked in 1629 on the Houtman Abrolhos while on its maiden voyage. Most of the three hundred and twenty-two passengers and crew were able to get ashore. A group led by the captain and Franciso Pelsaert tried to find a better supply of water on the mainland, but after no success headed north to Indonesia to seek help. Pelsaert returned to rescue the survivors and recover the gold and silver aboard the wrecked ship, but in the meantime a mutiny had occurred with over a hundred and ten murders. One group marooned on another island built a small fort out of limestone and coral for their defence from the mutineers. Justice was swift. A trial was held, some of the mutineers were hanged, and some taken back to Batavia for punishment. Of the three hundred and forty-one people who had boarded the 'Batavia', only sixty-eight eventually made it to the capital of the Dutch East Indies. Today, right in front of me were the anchor, cannon and some timbers of the 'Batavia', along with relics of the 'Zuytdorp', the 'Zeewijk' and the 'Vergulde Draeck'.

I had known of the misadventures of the early Dutch sailors, but I had never realised that the first European construction on the continent was a small stone fort on an island off the west coast of the country, built long before Cook's exploration, and one hundred and fifty-nine years before the First Fleet. Nor was I aware that the arrival of the first Europeans to the continent had been marked by a flattened pewter plate nailed to a post in 1616 by the crew of the 'Eendracht'. At least the island off the coast from where we had visited the police station at Denham now bore the name of Dirk Hartog, the ship's captain.

Without diminishing the work of James Cook, I was a little sad that more was not known about Hartog and the other Dutch sailors and merchants. So much of our history depends on our background. I was sure a little Dutch schoolboy would know more of Hartog and the Vereenigde Oost-Indische Compagnie than I had ever learnt at school.

As we left the museum and walked back to the restaurant precinct the white boat that had attracted my attention earlier in the afternoon was just leaving the harbour. It was some distance away, and it was still not possible to make out the name on the boat or the flag flying from the ensign staff. I was curious as to its home port. Probably some little country that registered boats cheaply. Most likely a tax haven. I asked Suzie to take a photo with her phone. Perhaps back at the hotel we could blow it up and work out where it was registered. I was curious about the flag with the Union Jack and the shield. The boat would be the new toy of some mining entrepreneur who had made a fortune selling dubious and far distant mining tenements to hopeful investors in newly floated mining companies. I always remembered the advice of a cynical financial commentator who had been through many a boom and bust. He suggested it was wise not to drill test holes on mining tenements. No test results meant you could sell the 'resource potential' time and time again into each new boom. Drill a hole and you would have to account for the knowledge that the supposed resource didn't exist.

"Have you ever been on a boat like that? I wonder what it would be like to have that sort of lifestyle?" Memories of our time in the Whitsundays came to me. I could see Suzie on such a boat. She had a manner and style that would look at home lounging in a chair on the polished deck, a glass of champagne in her hand.

"I was on a boat like that once. It was when we were living in London. My husband was good friends with a man whose father owned a boat very much like that one. Tony and I were invited to join a group for a week in the south of France. I have very mixed feelings of that week. The lifestyle was beautiful. The boat was wonderful. We had a great time. Most of the people on board were very nice but some we met were not so good. They didn't have any respect for others, or care about anyone else. And these weren't even bad people, they were all very respectable. No drug dealers or arms merchants. Just very successful businessmen and their wives or girlfriends. The other thing was the competition and envy between the boat owners. 'My boat is bigger than yours!' Thinking back to that time also brought back a memory of someone I met there who was not so nice."

"I wouldn't know. With work I've met a few men who have big toys but I have never set foot on a boat like that one. Apart from that beautiful launch that took us to Hayman Island. The best I have ever done is to fly out to mine sites with the directors in the company jet. I must admit I did enjoy avoiding the usual hassles of getting through the public airport terminal with its security and possible flight delays. A good coffee in the lounge at the private terminal, a short walk to the plane, and away. Then the large seats and the smiling service from the hostess with a whisky or beer. That had to change when mine sites became drug and alcohol free and the directors had to comply with the rules. After that the drinks would only arrive on the flight home."

We decided to go to a bar for a drink, then try a tiny restaurant that we had seen during our walk and catch a late train back to Perth. Whether it was the day, or the bar and its tapas, the music or the atmosphere of the little restaurant, we were much closer when we arrived back to our room at the motel. For the first time in many nights we touched as we lay together.

20 The Homestead

Suzie

Peter was very mysterious about our plans for the future. He would only say we needed to leave Perth, today, preferably this morning. All he would tell me was that he had made a booking before we had left Sydney and had been afraid our various visits to the police stations may have upset his plans. He made no mention of the coolness that had descended between us in Karratha and on our travels to Perth, or our decision to return separately to our homes. Fortunately the last vestige of that feeling had disappeared by the time we returned to the motel after our dinner in Fremantle. I felt we were now back to the possible happy relationship that we had when we commenced our travels.

He did say that we wouldn't need to use the tent for a few days. While he didn't admit as much, I think he was relieved to be back in a full size bed with solid walls around the room, not some thin mattress on top of the car and the hope that a flimsy piece of canvas would stop you falling to the ground if you rolled over too far. The thought of a large comfy bed and a clean spacious shower suited me. I had decided I preferred my bathroom and toilet close at hand and not after a walk in the dark to a community toilet. I had also decided that Peter was not really the camping type either. That was a good thing. I was not sure I wanted to spend the rest of my life with a man who would disappear into the bush and live in a tent as often as he could. My tastes were different. It didn't have to be five stars, although that would be nice. Three and half would do if it was with the right man.

We drove south on the motorway to Mandurah then took the Bussell Highway towards Margaret River.

Although he was driving it soon became clear Peter's thoughts had returned to our meeting at the police station two days earlier. It was the puzzle of the letters that was occupying his thoughts. He had decided that C D R M R must be an abbreviation.

"Probably a mnemonic for a phrase. Bit like EGBDF in music, you know Every Good Boy Deserves Fruit for the lines of the treble clef."

Peter's music teacher had a different saying to Miss Haufmann, my aging piano teacher at boarding school. She had taught me Every Good Boy Does Fine. I could imagine fruit being of more interest to a boy than being fine. Nor had I known Peter had learnt music. Had he learnt an instrument or was it just general musical appreciation? He had shown little passion for music and had mostly been disparaging of the hip hop artists or heavy metal that came over the radio. I doubted that I would get him to one of the operas I enjoyed.

He was also concerned about the beer. Did Magenta drink it herself, was it a gift, where did it go? Why the concern about the beer? What was it about the beer that kept the thought of it returning to Peter's head? From what I knew of him he hardly ever drank beer himself. I asked him to explain.

"Well if she didn't drink beer, and we know her preferred choice in Wyndham was vodka, plus there was an empty vodka bottle in the van, she must have bought it for someone. Had she met them before her death and given it to them? Or did whoever took the body also take the beer? If so who were they? Yet they left the wallet and the money."

"Are you sure it is 'they'? It could be 'he', or 'she'," I replied.

"Yes, but I still think there must be more than one, although one person could have carried her down to the beach and put her in a boat."

"So you think there was a boat?"

"There was no way anyone could have removed the body back to the main road and not left an indication—dust or tracks. There was nowhere to hide another car at the beach where Jimmy found the body, and there was no time for anyone to have driven in and then taken the body away. There was no sign of a burial or a body being hidden so it must have gone out to sea. Besides, that could also account for the leg being found in the ocean further south."

"But we didn't see a boat."

"True, but there was a cruise boat off the coast. I'm sure they would not have sent a zodiac ashore to remove a body, but perhaps there was another boat somewhere. Also the marks on the map. I didn't see the exact sites but from the questioning they must be on or near a beach—and remote. It could be that Magenta was going to follow down the coastline and meet someone at one of those places. Yet the van was to be returned to Brisbane. That's in the opposite direction. Perhaps they were alternate meeting places. If not the first, then the second, or the third. They were fall back plans. That they were near the ocean each time probably meant she was planning to meet someone coming from the sea. From a boat. Maybe that is why she was in Wyndham, but that plan was cancelled because of the police and customs. It still doesn't tell us what happened. Did they kill her, or just take the body after she had died? Did she have the beer for them?"

Peter was like Fred back at the station when the car, and the missing body, had been discovered. Then Fred had decided that there must have been more than one person involved. Peter now seemed to share his opinion. I was still undecided and thought of possibly one. "Perhaps he, or she, or they, took the beer as well as the body."

"It's possible. It's also possible that she didn't only drink vodka. She might have drunk the beer herself."

"True."

While Peter drove and tried to solve the puzzle he had set for himself my thoughts turned to Magenta. She was probably a little younger than my daughter Emma. Somewhere she must have a mother. I wonder if her mother knew what had happened, or where she had been. Probably not. Was her mother even alive? Perhaps she had died and Magenta was alone. Maybe there were other family members: brothers and sisters, or even a father who would mourn her. She seemed to be a girl that would drift off into a world of her own, rarely making contact with those who held her dear. Somewhere there might be a worried mother hoping, even praying, for a call to say, "I'm OK, Mum."

We didn't know why she was at that lonely beach when she died and whether it was an accident or murder. Our suspicions of a possible drug and alcohol overdose causing her death were based on one little white pill and the empty bottle of vodka. We had heard nothing from the police, but of course there was no body to test. Was she part of some drug syndicate trying to smuggle in drugs from Asia? Were the diamonds a payment for drugs? That seemed unlikely. Still I suppose someone could promise drugs, take the diamonds and then kill her and keep the drugs—if they existed in the first place. That still didn't explain her disappearance unless someone was trying to hide something. It certainly didn't explain why they would dismember the body. Then there was the police interest. They must have some knowledge of something that they were not telling us. Some fact that linked us to her disappearance.

I thought more about the woman. What was she like? She certainly had attitude. That showed in the way she dressed, the colour of her hair and the hairstyle. And her tattoos. She was giving out a message, 'I am me. I am an individual. I am different.' I could imagine her saying, "Accept or f* off!" What had taken her on that path? I couldn't imagine my son or daughter acting like that. Had Magenta come from a loving home or was she escaping from a difficult childhood? We would never know. Was she happy or was there some demon driving her? Again we would never know.

I thought again of my daughter. We had had our disagreements. We still did, but fortunately we were still close. I couldn't imagine her taking the path of Magenta. Was that just good luck on my part or was it the environment people grew up in? Then I thought of Peter's son. He was so like his father in many ways, yet he had taken a very different path in his emotional life. They had not been nearly as close as Peter had believed. Still I couldn't see Matthew being like Magenta. But we never know what life may bring us. I'd seen enough of my friends and their families to know that love and caring does not always bring happiness to either parents or children.

We drove on. We stopped for lunch at Busselton and found a convenient teashop. Then it was on to find our accommodation for our stay. Peter passed the map to me. We needed to find Caves Road. This was the first time Peter had ever relied on me for directions. From previous experience navigating for my husband I was concerned about how our day would end.

We entered the driveway and found ourselves looking at a large single-storey farmhouse. Farmhouse perhaps did not give it full credit. With its rambling shape, many roofs, and encircling verandah, it reminded me of the station homesteads of the Riverina where I had grown up. I realised Peter had chosen it for that reason. Back in Sydney when he was finalising our plans he had spent time researching the Margaret River wineries that he wanted to visit. He must have also spent time finding this beautiful B&B that he hoped would appeal to me. Deep down in the often gruff exterior there was a caring man.

After the silent hours spent in the car as we had driven south from Karratha, as Peter had tried to come to terms with his son's news, I was relieved that the warmth had returned to our relationship. I had made my decision to return to my family in Melbourne and put the adventure down to experience but had changed my mind, and now here, in this beautiful house with Peter relaxed and back to his old ways, I was again looking forward to spending time with him. I still didn't know if that meant 'permanently' or just 'on occasions'. This was certainly an occasion.

After checking in and finding our room we headed off for our first winery visit. Peter had planned to spend a few days going from one winery to another. The flaw in his planning was tasting wine and driving. Fortunately the locals had solved that problem. We could hire a car and driver by the hour.

Checking a map of the region he had picked up at the reception desk, Peter had found that we were close to a winery that he had heard of many years earlier. He had often enjoyed a glass, or several, of the red with friends. We decided we would make it our first visit.

The winery had taken its name from the nearby Cape that had been charted in 1801 by a French expedition and named in honour of two French brothers, a geographer and a cartographer of the 1700s. The French connection had returned with the winery now owned by a famous French company with interests in champagne houses. Peter was in his element trying the range of reds. The cabernet sauvignons, the blends in the Bordeaux style, the zinfandel. His only problem was the need to spit. I offered to drive back to the B&B, but he was concerned about retaining a clear head for later in the evening.

Returning to the B&B we changed and prepared for dinner at a restaurant in town. Our life on the road and the meals were having an effect on me. Squeezing into one of the two pretty dresses I had packed for the trip was becoming more and more difficult. I would have to watch what I was eating or I would need to buy new dresses. Being in the heart of the wine and food region of Western Australia a new dress was looking more and more likely. From the dress shops we walked past on our way to the restaurant it appeared the locals had anticipated the problem.

The restaurant was large. However the guests were dispersed behind screens and dividers in such a way that it had the feel of a much more intimate place. Rather than the noise of a big venue the talk was soft and subdued. The couples at the tables all looked as if romance was on their minds. We ordered, and at last Peter could drink the local wines.

As we were leaving I saw across the room a face that looked familiar. Gone was the polo shirt and shorts but it was the same shaved head. He was now wearing a suit and tie, and was with a group of similarly dressed men. It looked like some sort of business dinner, but I was sure he was one of the men we had seen in Broome talking with Magenta.

The dinner at Fremantle had broken the tension between Peter and me. Tonight we had caught the feeling from the restaurant. It was an evening for romance. That night we lay together and for the first time my feeling of uncertainty disappeared.

While I was waiting for Peter and our driver to plan the day's itinerary I ran through the photos that I had taken in Fremantle. When the photo of the white boat came up I remembered Peter's curiosity about where it was registered.

I tried enlarging the section of the photo showing the flag. Then I called Peter. The blue flag showed the Union Jack in the top left corner. A large shield in the central section of the flag had a lion. It was horizontal but definitely a familiar English style heraldic lion. Not rampant, but I could never recall the name for this particular form. Above the lion was a green turtle. I showed it to Peter and the driver.

"I don't know. The Union Jack and the lion says British. The turtle is strange. I'm not familiar with it, but it looks 'island'. Maybe the Pacific or more likely the Caribbean. Can you see the name of the boat and where it is registered?"

I played with the image again and zoomed in on the stern of the boat. There was the name: 'Sea Dreamer', George Town.

"Sea Dreamer. That's it! C D R M R. Sea Dreamer. That's what the initials stood for. It was phonetic. Magenta wrote C for Sea. She must have expected to make contact with the boat. But if that is the boat, who is Jason?"

21 Wineries

Suzie

Peter and Danny, our driver, had come up with a plan for the day. We would begin by visiting Voyager Estate and take a tour of the winery, then a tasting. Next a stop at a local coffee shop for a quick coffee break before heading to the second winery for a tasting and lunch in the winery restaurant. After a long lunch we would visit the art gallery at the winery before moving on to our final visit to a third winery. Today we would visit the big name wineries. Tomorrow Danny would take us to some of the interesting smaller family operations. I made the decision that we would not need to go out for an evening meal and asked Danny if we could stop off and buy some crusty bread, some cheese and a few bits and pieces—plus some soda water. Then if we did decide we wanted another meal we could just have a light snack in our room. Another night out and a new dress would be a necessity.

The first stop on our day's trip was at a beautiful white winery in the South African Cape Dutch style. Danny explained the Margaret River region had been the beneficiary of money from an earlier mining boom. To have a winery was the ultimate status symbol for some Perth mining entrepreneurs and they had ploughed their new fortunes into their wineries. That investment had supported the development of the region, the restaurants, and the specialist food producers that now existed.

The gardens and lawns around the buildings were beautiful. Yet as gorgeous as the buildings looked they were somehow out of place; it was like a transplant from another continent. Too pretty and formal for a land of scraggly gums and mallee. The formal werf garden was full of exotics showing a European and English influence. I loved the roses planted at the ends of the rows of vines. When I commented on them as we were tasting some of the winery's product it was explained to me that it was not just for show but was a management technique. The roses could indicate problems with disease and pests earlier than the vines themselves.

Our next stop was the famous Leeuwin Estate. With Peter's agreement Danny had phoned ahead and made a booking for the tasting and lunch package. He would return to pick us up when we phoned him, otherwise he would be back in five hours. Experience told him he would be back before Peter phoned. Long lunches were the norm.

On our arrival we were handed a glass of the Estate Brut and taken to see the originals of the artwork that appeared on the labels of the winery's premium wines. The works were a collection of the leading names in modern Australian art. I particularly loved the bold colour and patterns of John Olsen while Peter was attracted to the gentle work of Lloyd Rees. The winery was worth visiting just to see the works of art on display. Then we moved to the tasting area and commenced the tasting program under the tutelage of a knowledgeable guide. Unlike yesterday Peter was swallowing. I was more careful and decided it would be best if I only took a mouthful of each, and even then used the spittoon for some of those. By the third wine I was needing a break from terroir and tannins and the difference between French and American oak, and I looked around at the other visitors fronting the tasting counter.

At the far end a bald-headed man, standing alone, was tasting the range of wines that had been lined up in front of him. It was the man I had seen in the restaurant last night. Today there was no suit and tie, and he was casually dressed in a blue polo and tan chinos. I was even more certain that it was the same shaven head that I had seen talking with Magenta in the Roebuck Bay hotel in Broome. I pointed him out to Peter.

Seizing the moment I decided I would find out more about him. Taking a glass of wine I wandered off pretending to look at some displays telling the history of the winery. The walk took me to the end of the counter where the man was still tasting on his own. Noticing that he was tasting a red that Peter and I were also trying I asked him how he liked it. This lead to more conversation and I introduced myself, mentioning that I had noticed him at a restaurant last night.

"Oh, yes. I had a difficult day yesterday. That was the last of it. Perhaps I should have called it the 'Last Supper'. I was discussing a business deal but it fell apart. That was supposed to be the dinner to celebrate the deal but it turned into the wake."

I made a few polite noises of sympathy and wondered to myself what the deal might have been.

"I'm Eddie, Edward Markham."

I motioned to Peter to come and join us and introduced

him to Eddie. I made no mention that I had seen him in Broome and hoped Peter wouldn't mention that fact either. I wanted to find out more about Eddie before we went there. Since we were all interested in tasting the same range of wines we merged our tasting. Eddie obviously knew his wines and was interesting company. Little had come from the conversation apart from learning that he travelled a lot and was currently visiting the West. No mention was made of any business or where he had been. With our tasting finished it was time to move to the restaurant and on impulse I suggested he join us. I wanted to find out more about this man. Fortunately, he accepted.

We had expected to have a long lunch and so it was. The menu was worthy of the finest big city restaurants. Peter had difficulty choosing between the abalone and the cuttlefish with papaya, ginger and tamarind for entrée but was quite definite on the marron and pork belly for mains. I chose the venison carpaccio and Szechuan duck. Eddie chose the panko crumbed oysters with jalapeno dressing and a steak. The Estate wines came matching our choices of food.

Over the mains we discovered that Eddie was an advisor and facilitator consulting to businesses around the world on their financial arrangements. His speciality was international investments and he facilitated funds transfers from one country to another. When I asked where his home was he replied that home was wherever he was. He had an office overseas and a house but really his business was where his clients were. Officially home was where his office was based, but that was only for legal reasons. He travelled a great deal and was very rarely there.

He had a boat and often lived on it. These days with technology it was possible to conduct business anywhere in the world from on board. It was also useful for impressing clients. A few days on the boat was often an assistance in getting clients to commit to doing business. It also allowed him to move around the world as he did business.

Peter pressed him for more details of what sort of consultation he did.

"Financial consulting. Wealthy people who want to move funds from one country to another. I advise on the best ways of doing it and advise on the legal processes that must be followed. I arrange the banking and taxation requirements and assist with introductions to experts who can assist with investments."

Peter was also interested in the boat. Was it a yacht or motor cruiser?

"Motor yacht. Twin sixteen hundred horsepower diesels, plus units to power the generators and other gear. It's not sail. I think my clients prefer the security of moving when they wish, and not having to rely on the wind."

"It must be a big boat with those power units?"

"Yes. It has a crew of four including a cook and steward. Sometimes more if it is a big trip. It will sleep eight guests."

"Where is it now?" I asked.

"It's sailed down to Albany. I will meet it tomorrow. I was going to take a cruise for a few days with the people I was trying to do business with but that won't happen now. I will go down and meet it, then it will sail back to Perth and head north. I have some clients in Indonesia who might enjoy a trip. I have to fly to Melbourne and will meet it again in Broome or Darwin."

"Do you often sail from Indonesia to Australia?" Peter's question sounded innocuous but I now knew him well enough to see that there was more to the question than appeared on the surface.

"Every now and again I bring a few Indonesian or other South East Asian clients across to Darwin and down to Broome for a few days. Sometimes they fly home from Broome and I pick up a new group and sail back to Indonesia. They are important business people and they like the idea of a private cruise. It costs me quite a lot of money but it pays in the end."

I was dying to ask when he was last in Broome, but decided it may be better not to ask. I could see Peter was also interested.

"How do your clients like Broome? We were there on our trip down the coast."

"It's an interesting place. In some ways it reminds me of the wild west. It certainly would have been that once, though now it is much quieter. I think my Asian friends enjoy it for its multicultural history. It is so different to their home countries. So much empty space with no people. In some ways it frightens them. They are so used to being surrounded by masses of people. Even the wealthy who can afford some space and privacy can still be unsettled by the lack of crowds."

Four o'clock arrived quickly and in the doorway we saw Danny waiting for us. We had a choice. Another tasting at Vasse Felix, or a longer slower visit to the Estate Gallery. He would wait until five. I was relieved when Peter suggested the gallery. I think he had decided we had drunk enough wines for the day. I was very pleased that he had offered me an opportunity to spend more time viewing the artworks.

Eddie must have enjoyed our company. Maybe it was an escape from the failure of the previous day's business. Maybe he was just lonely and at a loose end. He asked if he could join us visiting the gallery.

It was only as we were parting that I noticed the letters under a small logo on his polo. It was an image of a motor cruiser and underneath were the letters G T Y C. I was curious by what they stood for. I thought it would be another puzzle for Peter to solve, and I was about to ask him when Eddie turned back to us and spoke.

"I will be in Albany for a few days. Why not come out to the boat and have lunch? If you are planning to do wineries tomorrow let's make it the next day. I'll send the zodiac in for you at noon. The main wharf. It is easy to find. The boat is called Sea Dreamer."

Peter and I looked at each other. This was an invitation we were not going to miss—even if it meant leaving Margaret River sooner than we had planned.

22 Big Boy's Toys

Peter

In Fremantle we had only seen the boat at a distance, but here, close up, it was so much bigger than I had expected. I had thought the boat had been all white but now we could see the narrow blue trim circling the hull just below the deck line. A similar blue line ran around the higher decks. The trim around the doors and windows were in shiny timber and brass. Seeing the size of the boat close up I realised Eddie's business deals must be very lucrative. His crew would also be kept busy polishing and maintaining the boat.

An attractive young woman dressed in white with blue trim on her blouse stood waiting to assist us to board. Stepping from the zodiac I felt a chill settle over me. With far distant Africa being the nearest landmass, the westerly winds blowing across the ocean can make Albany cold and windy in winter, but today the sun was out and it was not one of those bleak d ays. The sun shone from a blue sky with only a few high wispy clouds. The breeze was almost non-existent, but still I felt the chill. I looked across to Suzie and the smile that had been on her face as we were greeted by Eddie had hardened into one that was fixed and polite. It was as if she had the same sensation that I was feeling. Yet I could see no reason for it. Eddie was charming, the two crew members obliging, and the boat was immaculate.

As the zodiac had pulled into the platform at the rear of the motor yacht I could see the name of the boat, 'Sea Dreamer', and its home port, George Town, in the Cayman Islands. That would probably explain the initials Suzie had seen on Eddie's polo. GTYC. George Town Yacht Club fitted and would be the most likely explanation.

Eddie was standing on the main deck waiting to greet us and invited us forward to the bow where three glasses had been set out and a bottle of champagne was chilling in an ice bucket.

"Welcome aboard Sea Dreamer."

With the mention of the name I felt the hairs on my neck prickle. This was the name that Magenta had scribbled on a piece of paper left on the floor of her van. It would be unlikely to refer to anything other than this boat, but what could be the connection between a young hippy woman travelling Australia alone in a camper van and this luxurious, expensive boat? She certainly didn't look like the type of woman that would attract Eddie's attention, and yet he had been in Broome and she had been speaking with him.

After filling our glasses Eddie suggested we might like a tour of the boat. He was obviously proud of his possession and wanting to show it off. He opened doors and showed us three of the staterooms, while apologising for not showing us his suite with the comment he was not as tidy as he should be. His suite connected to a cabin which served as his office and gave him privacy should he need it. Opening a fourth door he showed us his office. A large desk in front of an impressive leather chair faced three comfortable armchairs. On the wall two television sets were mounted facing the desk while a big window gave a view of the ocean. The desk was bare except for a writing set, a telephone, and what looked like an ornamental paperweight of pebbly stone-grey interlocking shapes representing the states of Australia. Apart from the fact it was on a boat, it could have been a senior executive's office in an upmarket private bank.

The boat could sleep eight plus the crew. At present there were no other guests on board, but he was expecting to meet some friends in Broome as the boat was heading north to Indonesia and then Singapore where he hoped to do some business. Hopefully, more successfully than his meeting in Margaret River. Then we had a tour of the gallery, the engine room and the bridge before moving to the sun deck where a table was set for lunch beside the Jacuzzi. Aside from the boatman in the zodiac, who had disappeared as soon as we had boarded, and the girl in white we had seen no other crew, yet drinks and food appeared as if by magic. It was easy to imagine a very comfortable life on such a boat with staff who anticipated your every need.

"What length is the boat? I'd guess about twenty-eight or thirty metres."

"You're close. Ninety-seven feet, thirty point six metres."

"And what size motors do you need for that length?"

"Sea Dreamer has twin Cats. They're C32As. They each produce 1600 horsepower, plus there are twin Onan generators."

"What sort of range and speed do you get with them?"

"Range depends on the speed. Top speed is twenty-two knots but cruising speed is more like twelve. That gives a range of maybe sixteen hundred nautical miles. It depends on what you are doing."

"I think, yesterday, you said you had four crew."

"Yes, usually four, but it depends on how many guests are on board. There is the captain and another sailor plus a cook and a general dogsbody for the guests. Sometimes I have another person on board to assist with the guests, and if it is a big passage I will have someone to back up the captain."

"Where do you find the crew?"

"For a boat like this there are plenty of young people wanting to work just for the opportunity to travel. The problem is finding the ones who are willing to work, are capable, and are discreet. My guests don't want their life all over Facebook or the newspapers."

"I expect you would also need people who can get along together. The last thing you would need is a crew who are fighting with each other."

"Fortunately that rarely happens, although it did happen in Broome. Two of the crew had problems. One of them quit and left. I didn't have time to replace her. The three remaining had to cook for themselves until the boat reached Fremantle."

"I saw your cupboard for holding shoes. I hope ours are suitable." Eddie had made mention about wearing suitable footwear when he had invited us to visit the boat.

"Yes, they're fine. I recently had a problem with a young lady who came as a partner of a guest from Singapore with whom I was doing business. She was very petite and glamorous, and wore exceptionally high stiletto heels. They would have left indentations all over the deck timber. It really became quite difficult when I insisted she remove her shoes. She spent the entire trip in a sulk. I believe my guest will find a new partner on his return home. She was a very foolish young woman."

As we settled at a table on the sundeck the young woman we had seen on boarding came out of the galley bearing a plate of marinated shrimp and avocado on tiny circles of toasted bread and another plate with miniature empanadas.

"Margo has just joined us. She started work in Fremantle and I think you will see what I mean about capable. Her cooking is wonderful. I will be sad to see her leave when the boat arrives in Singapore. I guess I will then probably have to get used to Asian style food for a while. Unfortunately, the crew will get most of the benefit of her cooking as I won't re-join the boat until Broome. The important man is the captain. A good man is very hard to replace."

Margo's skills were certainly up to Eddie's description. The salmon in a nutty crust served as mains was delicious. Eddie's wine was also delicious, a five-year-old white from Chile. Somewhere on t he Sea Dreamer there was a sizable cellar.

"Suzie was intrigued by the letters on your shirt. I assume it is some club. George Town Yacht Club?"

"Yes. It is the George Town Yacht Club. The boat is registered in the Cayman Islands and I am a member, not that I am ever there very often. I have to turn up on the island occasionally to keep my residency in order."

"I suppose that explains the flag. With the Union Jack, the Lion and the Turtle?"

"Yes. The National flag of the Cayman Islands."

"Do you spend much time there?"

"Not a lot. Really it is just the base for my business. I seem to spend my life on the boat or in an aeroplane or hotel. That's business."

"What about a wife or family?"

I thought it was typically Suzie to be asking about family.

"My parents have both died, my wife divorced me years ago and my daughter went with her. I rarely see her these days. She has made her own life. I guess I am a free man."

"It must be lonely sometimes?" I thought typically sensitive Suzie. Perhaps he enjoyed the company of Margo. She certainly could cook and she was also a very attractive woman. I had difficulty seeing Magenta fitting the image no matter how well she could cook. Her style was so different to Margo and what we had seen of Eddie.

"I would need a very understanding woman to put up with me. I am so used to having my own way most women would find me a trial."

An understanding woman was what I would need in my life. I hoped Suzie would be that woman. She met the criteria of 'understanding', and she was also great company and still attractive. She was older than Markham but I could see he also found her company enjoyable. And he had the boat and the lifestyle. I wondered what Suzie would say if he made an offer.

"I'm sure there would be lots of women who would find you very attractive."

I wasn't sure what to make of Suzie's statement.

"Me, or the boat. I don't think that would prove to be a relationship based on a firm foundation."

"What do you do when you are travelling?" I thought I would steer the conversation back to more mundane matters.

Eddie turned from Suzie to me. "You mean when we are cruising? Lots of talking. Lots of drinking and eating. Sunbaking and the Jacuzzi. We have books, DVDs, satellite television, and I have a hobby. I have a small but well equipped work bench down in the engine room. I enjoy making models, animals, buildings, anything that takes my fancy really, and I sometimes cast or mould them in various materials such as acrylate resin. I'm particularly proud of the ornamental paper weight that I made for my office deck. We also go fishing. We have a big freezer on board if we get a big fish. There is a jet ski in the playroom and the zodiac. We can go onshore for picnics. You do have to pick the spot up north. There are too many crocodiles in some areas."

"What about sharks?" Suzie looked across at me as I asked the question.

"Not really a problem. I worry more about the crocs, although you still need to be careful. There are some bad places for sharks. I believe there have been some recent attacks north of Perth."

"Yes, when we were driving down to Perth there was somebody, or body parts, washed up on the beach. Locals thought it was a shark attack."

"I remember something in the papers about that. What happened?"

Suzie answered. "I don't know. I gather it is a mystery.

Nobody knows who the leg belongs to. Nobody appears to have gone missing. The media had lots of theories but no answers. I don't think the police know anything. You are very fortunate to have Margo as a cook. She is excellent at arranging meals. I wish I had a cook like her."

I was puzzled by Suzie's answer. We obviously knew who the leg belonged to, and we knew it was not bitten off by a shark. I had never heard of her wanting a cook. I thought she preferred to be in charge of the kitchen herself. She was a very capable cook and quite able to match Margo's meal. It was as if she wanted to change the conversation.

"Will you meet the boat in Singapore?"

"It depends on how I go in Melbourne. I hope to meet it in Broome, or if things take longer to arrange I may catch it in Darwin. I certainly hope that I can get back on board before it leaves for Singapore. How about coffee?"

We drank our coffees and it became apparent it was time to leave. Suzie excused herself and went to the gallery to thank Margo for her meal. Eddie and I continued chatting until she returned.

"Please excuse me. I must go to work. Some of my clients are just starting their day and they may have questions for me. Thank you for coming."

He showed us down to the stern where the zodiac was waiting for us. As we were pulling away Eddie waved and shouted a farewell to us. "I enjoyed your visit. Perhaps we will run into each other another time."

"Maybe in Sydney." Well it would be me in Sydney. We still had to discuss where Suzie would be.

"Take care of them Jason. Make sure they get ashore safely." With that Eddie turned away and disappeared below.

23 Jason

Suzie

"How long have you worked for Eddie?"

I thought Peter's abrupt approach was too direct. Sometimes a little subtlety and deviousness are far more effective. "How do you enjoy working on a boat like that one? It must be a very glamourous life moving from one part of the world to another."

Jason was more responsive to my question than he had been to Peter's. I wasn't sure if it was the abruptness of Peter's questioning but his reply to Peter's question had been very short. To my question he was more forthcoming.

"You certainly get to travel, however it's not so glamorous. Our cabins are tiny. They're not like the guest cabins. It gets boring sometimes, just hanging around and always being nice to the guests."

"How long have you been with Eddie?"

"It's been three years this August."

"From the sound of your voice you're not Australian. Where's home?"

"I'm from South Africa, but I haven't been there for years. My parents live in Port Elizabeth."

"I believe the southern part of South Africa is beautiful. I have friends who drove from Cape Town to Port Elizabeth some years ago. They really loved the trip. They also went to J-Bay. That impressed my son."

"J-Bay is good if you like surf, but I prefer boats."

"Did you start working on boats in South Africa?"

"Yes. I used to sail as a kid and then I decided to get away and see the world. I worked on a yacht that came over to Indonesia and I lived in Bali for a while before I got this job."

I could see Peter suddenly take more interest in our conversation, but he remained silent.

"What's Eddie like to work for? He seems very nice."

At this question Jason suddenly became 'discreet', and his answer gave little away. I decided to back off.

"I imagine there are probably lots of young men living in Bali who would like a job like yours. Probably lots of Balinese as well as travellers. It must be very competitive to get a good job?"

"Well it helps to speak English. Some of the locals are OK but they get jobs in the tourist industry. They prefer to stay near home. The fishermen don't scrub up enough for the international boat set, and they don't have the experience. Men with boats like Sea Dreamer can be very demanding. You do what they want and say 'Yes Sir' or you go."

"It must be difficult at times. You would have your own pride."

"The pay is good. Do your job and all is sweet."

"How many crew do you have on the boat? It must take a few to sail it. We only saw you and Margo."

"There is the captain. He is on shore for a few days' break. I think he went up to Perth. Margo and me and Pally. He's the odd jobs man. Does a bit of everything; whatever Eddie wants."

"I didn't see him on board?"

"When there are guests we are supposed to stay out of sight as much as possible."

"I gather the boat is going to Singapore. Eddie said something about picking up guests in Broome and Darwin before going on to Singapore."

"I don't know. I just do as I'm told and make up for it when I get a few days off."

"Did you get time off in Broome? We stopped there on our travels. I found it really interesting."

"I've had days off there before but this time I had to stay on board. We only stopped one night. Some guests left us in Broome."

There was something about his answer that made me decide it would be a good idea to change the subject. Not that there was any more time as the zodiac had pulled in alongside the wharf. Thanking Jason, we stood and waved to him as he returned to the boat.

I turned to Peter. "Well he was in Broome, and he has been in Bali. He was also 'very discreet' on some things. Do you think he knew Magenta?"

Peter may have been quiet while I was asking the

197

questions but he had been listening to the answers. "We have no idea they were there at the same time. He says he didn't go ashore in Broome but Magenta had his name and the name of the boat. Perhaps she was asking about him at the hotel. She might have expected to meet him there."

"What about Pally?"

"Maybe he is the other man we saw with Eddie. He was very tanned and had bleached hair. He looked as if he was a sailor. I would like to know what 'odd jobs' he does for Eddie?"

As we walked down the wharf towards the car I glimpsed a man dressed in a suit. He was sitting on a bench reading a newspaper. It was difficult to see very much of him behind the newspaper which was hiding his face, but in the brief moment when he lowered the paper and looked at us I imagined I had seen him before. I couldn't place where. It was strange to see a man sitting on the wharf dressed in a dark suit at that time of day. The other people on the wharf were all casually dressed, tourists like us, or locals out for an evening stroll, or maybe fishermen attempting to catch a fish off the wharf.

Sitting in the pub having a counter tea we discussed our day. We now knew who Jason was. With Sea Dreamer and Jason on the same scrap of paper found in Magenta's van it was unlikely to be any other Jason. However he was not the man we had seen with Eddie in Broome when they had spoken to Magenta.

"Who do you think was the other man we saw with Eddie

and Magenta in Broome?"

"Probably Pally. Or perhaps the captain. It could be another crewman we haven't seen. Maybe there were more than four in the crew; he could have left in Perth. Margo only came on the boat in Fremantle so there would have been another cook. She would have been the one that quit. Maybe Magenta was looking for the job?"

"The way Magenta was speaking to Eddie in the Roebuck pub it didn't look like a job application."

"You're right. It seems unlikely that she wanted a job. After all she had planned to return the van to Brisbane and had only booked it for three weeks."

"Perhaps she had decided to dump the van." From the shake of Peter's head I could see he didn't agree with my suggestion.

"I don't think that is likely. Hiring the van, the marks on the map. It points to whatever Magenta was doing being on land, not at sea."

"Could the man we saw with Eddie be someone else?"

"Possibly. He might even have been a local from Broome that Eddie knew. It appears he often passed though the town."

"What do you think of Eddie? I like him. He's an interesting and attractive man."

Peter's answer was slow in coming. "His business must be very good. I have no idea what a boat like that would be worth but it must be a lot. Plus the cost of running it: fuel and crew, and then maintenance. I read somewhere that you need to allow twenty percent of the value of the boat to cover maintenance and servicing each year. I don't know if that's true but it would be a lot of cash."

"Could he make that much as an advisor?"

"If he delivers the goods and has very wealthy clients it's possible. I expect he takes a percentage for his services."

"What sort of services?"

"That's a good question. The Cayman Islands are a tax haven. There are some people who want to move money into those sorts of places. Not all of it is legitimate. Maybe Eddie does a few questionable deals. By the size of the boat, perhaps quite a few questionable deals."

"Do you think he smuggles money in the boat?"

"I doubt it. Most of it is by electronic transfer these days. It is the paperwork that accompanies it that is suspect. Inflated invoices. False invoices. Still every now and again somebody is caught with suitcases of cash. Sometimes people use gold. I suppose he could shift gold or cash. Probably the boat gives him time to spend with his clients, or guests, in privacy while they organise their arrangements. I expect he would be very careful about maintaining respectability. He wouldn't want to attract attention to himself or his clients."

"Do you think Eddie has anything to do with Magenta?"

"Eddie said he had a daughter. Perhaps Magenta is his daughter?"

"No." I was sure she was not his daughter.

"You are very confident. Is that your female viewpoint?"

"The way they were talking in Broome was not father/daughter. I know that can cover a wide range of relationships for good and bad, but they are not father/daughter. Not even a rebellious daughter with a bad relationship with her father. Put it down to female intuition."

"Perhaps she and Jason were friends. They'd both been in Bali. But then that doesn't fit. You would write down the name of the boat if you didn't know it but I don't think you would write the name of someone you knew. Perhaps as an entry in a diary you might write, 'Jason, Sea Dreamer, Monday', but not on a scrap of paper. I think she was given a name and the name of the boat."

"We don't know that they were even in Bali at the same time. Jason was there three years ago. Magenta had just come from Bali."

"True, but Sea Dreamer appears to visit there often. It could have been on one of those stopovers."

"So is Eddie clean? Perhaps Jason and Magenta had some deal of their own, quite separate to Eddie?"

"It's possible. But then Jason could hardly decide to stop Sea Dreamer and take the zodiac into the beach and meet Magenta without Eddie's permission."

"We don't know Eddie was on the boat as it sailed south. He spoke of the crew having to cook for themselves. I got the impression he wasn't on the boat. He may have flown from Broome to Perth to meet people for business. We saw him onshore in Broome. He never said he was on the boat between Broome and Perth." My answer gave Peter more possibilities to consider. We were getting no closer to an answer.

"I think Magenta was to meet the Sea Dreamer in Wyndham. She was given the name which she wrote down as a mnemonic and Jason was to be the contact. Perhaps from a phone call. There was a call from Indonesia remember. The customs and police activity meant that plan got called off and she moved to Broome. Whatever they were planning couldn't be done in Broome so there was another plan. In fact, a number of contingency plans. Hence the three crosses on the map. Plan A, plan B, plan C. Magenta was waiting at the first cross and got bored, overdid the drugs and vodka and her body just closed down and she died. That left Jason with a problem."

"So he removed the body. Why not just leave it there?"

"I don't know. Perhaps they wanted to remove some clues. Jason, or whoever, I still think there would be two, took the phone but not the wallet. I admit I don't really understand it."

"So is it drugs, or is it money?"

"Or is it both? I don't know."

"Did you feel anything different when we boarded the boat?"

"I felt a chill. There was something that gave me the creeps. The sun was shining. It was warm. Eddie was charming. Everything was beautiful, but it was as if there was some malevolent spirit on the boat. I noticed your manner also changed."

"I didn't think you were into spirits." I was going to make a pun about Peter's love of whisky but it didn't seem very funny thinking of the boat. I had also felt something evil, or at least not good, as I boarded.

As we lay together in bed we continued to talk over our day. There was something about the boat. Something we had seen that was significant, yet neither of us could pin it down. Before we kissed and rolled into our favourite sleeping positions we had decided to return to the boat in the morning.

Lying, listening to Peter's quiet steady breathing, my thoughts turned to the future. Our relationship had improved since Karratha and Perth, and the phone call to his son. We seemed to have moved to a comfortable companionship. The passion and lust of youth were not there, but I enjoyed his company and I was happy to lie beside him in bed. I enjoyed his touch and being held by him. I enjoyed the sex that occasionally occurred. Soon our travels would be over and I would have to make a decision. Would I stay with him in Sydney, or would I return to Melbourne where my children and grandchild lived and where I would have to rebuild my house that had been destroyed by a fire?

After our breakfast it was time to put our plan from the previous night into action. I phoned Eddie on the number he had given Peter when we had met him at the winery. At first he had said it would not be possible as he was not on the boat but on the road to Perth to catch a flight to Melbourne. He would contact the crew and have them look for my earring. If they found anything they would phone me. Peter and I were prepared for that answer. I commenced the story of how the earrings were an old family heirloom. With one missing the set would be worthless. They held so much sentimental value for me. My great grandmother had been given them on the birth of her first child. By the end of my story I was almost in tears. It worked. Eddie agreed to arrange for someone to meet us at the wharf at three o'clock. He apologised for his earlier hesitation but he had had privacy issues allowing people on the boat if he was not there.

"Well that's done. Let's go out to the old whaling station. That's next on our to-do list." The wind had freshened this morning and Peter's idea appealed. It would be warmer in the car or inside a building.

What I hadn't expected was that much of the old whaling station at Cheynes Beach was in the open air. One day, late in 1978, the station just closed. Men who had worked for years in the industry no longer had jobs, and an industry that had operated for one hundred and seventy-eight years vanished from Australia. The last of the whale chaser boats now sat preserved on dry land, and the factory had become a museum to a past way of life. Where once an industry based on hunting whales had existed, today the industry was hunting tourists. At least now both whales and tourists survived.

Wandering the indoor displays I was pleased that the giants of the sea were safe, or at least safer, but at the same time I was sad that a way of life, with its excitement and danger, had vanished. Sitting enjoying a coffee in the warm cafe and looking out over the ocean I thought of the changes we all faced. Jobs that existed today could vanish overnight. Industries that we thought of as lasting forever could disappear. Hopefully they would be replaced by new businesses that we had not yet even dreamt of. Still, there would be huge disruption to many lives. Should we keep old industries going even if the taxpayer had to support them forever? Perhaps we should let them die and concentrate on the new businesses of the future?

What neither Peter nor I had realised was that the old whaling station was now surrounded by a botanic garden. We ignored the cold breeze to walk the pathways and see the vast variety of local plants, many of them the wildflowers for which Western Australia is famous. I think I enjoyed the garden more, while Peter preferred the whaling museum.

When we walked back to the carpark there were still six or seven other cars parked there. All except one was empty. In a small red Toyota, a man had reclined the seat and was lying back asleep. He was wearing a dark grey suit. This time there was no newspaper and I suddenly realised where I had seen him. It was the older man from the police station in Perth.

"Peter, don't do anything obvious but look at the man in the red Toyota. It's one of the men from the police station in Perth. I think his name was Newman. I'm sure I saw him at the wharf when we got out of the zodiac. What does it mean?"

"Our feelings at the police station were right. For some reason we must be under suspicion."

"What do we do? Do we go and talk to him?"

"I think just ignore him. Pretend we haven't noticed. We have nothing to hide. They have no reason to do anything to us."

The zodiac was waiting for us at the wharf at three pm as promised. Again the boatman was Jason but today he was far less chatty. I felt Eddie had only agreed to our visit under duress and really would have preferred us not to be there. I thought his feelings had been passed on to Jason. There was no chat as we motored out to Sea Dreamer.

Unlike our last visit, this time there was no one to assist us when we arrived at the boat. It was not really a problem to clamber on board but the difference to our previous welcome was noticeable. As I had asked, Jason took us first to the gallery. Talking with Eddie I had suggested the earring may have been caught and fallen out when he had shown us the large game fish stored in the bigger of the two freezers. As I leant over pretending to search for the missing jewellery I felt Peter close behind me.

Finding nothing, I suggested perhaps it may have fallen from my ear when we were having lunch. Jason led us up onto the sundeck and I ferreted around the chair I had sat in the previous day. As I was running my hands over the folds in the fabric of the chair Peter started to chat with Jason.

"Where's everybody today? The boat seems deserted. I know Eddie said he would be flying to Melbourne but where are the rest of the crew? I thought you would have free run of the boat with the boss away."

"Here it is! Thank heavens I found it. It has passed through my family for four generations. I was devastated when I realised it was missing." My exclamation cut off any reply from Jason, but Peter's question had held Jason's attention as I dropped a cheap blingy earring I had bought earlier in the day into the fold of the chair.

"Well that's good. Now I'll take you back to shore. Then I'll phone the boss and let him know you found it and are off the boat. He wants a report."

24 Suspicion

Peter

"You should have told us the truth."

Suzie and I both turned at the sound of the familiar voice. It was Adamson, the younger police officer from our interview in Perth.

"What do you mean?"

"You didn't tell us that you knew Markham, or you knew about the Sea Dreamer."

"We didn't know him. We only met Markham a few days ago at a winery, and we didn't know that the Sea Dreamer was his boat."

"You seem to know the boat quite well. You have been on it twice in the last two days."

Adamson's knowledge of our movements confirmed Suzie's suspicion that we were being watched. She had thought she had glimpsed the older police officer when we had returned from our lunch on Sea Dreamer, and had become convinced when she saw him again at the museum. The police must have known where we were to be waiting for us on our return from the cruiser the second time. I was puzzled why they would be interested in us. But then we had both had the feeling that we were under suspicion when we had left the station in Perth. Perhaps they had already solved the puzzle of the initials and that was why they were here. But was it us or were they watching the boat?

"We only realised what CDRMR meant when we looked at a photo Suzie had taken in Fremantle and we saw the name of the boat. That was the day after we spoke with you."

"So you saw the boat in Fremantle?"

"Yes, but only in the distance. At that time we didn't know its name, and we certainly didn't expect to have lunch on it in Albany."

"Did you see the boat in Broome?"

This time Suzie answered. "There was a big white boat out in the bay. It could have been Sea Dreamer but I don't know. I just thought it was a cruise boat for wealthy tourists."

"And have you ever seen Markham before?"

"We saw him in Broome, at the Roebuck Bay Hotel. He was one of the men talking with the woman and another man."

"So have you met Jason, your Argonaut man?"

"Jason is one of the crew. He just brought us ashore in the zodiac. He also transferred us to and from the boat yesterday."

"And where is Markham now?"

I answered. "Apparently he is not here. I think he is on the way to Perth. He spoke of catching a flight to Melbourne today. Some business deal. When we phoned him to ask if we could come out to the boat to look for Suzie's lost earring he told us he had already left. He was rather cool on the phone. Said he had had to go away on business and was not on board. That he preferred only having visitors on the boat when he was there. It was only after Suzie insisted that we were leaving soon and the earring was part of a very special sentimental set. It had been handed down through her family for generations. Finally he agreed and said he would send the boat in for us."

"So the boat picked you up?"

"Yes."

"And?"

"Jason picked us up. He was even less friendly than yesterday. When we got to the boat he was with us all the time. It was as if he had been told to watch us. It was uncomfortable."

"Did you find the earring?"

"Oh, yes. That wasn't hard." I didn't mention that Suzie had dropped it in the fold of a chair just before she had pretended to find it. "As soon as we found it Jason brought us back to shore. I'm sure you would have seen that."

Adamson made no comment so I decided it would be my turn to ask questions. "What is this all about? Why are you watching us? We can hardly help you if we don't know what it is about." Until the police were open with us I decided we would not tell them of our suspicions.

"We are not watching you."

"Well what was Newman doing yesterday when we came

back from the boat? Why was he out at the whaling station when we went there? If you are investigating a death or Markham why are you following us?"

"I hope you didn't bring anything else back with you."

"What do you mean?"

"I think you need to be very careful."

"Why? We haven't done anything. We have no idea what this is all about."

"I would stay away from that boat if I were you. You could find yourself in serious trouble and not just with the police."

25 A Warning

Suzie

'You are in danger. Leave town now. Don't talk to anyone. Go home!'

I showed the folded note to Peter. The woman at the hotel reception desk had passed it to me when I asked for the key to our room.

"Who gave you this?" She answered my question by telling me that she had only just come on duty and had found the note in the pigeon hole when she reached for our key. She thought it had probably been put there by the morning shift receptionist. If it had been there when we had left the hotel for our sightseeing drive around Albany it would have been given to us when we had handed in the key.

"Could it have been a phone message?" Even as I said it I realised how unlikely that would be. You would be very silly to phone through a threat, ask the hotel operator to write it down and not expect to attract attention. Our receptionist thought it unlikely. Any phone messages would be on a hotel message form. This note was a larger sheet of paper. More likely someone had left it with the receptionist or perhaps left it lying on the counter. Folded, the warning would have attracted no attention. We decided to go to our room and consider what it meant. A cup of coffee would also help my nerves. Someone was either trying to help us—or frighten us. Which it was I didn't know, but it certainly was doing the latter.

The four short lines were brusque and to the point. It was written on a piece of ordinary paper that could have come from anywhere. The text was printed—more scrawled—in large red letters. It looked like the writer had used a fine marking pen rather than a biro. The sheet had been folded in three and both my Christian name and surname were neatly printed on the outside of the fold.

"Who would send this? Why? What do we do?" I looked at Peter but he seemed as puzzled as I was.

"I don't know. It must have something to do with Magenta. What else could it be? But I have no idea how or why. Is it the police? Is it Sea Dreamer? Markham? Jason? Who else could it be?"

"How could we be in danger from Magenta? We don't really know anything?"

Peter shook his head. "Perhaps someone thinks we know more than we do. The police seem to think so."

"What do we do?"

Before either of us could answer the phone rang. It was the receptionist from the front counter who had given me the note. She had spoken with the morning duty clerk who had told her that the note had been left on the counter. She had recognised the name and put it with the key. She had not seen who had left it as she was in an inner office doing reports. No one had rung the bell on the counter or called out for service. However a man had come in at about nine-thirty and asked if either I or Peter was available. When told we were out, he left. He had not left a message.

Was it two people, or was it the same one? I looked across to Peter. I could see he was trying to make sense of this latest news.

"Which came first: the visit or the note? That could make a difference. Perhaps we should talk with the morning receptionist."

While I agreed with his suggestion I thought it was unlikely that someone would leave a threatening note and then come back. Maybe he came looking for us, then when he didn't find us, thought about it, and decided to come back to leave the note. But would you come to threaten us in person? I decided it had to be two different people. That seemed more likely.

"Let's go and see the receptionist and track down the person who saw the man. Perhaps she can give us a lead."

"So you are not leaving town?"

"Not yet. What about you?"

I was more concerned than Peter. "I'm worried. I don't like threats, but talking to a hotel worker shouldn't be too dangerous."

The thought did cross my mind that we had been seen going onto Sea Dreamer, and Adamson had been waiting for us when we left the boat the second time. Perhaps we were still being watched. But then it was hardly likely that the police would leave a threatening note written in red. Still, these days, with the amount of money associated with drugs, not all police were honest.

From the sounds coming out of the unit the morning receptionist from the hotel was watching television and talking on the phone when we knocked on her door. A young woman I had noticed earlier in the day at the hotel opened the door. She had already changed out of the black and gold hotel uniform and was dressed in a bright comfortable top and yellow trackies. A tray with a cup of coffee and a half eaten salad sandwich sat on the table beside her chair. A mobile phone was in her hand as she opened the door. On the television a repeat of an old Agatha Christie mystery was playing. I recognised the story having seen it so many times. Perhaps for this young girl it was a new show. Or maybe it was just background noise as she texted or checked Facebook. The thought flashed through my mind. How would Hercule Poirot solve our problem? Unlike the television show our problems were happening in real life.

After introducing ourselves and thanking her for agreeing to see us, Peter began by asking the questions. "When did you find the note on the counter?"

"It would have been a little after nine. There was a lull in people checking out. The ten o'clock rush hadn't started and I was in the back office preparing accounts."

"You didn't see who left it?"

"No. I just saw it on the counter when I came back. I saw the name, looked up the register, and put it with the key so you would get it when you came in."

"Did you see anyone around the hotel?"

"No. The only person was one of the cleaners. I asked her if she had seen anyone leave it but she had just come down the stairs. She hadn't seen anyone."

"What about the man who was looking for us?"

"Yes. He was an older man. In a suit, but a bit scruffy. Looked as if he would be more comfortable wearing something else. Not well groomed, if you know what I mean. Bit old-fashioned looking."

"Was that before or after you found the note?"

"After, definitely after. He asked for Suzie Benedict by name. I remembered it was the same name as on the note."

"How old would you think?"

"I'm bad on ages. Older, like my dad. Maybe fifties, late fifties. Younger than you."

"Would you recognise him if you saw him again?"

"Probably. He was … He didn't really stand out. Just normal looking, but I think I would recognise him if I saw him again."

"What colour was his hair?" I hoped that I might be able to get more information than Peter.

"Ah, brown maybe with a bit of grey around the sides. He was taller than me."

That could have been most of the male population. Our informant was about five foot three. "What colour was his suit?" Perhaps clothing and colour might have had more impact on our young woman.

"Grey, with small stripes, and he had brown shoes and a blue tie."

Peter looked at me. We had seen a man in a grey striped suit and brown shoes twice before. He had even worn a blue tie. If it was him, it could solve one part of the mystery.

As Peter was driving us back to the centre of town I asked him, "Do you think the man who called at the hotel was Newman?"

"It's possible. Even probable, but why would he be calling on us?"

"Maybe he was going to say we were no longer of interest to them and we could leave."

"Perhaps. But then what about the note at the hotel? Who left that? I don't see the police leaving a note telling us to get out of town. Unless the second visit was to back it up in person. But that doesn't seem likely. Why would we be a problem to them?"

"Do you trust them? I have an uneasy feeling about Adamson."

"Is this your women's intuition again?"

"Call it what you like. I just get a funny feeling when we talk with him."

"I agree. He certainly knows more than he is letting on. I think he knew about Markham and the boat. I just don't see where we fit in."

That night I went to bed very troubled. Our problems seemed like a tangled skein of twine: all ends but leading nowhere. Yet beside me Peter slept soundly. The only noise to break the silence of the room was a small *pop pop* from his snoring. The image of an old-fashioned coffee percolator came to mind.

26 Red Lipstick

Peter

On the drive back to our hotel I had an uneasy feeling that all was not right.

It was unlikely that the police would leave a note to tell us to leave town. They could just have a talk with us. Why not just contact us and arrange a meeting? Adamson had done that before.

From the description it certainly could have been Newman, the older policeman, who had called at the hotel. When we had seen him in Perth he was wearing a grey suit and had a blue tie. He looked as if he lived in that same suit. I had no idea what colour his shoes had been but Suzie thought he had been wearing brown shoes in Perth. Perhaps he had come to warn us. But then why would he do that? It seemed unlikely. If he had left the note, why not wait and see us? And why not sign the note? It was all very strange.

The more I thought about it the more worried I became. Somewhere out there, in this town, someone was giving us a very strong message. I was sure it wasn't just advice but more a threat. 'Leave town. Don't talk to anyone.' They knew who we were and where to find us. They could be checking to see if we were leaving town or talking to anyone. What would they make of our visit to the hotel desk clerk?

But why would they call and ask for us when we weren't in the hotel? If they were watching us they would know we weren't there. Perhaps that meant the message and the visit were from two different people. If Newman was the visitor, then who left the note?

If the note hadn't come from the police, and that appeared probable, then it must have something to do with Sea Dreamer. But was it Markham or Jason, or both? I began to feel paranoid and started checking the rear view mirrors in case we were being followed. There was nothing.

If we did go to the police we would have to find Newman or Adamson. Walking into a local police station with our note and trying to explain our situation would not work very well. I remembered the response we had received in Denham and Carnarvon. Yet the note said not to talk to anyone. The police were not just anyone. They were probably whoever was behind the note did not want us to see.

Then there was Suzie. I didn't want to get her in trouble. She had enough problems after our troubles in Ballarat. Perhaps we should take the advice and leave.

We decided we needed a coffee and found a shopping centre, parked the car, and we went off to find some likely café where we could discuss our thoughts. The warning and the knowledge that someone was looking for us didn't make any sense. We had done nothing and we knew nothing that should concern anyone. The disappearance of a body from a beach south of Broome was common knowledge, as was the finding of a leg south of Carnarvon. The police were investigating, and we had told them all we knew. Going home early would change nothing. We were no threat to anyone.

Walking back to our car after the coffees I could see red marks on the windscreen. My first thought was it was a nasty prank by a graffiti artist or possibly a person with a grudge against the company who had hired us the vehicle. Getting closer I could make out the image. It looked like four words, yet there was something peculiar about their appearance and from the distance I couldn't make them out. Coming closer I realised some letters were reversed and suddenly I understood the message. Suzie obviously hadn't yet realised what the words were.

"When I unlock the door, sit inside. It will make sense." A look of concern immediately came over her face.

"'Your life. Leave now!' Who would write that?"

"Maybe the same person who left the note at the hotel, or perhaps it is someone trying to warn us."

"Are they trying to give us a warning, advice, or is it a threat?"

I didn't know whether I should tell Suzie, but to me it was more like a threat. Then again, I could hardly pretend that it wasn't there in dark red scribble on the windscreen, and she was smart enough to realise that it was more than a warning. It was definitely a threat.

"What do you think it is written with? It isn't a texta or a spray can. Could it be lipstick?"

Suzie dabbed a finger on a thicker section of the text. "Yes, I think it's probably lipstick."

"So did a woman write it?"

"Don't jump to conclusions. I wouldn't ruin my lipstick writing like this. It could be a man wanting us to think it was a woman."

"Margo had red lips the same colour as this."

"Oh you noticed did you? It matched her fingernails."

"So it could have been her?"

"Or someone who used her lipstick. Anyway it's a common colour with girls these days. You could buy it anywhere."

"Do you know what puzzles me? The way it was written to be read from inside the vehicle. It's not easy to write a mirror image like that without practising. When I was a kid a few of us had a secret society and we used to write notes to each other in reversed writing. You really need to practise to do it. Whoever wrote this warning must have practised it a few times. They would hardly be likely to go around doing it all the time. That means it's not some spur of the moment warning."

"They must also be watching us. We were only at the coffee shop for half an hour."

Suzie's comment meant more than she had realised. Since we had gone from the hotel out to the suburbs to interview the desk clerk and come straight to the shopping centre, it meant whoever had left the message must have been following us. They would have no way of knowing that we would stop in this particular shopping centre. We hadn't even known we would stop here ourselves until we decided on a cup of coffee. They must have been following us ever since we had left the hotel to visit the receptionist. Somewhere in the carpark there was a vehicle that had followed us from the hotel. It also meant they were probably watching us now. I glanced around the carpark but it looked as if every third car was a red car, many of them Toyotas.

"How do we get lipstick off the windscreen? You're a woman. It's not a problem I usually have."

"Metho might be best, or eucalyptus oil, and some tissues."

"Do you want to go back to the shops and buy some?" As I said it I changed my mind. If we were being watched perhaps it would be better if I went with her. "I'll come with you."

The metho and tissues eventually worked and the message disappeared. Now we had to make a decision. Do we take the advice, or do we visit the police?

27 Noisy Scrub-Birds

Suzie

A friend of mine had once lived in Albany many years ago. I had always been intrigued by her stories about the little Noisy Scrub-bird. To me the name had seemed so evocative of the Australian landscape, and I was curious to hear its call in its native habitat.

Peter and I had discussed the lipstick scrawled threat and decided that if we were typical tourists, well away from any likely contact with unknown persons who considered us a threat, we would not be in danger. I felt he wasn't happy walking—or driving—away from the threat, and I also felt uneasy. I didn't like the thought that someone bore us ill feelings. It brought back memories of Bernard Mayne and Ballarat, but Mayne was dead and his son was in prison. It was hardly likely to have anything to do with them. Besides, we were on the opposite side of the country. I was sure whoever was sending us a message was concerned about something more recent, and that it had to be somehow connected with Magenta.

We decided to drive out to Two Peoples Bay, find the birds I wanted to see, then drive on to Bremer Bay and once again camp overnight in our tent on the roof of the vehicle. We both felt that our plan should put at ease anyone who was taking an interest in us. After all we would just be tourists, and we had left town.

Driving into the Visitor's Centre of the National Park it looked as if we were the first arrivals for the day. No other vehicles were in the carpark and the centre itself was closed. I had already researched what I wanted to do so Peter and I began the walk that would take us through the peppermint woodlands, past lookouts over the bay, and return us to our vehicle. Along the way I hoped to see and hear the bird I had come to find. My friend had warned me I would hear the bird, but seeing it could be another matter.

The Noisy Scrub-bird had been thought to been extinct for seventy-two years until it was re-discovered fifty years ago at this very site. Now efforts were being made to preserve them and establish populations in separate protected areas. Even today the population was still very small.

Our walk took us to various lookouts over the bay. Below us the waters were multiple shades of blue, made even more beautiful by the white sand and rocks on the headlands. At times a solitary potoroo scampered along the path in front of us as we walked. In the distance we could hear the distinctive cheeps that became faster and faster towards the end of the call. At times the bird varied the pitch of its call, but nowhere could we see one. I had been warned trying to see the bird was difficult. Its brownish colours were the perfect camouflage for the shy elusive bird in its natural habitat of shrubby undergrowth and plant litter carpeting the forest floor. From its singing it was difficult to know if the bird was on the move or if it was using its vocal skills to confuse those trying to locate it. My friend had also warned me of that particular trick of the bird.

We were heading back to the car when at last I saw a scurrying brown bird cross the path in front of us. I had seen the bird! Back at the Visitor's Centre I spoke with a ranger who confirmed that I had really seen the Noisy Scrub-bird and not a close look-a-like that also inhabited the park. While my description was not good enough for him to say what sex it was, he also told me the birds I had heard would be the males. The females were silent. I did hear Peter's comment, "Unlike humans!"

By the time we drove out of the carpark on our way to Bremer Bay a few more tourists had arrived. I checked to see if any were in a small red Toyota but none were. Two were caravanners with their big four-wheel drives and vans, another a blue tray back with ladders on the rack, a fancy black utility with a cover over the tub, a white sedan, and an aging Kombi with surfboards. I didn't see the owner of the Kombi to discover if it was someone reliving their youth, or if it was a young person going retro.

As we came closer to Bremer Bay the clouds began building up. The radio was forecasting overnight showers. Nevertheless Bremer Bay was as beautiful as the postcards in Albany had shown it. Only this afternoon the sea was a darker shade of blue than I had been led to expect; a reflection of the heavy dull clouds suggestive of the forecast rain.

After driving through the small town and finding the beach, we returned to the closest caravan park and checked in. We found our site and Peter erected our tent. I felt a tinge of sadness at the thought that we may not have many more nights in our little camp. I was still not a camper; I doubted I would ever be one. My preference was definitely for motels, but I had grown fond of the thought of climbing up the ladder to sleep in the tent on top of our vehicle. Maybe I was not fond of the actual climb and bed, but of the memories it held of our time together.

After he had set up our tent Peter put out our chairs and table and opened a Margaret River wine we had purchased while I prepared our meal. Parked opposite was a large caravan and four-wheel drive Nissan. The roof rack on the Nissan was loaded with a small aluminium boat, and fishing rods leant against the van. I could smell the cooking fish as I prepared our casserole from packets purchased in an Albany supermarket. As the caravan's owner walked past our campsite he spoke to Peter and soon they were in conversation about fishing and travels. He then invited us to join them. Tonight they were having the catch of the day, bream freshly caught only twenty minutes earlier. With our meal already cooking we declined their offer but accepted the invitation to join them later for a warming port.

Our new friends were from Sydney, and unlike some of the other caravanners we had met previously, were not doing a circumnavigation of Australia. Rather they had planned a barbell shaped route that had the long Nullarbor crossing between the two ends where they would take different roads on their return travel. Along the way David was enjoying the range of fishing. Meanwhile Jenny caught up on books she had long wanted to read but had never found the time she needed to settle in and enjoy them without distractions.

The evening passed pleasantly as we sat around the fire with a glass of port—or two—and we learnt of their adventures crossing the Great Australian Bight. While we had driven from Darwin to Bremer Bay and passed through remote areas, their experience with the long straight stretch of road was something we would not do. Our return would be on the red eye special from Perth.

Peter told the story of the disappearance of Magenta without mentioning the police interest in us or the threat we had received. It was interesting to hear the comment, "Oh, it will be drugs, for sure." For so many people all the problems of the world could be traced to drugs. I had to agree. It seemed the most likely scenario.

Feeling warm and relaxed we left our hosts and climbed the ladder to our tent. Perhaps for the last time.

The sun rose to a fine morning. However, while it was shining in a clear sky, it lacked warmth. The night had been wet and cold. In the north of the state the problem had been how to stay cool. For a woman from Melbourne even a cool day in the north was hot. Here in the south, the temperatures were more like those I was familiar with at my home. Only I was normally in a warm house under my favourite blankets, and here I had only a canvas tent and a thin blanket between me and the elements. I was glad to have Peter's warm body close to mine.

We breakfasted and packed away our gear in preparation to return to Albany. We had decided we would drive back to Perth, return the hire car and fly east. Would we separate and I fly back to my family in Melbourne, or would I stay in Sydney with Peter? We still hadn't resolved that question. We could not put off the decision much longer. I sensed Peter wanted an answer but I still didn't know what I really wanted. He suggested we take a final walk along the beach. I knew that he wanted to bring the question to a conclusion.

This morning the waters of the bay were a light blue. The

white sandy beach clean and as yet unmarked by another human presence. Above us the sky was an even lighter shade of blue. The morning was cloudless; the rain clouds of the previous night had already completely vanished. We were alone on the beach. We walked on, neither of us wanting to open the conversation that we knew we had to have.

I took off my shoes, rolled up my jeans and walked along the edge of the ocean with the final inches of surf running in and out over my toes. The waves gently rolled in and away leaving little patterns in the sand. Peter walked along beside me but just staying above the waterline.

"Peter."

"Yes?"

"What are we going to do?"

"I think that will depend on you."

"I'm so unsure. I do like being with you. No, it's more than that. I want to be with you. I'm just unsure how it will work. Will I be able to adjust? I've been on my own for so long now. I'm probably too set in my ways."

"I would have thought that it was more likely me set in my ways."

We found a convenient rock and sat. We talked, and finally opened up about our deepest concerns. If we did live together how would we share our lives? The day to day issues? Our families? The freedoms we had both grown used to? We talked over our experiences travelling together. The little habits that irritated each of us. At least we were still together, unlike some of my friends who had parted, either in anger or disappointment mid road-trip.

For the first time Peter lowered the guard on his emotions and told me of his feelings. I had suspected much of what he told me, but to hear him say them was a very special moment. I realised how sensitive he was underneath his matter-of-fact nature. I realised how much my decision could affect him.

Eventually we walked back along the beach to our car. We were hand in hand.

We returned from our walk in the knowledge that we had, at last, made our decision. Peter turned the key on the four-wheel drive and we moved off leaving behind the beautiful blue water, the white sand, and the tumbled rocks of the bay. Just as we were about to drive out of the campground we saw David and Jenny, with whom we had shared the previous evening, returning from the campground office. We pulled up, and leaving the car running, went over to make our farewells and arrange to meet again in Sydney. I was just giving Jenny a parting hug when I heard a massive sound and felt a buffeting wind. I turned but there was no sign of the white four-wheel drive, only a blackened blazing wreck where it had stood seconds before. From the corner of my eye I thought I glimpsed a small red car driving away.

28 Paranoia

Peter

I stood looking at the burning wreck of the car. Only a few moments ago we had been sitting in it ready to drive back to Albany. Now all that remained was a tangled wreck with flames coming from the engine bay, and a black hole in the ground where it had once stood.

The whole thing was unreal. I couldn't believe it. It was as if we were viewers watching some bad movie. I looked at Suzie. She must have been feeling the same as me. There was a look of disbelief on her face. At least she was unharmed.

"Watch out, I've got an extinguisher. I'll put out the fire." It was David who had responded first. I was still standing in a state of shock.

"Be careful. It could explode!"

"The vehicle's diesel isn't it? I won't have enough foam for the vehicle. It's too late for that anyway. I just want to stop the fire from spreading. Get the office to phone the police. They should be able to contact the local fire unit."

For the first time since the explosion Suzie responded and ran towards the campground office. I was still standing looking at the car trying to make sense of what had happened. Was it an accident or was it something more sinister? I couldn't believe it was an accident, yet it was just too much to accept that it was a result of the threats we had received. Here, in quiet Bremer Bay, where nobody knew us. Away from anything to do with Magenta, or Sea Dreamer, and whatever connection they may have. It was only then that I started to shake. David came over to me and put his arm on my shoulder. "Thank God you stopped and came over to say goodbye. If you had been sitting in the car you'd be history. You would have been two minutes down the road when the car would have exploded. What happened? Did you leave a gas bottle turned on?"

I replied automatically without even looking at him. "No. I'm sure I turned it off after we had a cup of tea at breakfast. Before we went for a walk down to the beach. We packed the vehicle ready to leave. I'm sure I turned it off."

"Perhaps there was a fuel leak and fuel got on the hot motor."

David's suggestion was a possible explanation, but then diesel motors don't explode like that. The diesel will burn but not explode like petrol. It had to be something else. It had to be a bomb of some sort. A bomb set to go off when we were in the vehicle. A bomb that was meant to kill us. I looked at Suzie as she came back from calling the police. I wondered if she had reached the same conclusion. David wouldn't, because he didn't know about the threats that had been made to us.

A police car arrived closely followed by a fire unit. Not that there was anything the two firemen could do. By this time the wreck had burnt itself out and we could approach the still hot metal remains of the once white car. It was obvious that all our clothes and personal effects had been incinerated. Suzie's purse and phone had been in her handbag lying on the floor under her seat. There was nothing left of them. Our bookings for the flight back east had been in a folder in the driver's side door. Gone. Our clothes, our cameras, everything burnt. All we had left was what was in our pockets, my phone, my wallet with some cards, a little over a hundred dollars and my driver's licence. Suzie had nothing, everything was in her handbag and that had been incinerated.

The policeman who had responded to Suzie's call was sympathetic and concerned for our wellbeing. Like David he assumed that the problem was probably a leaking gas bottle. I gathered that gas bottles, camping, and fires were a common occurrence. I was sure I had turned off the bottle, but even if I hadn't it still didn't explain how the gas could ignite. There would have to be an ignition source. I doubted the idea of gas or fuel spilling onto a hot motor or exhaust. Perhaps a short across some electrical wiring might create a spark to ignite the gas. But I was sure I had turned the gas off! And diesel doesn't explode. I'd used diesel on fires with my work in bush camps. It burnt, but it didn't explode like petrol.

The two firemen hooked their unit onto the wreck to drag it to the verge so others could again make use of the road. Under where the driver's seat had once been there was a hole in the roadway. That was not the result of a gas blast but the down blast of an explosive. I had spent enough time in mining camps to recognise the pattern. Most of the blast had been directed up into the vehicle but some had gone down into the roadway itself.

I could see that my explanations would have no effect on

Magenta

the young policeman. Gas explosions happened. That was the cause. That would be his report. At least he agreed to give us a letter reporting the accident for an insurance claim. I used my phone and took a photo of the wreck. I may need it when I tried to explain to the hire company why we couldn't return their vehicle. At least I had my phone. That would be useful. Suzie's was a small burnt mess of plastic.

Our next problem was how to return to Albany. There we would be able to arrange to hire a replacement car and return to Perth and home. I would have to see what we could do about replacing our airline tickets. But first I would need to buy some clothes. My cards would be useful. Suzie would need new clothes too.

Then a more important thought came to mind. Should we also disappear? The plan was to kill us. Perhaps we should stay dead. But then, perhaps we were being watched, and whoever planted the bomb knew we were still alive. I looked at the group of bystanders who had collected around the wrecked car. Was one of them the perpetrator?

"Don't worry, Jenny and I can take you into Albany." I was grateful for the support of our new friends. Then suspicion came into my head. Perhaps they were the perpetrators. Was it a trap? I immediately put the idea out of my mind. They were already here in Bremer Bay, long before we knew where we would stay in the town. No one apart from Suzie and me knew of our plans. They couldn't have known we would park next to them. I was becoming paranoid! Whoever had done it must have followed us. I looked around to see if any of the vehicles were the ones we had seen at Two Peoples Bay, but none of them were the same.

David and Jenny dropped us off at the hotel in Albany and left to return to their caravan at Bremer Bay. Suzie and I went shopping to buy the basic necessities we would need until we returned home. Buying replacement clothes seemed to be becoming part of our life. We had had to do the same thing after the firebombing of Suzie's home.

We also made a decision that rather than rent another car, we would take the bus back to Perth. That would be less stressful, and we would be surrounded by people. I was still concerned that whoever was behind the attack may have another attempt. We discussed whether we should contact Adamson. If Suzie had seen the red car, did that mean the police were involved? We couldn't decide what action we should take.

One thing I wanted to do before it became dark was to go to the harbour to see if Sea Dreamer was still in port. The mooring where it had been was empty. Sea Dreamer had left early in the morning. No one on the wharf knew where it was heading. Anyone who was on Sea Dreamer when it sailed could not have planted the bomb, but did it leave with a full crew?

29 Deathly News

Suzie

My feelings of apprehension and anxiety of the previous day were still with me when I woke in the morning.

We were having a quiet breakfast in our room and as usual Peter had turned on the television to catch the early news. It was one habit of his that I found a little annoying. The news reports were usually full of murder and mayhem all around the world, and the local news was hardly any better. I preferred the stations that had lighter, more trivial, segments with less violence. At least the day could commence on a positive note.

Suddenly our attention was drawn to the television by the word 'Markham'. The story had just finished and all we could see on the screen was some smart, expensive looking high rise building. It was too late to learn more. We would have to wait half an hour for a repeat of the segment.

As we waited and finished our breakfast we planned our day. First we needed to buy some more clothes. Our shopping of the previous afternoon had been sufficient for the basics for one night but we would need more. Whenever Peter was around I seemed to need to buy new clothes. After the fire at my house in Melbourne, then the sudden plan to travel north when I had packed expecting a few weeks of winter in Sydney, and now again after losing everything in the car explosion. Then we had to arrange our trip back to Perth. Also I wanted a new phone and a handbag. I was lost without the two necessities of a girl's life.

I thought of phoning my children in Melbourne and telling them I was safe, but then that would only cause them to wonder why I wasn't safe. I decided it was better not to worry them. It would be better to wait and tell them the full story when I returned home.

At last the eight-thirty news segment began. We waited, hoping the news of Markham would not be replaced by the latest report on an injury suffered by a local football hero. That proved unlikely. A badly injured body had been found beside the pool on the third storey of an upmarket apartment building in Melbourne. It appeared from the injuries the body had fallen from a balcony much higher up the building. Police had identified the deceased as Edward Markham, an international business consultant and fund manager based in the Cayman Islands. Enquires had shown he had only recently arrived in Melbourne and was due to meet with clients. He was known to have a heart condition and it was surmised that he had been on the balcony, leaning over the rail when he had a fatal heart attack that had caused him to fall over the rail to his death. Security cameras in the building showed he was probably alone in the apartment and there were no suspicious circumstances.

"Did you know of his heart condition?" Peter looked across the breakfast table to me.

"No. I thought he was in good health. When you were talking with Margo in the galley he did tell me that he had just had a full health check for his fiftieth birthday. He said he came through fine. No problems."

"Could he have been covering up?"

"Who knows, Peter. I thought he was telling the truth, but some people don't like to admit a problem to anyone. Sometimes it's bad for business. Do you think it might not have been an accident?" To me Eddie had been in good health.   He wasn't obese, he looked fit, he had gym equipment on the boat and looked as if he used it. But then I've had, still have, friends with heart problems. It seems to be the disease of the day amongst the people I move with. "Do you think there is something suspicious about his death? The police don't think so. A few moments ago we had Eddie and the Sea Dreamer trying to kill us, and now you seem to think he was killed." I had to admit I thought Peter's idea was completely unfounded. We had nothing to link any of the events together.

"Perhaps somebody was upset with his management of their money. Some of it could have come from very dubious activities. Perhaps even drugs. I don't imagine drug bosses would take kindly to someone crossing them. People seem to be killed for lesser reasons."

"True."

"Suppose Eddie went to Melbourne to tell some crime boss he had lost his money."

"You think the boss gets annoyed and has him bumped off? Peter, you have been watching too many bad movies. If Eddie is killed, how does the boss get any money back from the business?   You would be better to kidnap and use threats."

"Perhaps the boss wanted to set an example?"

"Now I'm sure you watch bad movies. If I lost money I would try to get it back first. Then I would bump him off—if I was that sort of person. But I'm not, so perhaps I shouldn't make that conclusion. Anyway, none of that explains the bomb in our car. I don't see how they can be linked." My husband, ex-husband, always used to say follow the money. He was good at that, as well as following any pretty skirt that passed his way. "Well? Who benefits from Eddie's death?"

"Someone he owes money to? Perhaps he couldn't meet a redemption. Killing him wouldn't get you your money back unless whoever takes over the business is more agreeable. Perhaps it is somebody who owes him money who wants to make the debt disappear."

Peter's suggestion was a possibility.

"Who would be next in line. His wife? He did say he had a daughter. She would be more likely than an ex-wife."

"Possibly he had partners. He did say that someone ran the investment side of the business. I got the impression Eddie was more involved in transferring money, not the actual funds management. Maybe his partner wanted him out. There are some very dodgy business practices operating in some tax havens. From this distance, with no information about the actual happenings, we can only make guesses. Very uninformed guesses."

While Peter's thoughts were on a money trail I couldn't get away from the possibilities of drugs. "Could there have been drug money involved?"

"Maybe. I don't think Eddie would have been greatly concerned where the money came from. I thought he might have even been smuggling drugs himself. That would explain some things. He could bring drugs in from Asia. Magenta was to pick them up in Wyndham but the police and customs frightened them off. Broome was too visible so they arranged for another rendezvous. That was where she died from a drug overdose, so that failed. Perhaps they offloaded the drugs somewhere else, Fremantle or even Albany. That could explain the police interest in the boat and us. Maybe they thought we were the couriers. We have been following the boat all the way down the coast. My God, they thought we were part of the network!"

"So why would the police try to kill us?"

"You're right. That doesn't make sense. Nothing does. Eddie knew we were not part of any deal. Even if the police thought we were they would hardly need to kill us. They could just arrest us."

"Unless they knew that we had the drugs and they knew where they could find them and keep them for themselves."

"Corrupt police? But Suzie, we don't have any drugs. We don't know where they might be. They would hardly blow up the car if they thought there were drugs in it. We don't even really know this is about drugs. It is all just supposition."

Peter was right. Really we were just creating a fantastic story with no solid facts. The one fact we knew was someone had tried to kill us. It had to be because we knew too much. We must know something that they don't want made public. No, that was not quite correct. They must think we know something they don't want made public. But what is it? And who doesn't want it made public? Eddie? His friends? His killer? The police? We still had no idea of what or who.

30 Unexpected Texts

Peter

When we had checked the harbour on our return to Albany we'd found the beautiful white boat was no longer anchored offshore. Chatting with the fishermen on the wharf we'd learnt it had suddenly sailed early that morning. The same morning our car exploded at Bremer Bay. The previous afternoon it had pulled into the wharf, taken fuel on board and then vanished in the early morning before the sun had risen. No one had any idea where it was heading. We had tried the Harbour Master's office to see if we could learn more but it was closed. At least this time there was no sign of a little red Toyota. I didn't know if that was a good sign or not.

Watching the morning's television report about Markham had again brought to mind the boat. I would have loved to know where it was going. It had left before the news that Eddie had died had been broadcast, so it was probably acting on his last orders. The captain may not even know his boss was dead. I assumed they were just continuing with the old orders. Then again, perhaps they already knew he was dead. Perhaps someone else was issuing instructions. On the other hand, if they were involved in the bombing of our car they have may have wanted to get away before any questions were asked. There wouldn't have been time for someone to set off a bomb and get back to Albany before the boat sailed. So if it was anyone from Sea Dreamer they must still be onshore. Perhaps they don't even know we are still alive. I told Suzie of my thoughts.

"The explosion of our car was on the news last night. They had four or five TVs on the boat. If they watch TV they would have seen, or heard, we were uninjured. They would probably also know of Markham's death by now."

Suzie was right. Any plan to pretend we had been killed had fallen over within hours thanks to the radio and television news services. That plan had not even lasted until we had arrived back in Albany. What had surprised me was that we had not had a visit from the police. They had been watching us since we had gone aboard Sea Dreamer—we suspected it was their red car at Bremer Bay—and yet since then we had seen no sign of them. That was troubling.

"From Albany the boat has three options. North, back to Fremantle and then Broome. East around the Great Southern Bight, or west to Africa. That last option seems unlikely. The boat was due to go back north. I think that's where it is heading, even if it eventually plans to head for the Caribbean. The question is, will it stop at Fremantle, or bypass it and take on more fuel further up north? I think the best thing we can do is visit the police in Perth. They must know we are alive. They must also know about Markham's death. Perhaps this time we will get some answers."

"Do you think the police might know who set off the explosion? If they were in the red car they might have been watching us and seen who did it." Suzie's comment made sense but only led to another concern.

"What troubles me is if they were watching us why didn't they do something to prevent it, or at least warn us?"

"Maybe it wasn't them in the red car."

"Two red cars?" I hadn't given that any consideration. "I suppose it's possible. But why? If it isn't the police, then who is it? Even accepting that Markham's death wasn't an accident, it still doesn't give anyone a reason to try to kill us." I was just about to say to Suzie that if someone was connected to Markham's death and the unsuccessful attempt on our lives, they may have another try. I stopped myself from speaking just in time. There was no need to add to Suzie's fears. "Let's go down town. We have to do some more shopping. I'm getting sick of living in these clothes. I need some new jeans and some shirts. Besides, I need some new pyjamas. I couldn't find any when we went shopping last night."

"I thought you looked quite good without PJs. You didn't have a problem last night."

"That's all very well for you. I noticed you were carefully wrapped in a towel until you hit the sheets." Suzie had very discretely wrapped herself in a large bath towel until she had slipped into bed. Not that it mattered once we were together.

"Peter, it's not that I am a prude, but more I'm at an age when some parts are better covered. OK. Today I promise you I will buy a slinky nighty when we go shopping, but only if I can select some pyjamas for you." As I said it I wondered if choosing his pyjamas would be a step too far. He may not be ready for that just yet. "In any case you will have to pay for the nighty. You're the only one with a credit card and access to cash."

With Suzie beside me I had quickly found myself a pair of jeans, another pair of slacks and two shirts. Socks, underclothes and a new jumper and my shopping was complete. The only thing left was toiletries at a supermarket. It was not so quick with Suzie. Each item was picked up, turned over, considered and compared to another. I had never enjoyed shopping. You knew what you wanted, found it, bought it, and left. I have never met a woman who adopted that approach.

Eventually I found a seat that had been thoughtfully provided by the shopping centre for husbands, or partners, to sit while they waited. At least there I could be comfortable while I was bored. I had been sitting waiting for ten minutes and just about to visit the newsagent to buy a magazine when my phone buzzed with a text message. 'Tell your friends to give us the package!' Friends? Package? The message was like everything else that was happening to us. It didn't make sense. Who were our friends? We didn't have any. What package? We didn't know of any package. What package could our friends have? I was puzzling over the message when Suzie returned. She saw my troubled look, and I couldn't hide the message from her.

"Is it the police or someone else?"

"The police would hardly phone up with a message like that. They would just pick us up for a chat."

"Then they must be someone else."

Suzie was right. It would seem to confirm our suspicions that some other person was interested in us. They knew we were alive and were once again threatening us. I decided it was time to phone Adamson. I didn't really trust the police. There was something suspicious in their behaviour, but at least we should be safer. I searched the call log to find a contact number for Adamson and dialled.

"Adamson's phone. Who's speaking?" The voice wasn't Adamson's.

"I want to speak to Inspector Adamson. It's Peter Jamieson."

"He's not available at the moment. Can I take a message?"

"Just tell him to call as soon as possible. We need to speak with him urgently."

"I'll pass on the message. Thank you." The phone went silent.

Seconds later it flashed again. Another text. 'Very wise! Don't do anything stupid. We know where to find you if they don't deliver.' I looked around the shopping centre. People were all going about their business. Nothing unusual was happening. Nearby a woman with a small child in a pram was typing on her phone. A group of young women were sitting drinking coffees and playing with their phones. Two men were talking together and one held a phone in his hand. In a doorway three men were standing chatting, two of them held phones in their hands while the third was talking on his phone. Everywhere men, women, and children were holding mobile phones. Surely one of them must have been watching me, seen me make a phone call and assumed I had contacted my 'friends'. Unless they were watching they could not have known I had made a phone call. Fortunately, they would not know I had phoned the police and not my 'friends'.

"What do we do now?"

I didn't really know how to answer Suzie's question. We had phoned the police but they didn't appear interested. I wasn't even sure that the message would be passed on to Adamson. It was surprising that he didn't have his mobile phone on him. I had no idea what response we would get in that area. At least whoever was sending me texts would be expecting a result from my phone call. That would give us time, but eventually their patience would run out and we would be in trouble again. I still couldn't work out why whoever it was behind all this had tried to threaten us, then tried kill us, and now were back to sending us messages. It must be the same people. We could hardly have the police and two other different parties on our trail.

I was also puzzled. How would they have my phone number? The police had it. Markham had had it but he was dead. Perhaps he had given it to someone. Did someone on the boat know it? Nobody else would know it. Unless they had somehow got it from the reception desk of the hotel. Perhaps we should just leave Albany. Go to Perth and visit the police station.

But first I wanted to see if we could identify our watcher. In one respect we were lucky. The shopping complex was only one storey. Nobody could be standing in a gallery looking down on us. Of course whoever was watching us may have decided to leave after sending the two texts. However I had a feeling, a gut feeling, that they still had an eye on us. Maybe the watcher had changed duty with a mate. That was a possibility, however the new person would still have to be where they could see us. Even hiding behind a pillar or display board they would need to keep us in their eyesight. If they could see us, possibly we could see them.

Suzie and I sat and looked around us. There was constant stream of shoppers passing by us.

"I think you can cut out the workers in hi-vis vests, and the school kids. The first are too visible to be hiding and the second are hardly likely to be candidates to watch us."

Suzie was right. We could also cut out mothers with small children. It was also unlikely anyone pushing a shopping cart would be following us. I thought we could count out groups of three or more people who appeared to know each other. I couldn't imagine a surveillance team standing together talking.

I decided we should move. "Let's go to the food court and get a coffee. We will see if anyone follows us."

Sitting drinking our coffee we again scanned the court for familiar faces. At one table several men we had seen before were chatting. One held a phone in his hand and appeared to be reading a text. The other walked over to a counter and ordered coffees while his companion sat watching the passing parade. Another man was standing outside a jewellery shop. I recognised the expression of boredom on his face. Either he was a good actor or he was genuinely waiting for his wife.

We would need to go somewhere that they would also have to move to keep us in view. Somewhere they couldn't hide and some place where there wouldn't be masses of people to hide amongst. I looked around the complex. There was a large crowd of people standing outside the movie multiplex. If we could identify a prospect, then pass through the crowd at the movies to another quiet spot and we still had the same tail, we would have identified our man or woman. The only problem was the multiplex was in a dead end. We would have nowhere to go.

"What about the passageway to the toilets? I noticed that it has two entrances from different arcades. If we go down one passage anyone following us would have to do the same or we could walk out the other end and they would lose us."

The only problem with Suzie's idea was that our watcher may not know the layout as well as Suzie and assume we had gone to the toilet and wait for our return. I decided that the multiplex offered the best option. We would walk down to the cinema, mingle with the crowd, watch for anyone who followed us, and then retrace our steps without actually entering the cinema. It would be unlikely that another person would do the same.

As we left the food court I noticed a man who had been chatting on his phone get up and leave a half drunk cup of coffee and follow us. This looked promising. Perhaps we had identified our man. We joined the throng in the foyer of the cinema and saw the man waiting outside. Then a woman approached him and kissed him. He took cinema tickets from his pocket and they entered the cinema.

My attempt to find whoever was watching us had proved unsuccessful. We had identified no one.

We left the shopping centre and started our walk back to our hotel. Everywhere I looked there were red cars and people on mobile phones. Glancing in windows of shops I tried to find reflections that might show a man or a woman following us. Nothing. When we arrived back at the hotel I half expected to find a note waiting for us, but there was no note.

That night we went to bed, Suzie in a slinky pink number,

and me in blue tartan pyjamas I had chosen for myself. Neither of us slept much.

31 A Safe House

Suzie

Peter and I found the Visitor's Centre housed in the old railway station overlooking Princess Royal Harbour and checked in for our coach service to Perth. We had decided that it would be easier to travel by coach than to arrange another hire car given our history. When we arrived in Perth we would have some explaining to do to the hire company about where their car was, and what had happened to it. Besides, I didn't think either of us really wanted to drive. All we both wanted was to get home as quickly as possible.

The blue and white TransWA coach was already waiting in the terminal and the first passengers had commenced boarding. We joined the line and stepped up into the cabin and found our seats. In our hands we carried our newly purchased clothing and personal effects, all jammed into two small stripy plastic bags.

The atmosphere as we sat waiting on the bus for Perth was so different to our drive south. A week ago we had expectations of relaxing visits to wineries and the numerous tourist sites that we had seen in brochures. Then we had been carefree, but now there was an edge to our travels that we could not escape. Even the chatty driver and the half-full bus of relaxed locals and tourists heading north could not erase our sense of tension. I noticed Peter surreptitiously glance around the passengers on the bus and those still boarding. I thought he was looking for someone; someone who was following us. Then his eyes fell on a big tanned man in a singlet.

"Didn't we see that man in the supermarket yesterday?"

I turned and followed his eyes. Outside the bus station office there was a well-built man wearing an orange and yellow singlet. In his hand was a large pink suitcase. I was sure he was the same man we had seen in the supermarket yesterday. As we watched a young woman came out of the ticket office pushing a baby in a stroller and walked up to him. Together they approached the bus, and the man took the pusher and gave it and the suitcase to the driver to load into the luggage compartment. Then the man and the woman embraced and mother and child climbed aboard the bus.

I turned to Peter. "I don't think he is any concern of ours."

Sitting in the coach watching the countryside flow past should have been relaxing, but neither of us could escape the feeling that all was not well. Our fellow passengers were a varied lot. The backpackers were obvious by their youth and their tanned complexions, plus their immense packs complete with bedding strapped to the frame that they had stowed in the luggage compartment. Others were more like Peter and me: an older group. A few could have been retired couples on holiday, or perhaps visiting children or grandchildren. The remainder I assumed were locals. They were a very mixed group. Most were dressed casually, some very casually. Not one looked like a business person heading to the big city for conferences, buying trips or meetings. I guessed such people probably drove themselves to Perth and did not take public transport.

At Katanning the coach pulled into the roadhouse. Following the driver's advice we fronted the counter to buy coffees and some pre-packaged sandwiches enclosed in hard plastic cases. I thought of how different it was to our lunch with Eddie Markham at the winery just a week earlier, but now Eddie was dead.

As we waited outside the bus eating our sandwiches and drinking roadhouse coffees a number of cars pulled into the service station. Two men emerged from a blue ute and started walking towards the bus just as Peter's phone rang. At the same time another two men appeared from a white car and walked over to the bus driver and started talking with him. I could feel Peter's hand on my back and felt myself being propelled towards the bus.

"What are you doing?" I asked.

"Just get on the bus. I'll explain then."

Once we were seated Peter told me about the phone call. It was Adamson with instructions to get on the bus immediately. Not to ask questions, and just do it, immediately. I looked out the window. The two men were still talking with the bus driver. It looked as if they were asking him questions. The two men from the blue ute had moved away and stood beside their vehicle talking to each other, however their eyes never left the bus driver and his companions. "What's this all about?"

Peter answered. "I don't know. That's all Adamson said. Then he hung up."

"How would he know we were off the bus?"

"He must be watching us! Otherwise he wouldn't know. Where is he?"

We looked around the roadhouse carpark. There was a red Toyota, but an aged couple were leaning against it eating ice creams. People were coming and going from the roadhouse café carrying drinks and food but none were Adamson or Newman. Another couple had set up a thermos flask and cups at a table under the shade of a tree. Nowhere was there any sign of the detective.

"Phone him back. Ask him what it is all about." As Peter took out his phone the two men moved away from the bus driver who took his seat and started the motor. The door closed and the coach moved off. The two men who had been speaking to the driver walked to the white car and followed the bus out onto the main road. I lost sight of the men in the blue ute.

Peter's phone rang again. He answered. I couldn't follow the conversation from his replies but his face grew concerned. He nodded as if in agreement but I had no idea what he was agreeing to. Then he put the phone away.

"Adamson says we are to stay on the bus when it stops at Brookton, wherever that is. He says there is a planned ten-minute toilet and coffee stop there. We are not to get off the bus for any reason. There will be two men who will get on the bus. They will be wearing suits. Ignore them. If anyone else gets on the bus don't talk with them. If we have a problem the men in suits will be there to protect us. When we get to the bus terminal in East Perth two uniformed police officers will meet us. We are to go with them. They will take us to a safe hotel. Stay in our room, order room service. We are not to go wandering outside. He said he will contact us again tomorrow and arrange to meet us."

The next two hours in the blue and white coach passed slowly. I leant against Peter's shoulder and tried to relax, but try as I might I looked at every car that overtook us. I kept wanting to turn around and see if the blue ute was still behind us. A blue ute with fancy wheels would surely want to pass a slower moving bus, especially one that that stopped briefly in every town along the road. There was no sign of either the ute or the white car. I wondered if they had taken the more direct road to Perth.

Any other time our trip would have been enjoyable. From experience I knew Peter would have found much to interest him in the countryside flowing past the bus's windows. Yet today neither of us gave the view a second thought: our minds were on Adamson's message.

The bus was on schedule when it pulled into the Roadhouse in Brookton. Most of the passengers disembarked, some to find coffee and food, some to find the toilets, and a few diehards a quiet spot to have a cigarette. As instructed we stayed in the bus. Just as we had been informed two men in suits boarded the bus and took their seats several rows in front of us. We didn't acknowledge them, and they didn't speak to us. Still no sign of the blue ute or the white car. The bus moved off again. In front of us the two men in suits sat quietly. We could hear them speaking to each other in low voices but could not make out any of the conversations. They were constantly checking their phones. I wondered what phone messages they were receiving, or perhaps they were just playing games to kill time.

It was late afternoon when the bus pulled into the East Perth terminal. Standing waiting for the bus were the two uniformed police officers Adamson had promised. They approached us as we stepped down from the bus and politely lead us away to a marked police car. I could see the look on the other passengers' faces as we were led away. Even I felt it was as if we were being arrested—quietly but firmly.

The drive to the hotel only took a few minutes. In the car Peter's questions about our circumstances had gained little information. The hotel we were taken to was functional and unexceptional. The sort of hotel that business owners use when it is their own money paying the bill and not some large corporation's expense account. Both policemen accompanied Peter and me to the reception desk and then to our room. The instruction not to leave the room was repeated along with the suggestion that we use room service for a meal. The suggestion of a meal was attractive. I realised I had only had a coffee and two sandwiches all day.

"How do we know that the room service will be safe?" I thought Peter's question was a bit over the top.

"Don't worry, one of us will be in the hallway, and the other in the adjoining room. You will be safe." The darker policeman's words made me worry even more. Why were we unsafe? How unsafe were we? The feeling that we were under arrest returned. Peter must have had the same thought.

"Can't you explain what is going on? We are being treated as if we are being detained yet we have done nothing."

Again it was the darker officer who answered. "I'm sorry. I really don't know myself. Our orders were to pick you up at the bus terminal and bring you here. We are to provide for any of your needs and make sure nobody sees or speaks with you until we have further orders. It was particularly stressed that you were to talk to nobody. I'm sorry but that is all we know. Can I arrange for some drinks and food to be brought up for you?"

"How long are we to be locked away?" Peter tried again with a further question.

"I don't know. Obviously something is happening and they don't want you involved. I expect that tomorrow will bring some answers to your questions. What would you like for your evening meal?"

"I hope it's not our last supper."

I didn't think Peter's comment was very appropriate.

The police had arranged for two meals from a local restaurant to be delivered, along with two bottles of Margaret River wine, a red and a white. My chicken was enjoyable, and Peter devoured his steak with gusto. I wasn't sure the police budget stretched far enough for the workers as our guards appeared to have hamburgers and cokes from the nearby fast food outlet.

Sitting back in an armchair drinking our third glass of wine, we reviewed our situation. The gaolers were friendly, the food pleasant, and the room basic but comfortable. The television programs were less so. We turned on the evening news in the hope that we might learn something but it was the usual wars, politics, car crashes and footballers' injuries, nothing that might explain our situation.   Eventually we found a channel with an old movie and settled back in bed to watch it. It felt good to have Peter stretched out beside me. I felt comfortable and relaxed until I thought of the two men waiting outside. Who were they keeping away from us?

By the fourth glass of wine we had given up asking questions. The romance of the movie had got to us both; even Peter had succumbed. We settled in for the night. Tomorrow we would find out what was in store for us, but tonight there was just us.

32 Diamonds

Suzie

"Where are they?"

Inspector Adamson's question took us by surprise. "Where's what? What are you talking about?"

"The diamonds?"

I was puzzled by his question. Peter made no comment. "The diamonds? We told you about the diamonds that Magenta bought. How would we know what happened to them? Your police officers must have searched the car."

"I'm not concerned about two little diamonds. I want to know what happened to the five million dollars' worth of diamonds that Markham had."

"Five million dollars of diamonds. What are you talking about?"

"We know Markham was given a parcel of uncut diamonds that had been stolen from a mine site over a number of years. He was to take them out of the country and exchange them for five million dollars US in the Caymans Islands. The money was to go into an account with his partner's funds management business. We have found out Markham was to receive a fee of half a million dollars for his efforts. The diamonds have gone missing."

Adamson ordered coffees for three and told us a story of diamonds and drugs.

"We have been working on a case of uncut diamonds disappearing from the mine near Kununurra. It has been going on for a number of years. Finally we got a lead on the group responsible. They had discovered a flaw in the mine's on-site security and were making use of it to smuggle out small quantities of stones. When the opportunity arose because the members were all in certain work positions they could remove rough stones before the final sorting. The mine management knew small quantities of the diamonds kept going missing but had never been able to find who was responsible, or how it was being done. Eventually we had a breakthrough and could follow their trail.

"Obviously they couldn't sell the stones on the streets of Kununurra but they found a contact who would take them. They accumulated stones on behalf of a buyer in Melbourne. When ready a parcel of diamonds would be passed to Markham on one of his trips to Broome, and he would transfer them to the Cayman Islands where he would hand them over to a gem dealer for cash. The cash would be invested in one of his partner's funds on behalf of the Melbourne businessman. We believe he had done several similar deals previously. Certainly at least one twelve months ago.

"Masters was a different story. Initially we didn't know where she fitted in. From what we have found out she was in Bali and given the job of flying to Australia, hiring a van, driving to Wyndham, picking up the drugs from Sea Dreamer and then delivering them to a contact in Brisbane.

She had nothing to do with Markham or the diamonds.

"The drugs seemed to be a separate deal conducted by the captain and some of the crew on the side. We don't think Markham knew about it. The last thing he wanted was any police attention given his own deals with clients who wanted privacy.

"When Masters got to Wyndham she saw the police and customs and phoned her contact in Bali. Her contact must have contacted the captain of the boat and told him to avoid the town. Somehow the captain must have convinced Markham to change his plans. Perhaps he had some story about the tides and it not being a suitable time to berth.

"Anyway the boat went on to Broome. As had been arranged, Markham was given the diamonds, but the crew were unsuccessful with their arrangements to get the drugs ashore. Markham had booked to fly from Broome to Perth so the crew then came up with a new plan. Without Markham the boat was free to run the drugs ashore to Masters at an agreed meeting place, so they gave her a map with some new drop off positions. That left the cook on the boat. She was the only one not in the plan. The crew made life so difficult for her that she quit the boat in Broome. We eventually managed to track her down. She had no knowledge of any of the various activities occurring around her."

Adamson's explanations of the two different activities explained some things but left many questions. I was puzzled. "Why did Magenta have the boat's name and Jason's? Surely she would have known them."

"We don't know. I would have thought she would know the name of the boat before the planned meeting in

Wyndham. Perhaps she didn't know the name of the person she was to meet. Perhaps she just scribbled down the boat name to link Jason to it. Some things you never know! Anyway, by the time Jason landed in the zodiac she must have been dead. Mix the drug we found on the floor of the van with too much alcohol and your heart slows down and stops. With the tablet found on the floor it would be reasonable to say she was using that drug. Maybe she got bored waiting and decided to get a high and drink her vodka as she was listening to her music. She may have taken a number of tablets. Without a body and a forensic test we can't know for sure, but it is my best guess.

"When I interviewed Jason he told me he panicked and took the body back to the boat. He was afraid that leaving it in the car might lead to questions. He didn't know that your ringer from the cattle station had already seen the body. They decided to put her in the freezer but to do that they had to cut off her legs. They were hoping to throw her to a crocodile but didn't see any. Then they saw they would pass Shark Bay and decided to throw the body overboard there. The sharks must have got most of the body but two legs made it to shore."

"But the car was locked. The keys were in the ignition when Jimmy found her. The car was locked and the keys were lying on the floor when we went back with the police. How did Jason get into it?"

"Like you, Peter, that had us puzzled. Until Jason told us that the rear door wasn't locked. Apparently it was shut, but not locked. Masters must have locked the other doors manually from inside but not the rear door. Jason opened it and climbed through the van and unlocked the driver's side door to remove Masters. Then when he was leaving he left the rear door open, pressed the central locking which locked the closed doors, threw the keys into the car then closed the rear door. It automatically locked once it was shut.

"At this stage we were still following the diamonds and hadn't come across the drug connection. It was only when word started to spread in Perth that someone had drugs for sale that we first learnt of the connection of drugs to Sea Dreamer. Apparently Masters, or as you call her, Magenta, was the only one who knew where the drugs were to be delivered. The boat's crew were just transport. With Masters dead they decided to sell the drugs themselves. Unfortunately for them word got to the man in Sydney who was wondering why his drugs hadn't arrived in Brisbane as planned. He was not happy to learn someone in Western Australia was trying to sell drugs that he believed should be his. That night two men were on a plane from Sydney to Perth.

"Markham knew nothing of this. As far as he was concerned he had the diamonds and they would be delivered as promised. Suspicions about his boat and drugs would be the last thing he wanted. He had too many prominent businessmen and politicians using his services to run the risk of attracting police and customs interest in his activities. What he did not know was the man with whom he was planning to do business in Melbourne also had business associates in the Sydney drug trade. Markham's client was ostensibly a legitimate businessman, but had other not so respectable interests on the side. That had never worried Markham in the past, but this time his client had an angry Sydney associate involved in the drug industry who held Markham responsible for the loss of his drugs and thought he had been double dealt with by Markham. He wanted his drugs and Markham punished as an example to others. The

Melbourne businessman now became worried about whether Markham might do a runner with the diamonds and agreed to let his friend take revenge—provided they could recover the diamonds first. Then Markham could disappear.

"We don't know what happened exactly, but something went wrong. Markham knew nothing about the drugs, but probably the heavies didn't believe him. It was likely Markham fell, or was pushed or thrown over the balcony. Apparently before revealing where the diamonds were hidden. I expect the men sent to talk to him were more concerned about the drugs than the diamonds. No one seems to know where they are."

Peter shifted in his seat. "The report said there were no suspicious circumstances. There was nothing on the CCTV cameras."

"Not every police officer is honest. Drug money can corrupt some people. Files disappear, or can be altered. Sometimes you only find what you are looking for."

"What about the coroner's report? I'm sure there would have to be some sort of an inquiry into Markham's death."

Adamson again looked steadily at Peter as he answered his question. "The coroner is given the information. It says there are no suspicious circumstances so the report is straight forward."

"What about the doctor? He would have to sign off on a heart attack."

"True, but pick the right doctor and it isn't a problem. Besides, he might even have had a heart attack by the time he hit the ground."

I shuddered at the thought of Eddie falling to his death. I had found him very charming and had enjoyed his company. I knew Peter also liked the man even if he had been a little jealous of my flirtation with Markham. It seemed so sad that no one was concerned about his fate. What of his daughter and ex-wife? Would they grieve for him? Would the people who had caused his death ever be held to account?

Peter asked, "So where do we fit into all this?"

"You were another puzzle. We didn't know why, but you always kept turning up. In Wyndham, Derby, in Broome, the beach where Masters died. Again in Fremantle, then with Markham at the winery and on the boat twice. You didn't seem connected to the diamond deal but it began to look as if you were involved with the drugs."

"Who, me!" I was sure my voice showed my horror of being considered a drug mule.

"You wouldn't be the first little old grey-haired grandmother to be involved with drug importation, believe me. Drug mules come in all sorts and sizes. Besides, we weren't the only ones suspicious of you. The two men from Sydney sent to find and collect the drugs also thought you were suspicious. That's why your vehicle was bombed. They thought you were working for rivals so they decided to remove you. They had seen you with Markham and saw you go out to the boat several times. They assumed you were trying to do a deal. Your death would remove competition and send a message to the crew on the boat to do as they wanted—or else."

"Did it work?"

"Definitely, Peter. It certainly worked. When you weren't

killed they decided to contact you again. They thought you would contact the boat. They were following you yesterday. We were afraid they may have another attempt on your lives. That was why we took you into care.

"This morning the captain of the boat reluctantly handed the drugs over to them in exchange for a very small payment. After that we picked the crew up. They are not very chatty, apart from Jason who is afraid we will charge him with Masters' death. I think the visit by some hard men from Sydney has made them tongue-tied. The thought of being in the same prison yard as those Sydney men worries them. Nevertheless we have been able to get some information from them. They were very keen to tell us that Naomi Masters was dead before Jason found her."

"What about the other two?"

"We picked them up with the drugs in their possession. Almost twenty kilos of ecstasy and other things. The crew had hidden the drugs in the fuel tanks. Even after the packages had been cleaned down they still stank of diesel. The lab hasn't finished a definitive analysis of what they all are. We know who was behind the importation but I doubt if we will ever get sufficient evidence to prosecute the main man. Nor have we found the diamonds."

Peter's face showed the quizzical look that sometimes would come over his face when he was thinking. Finally he spoke. "I assume that the bad guys must have tried to get him to say where the diamonds were before they killed him."

"We assume so. They asked the captain of the boat about the diamonds but he knew nothing."

"What exactly are you looking for?"

"Markham was given a small parcel wrapped in several layers of paper with the stones in it. They were rough, uncut, and unpolished stones of various sizes. Not the sparkly gems we usually think of as diamonds. More like a handful of gravel."

"He would hardly be likely to take them with him so I would expect them to be on the boat."

"We have searched it already. We could find nothing."

"Did you check the safe?"

"Of course. We took a locksmith along to open it and checked. There were no diamonds."

"Did you find a second hidden safe?"

"No, is there one?"

"Probably. I would think Markham would have more than one secure place for valuables. Perhaps we should have another look at the boat."

33 Sea Dreamer

Suzie

When we arrived at the dock in Fremantle a police boat was waiting to take us out to the Sea Dreamer. Somehow the glamourous appearance of last week had vanished and the boat had already taken on a forlorn look. A little like an empty house that has not been lived in for years. The young policeman on guard duty helped us on board and the police boat moved off to its next assignment.

"What will happen to the boat now?"

Adamson answered me. "No idea really. At present it is evidence. Eventually it will be released. I suppose Markham had a will. Perhaps a finance company might take it over. Who knows? One day the port fees will be paid and the boat will disappear. There is a safe in the cabin Markham used as an office but we have had that opened and the diamonds were not there."

"Did you check all of his suite?" Peter was padding around the salon, poking into cupboards and running his hands over bulkheads. It looked as if he was trying to find some secret compartment.

"Yes."

"What about the bridge?"

"The same."

"And his office?"

"Look for yourself."

We went into what had been Markham's office and again Peter searched around the room. Finally he sat down at the desk and started to play with the paperweight puzzle of Australia lying on the table. He seemed to be in deep thought as he played with the puzzle, removing the moulded shape of each state from the wooden holder one at a time, looking at it, and then replacing it in its correct position. "What about the store room? If you were going to carry large quantities of gold or cash you may need a larger safe, or a strong security locker. I wonder if there is anything down there, perhaps hidden behind the big freezer where they must have put Magenta's body. There could be space between bulkheads."

I shuddered again at the thought of the young woman's penultimate resting place.

"Take Suzie down to show you which one. You will need the guard as well to move the deep freeze. I expect it will be heavy. I'm not much help. My back has been causing problems ever since the camper was blown up."

I looked at Peter. His back had seemed in fine shape this morning when we had woken.

The freezer was impossible to move. It had been securely fixed to the deck and the bulkhead behind it. If Markham had a secret hidey-hole there he would need an angle grinder or oxy torch to move the freezer and access it. We returned to the saloon. Peter was standing looking out over the harbour.

"Any luck?"

Adamson had already let me know what he had thought of Peter's suggestion. He didn't need to speak for Peter to know the answer.

"Well the diamonds have either got to be on the boat or Markham moved them. Do you have any idea where he may have taken them?"

Adamson's reply to Peter was curt. He had had enough of searching. He called up the police launch to return us to the wharf. For some reason he seemed to hold Peter responsible for the wild goose chase.

"Will you need to see us again or are we free to return home?"

"No Mrs Benedict, you are both free to travel. If we need you we will contact you, but I don't think it will be necessary. I will have a car drop you at your hotel."

As the taxi took us to the airport to catch the red-eye special back to Sydney, I thought of our road trip. It had been far removed from what I had expected. When I had flown to Sydney worried about Peter's whereabouts I hadn't given too much thought to what I wanted with the rest of my life. I knew Peter was special to me. After all, that was why I had flown to Sydney to find him. Still, I hadn't thought beyond that, or considered the decisions that I would have to make. Even when I had agreed to take the holiday with him I had avoided making the real decision. It had seemed like a good way to find out more about him. Now, after a trip through the north and west of Australia, finding a body that had disappeared, visiting so many interesting tourist sites, family shocks, long lunches at a beautiful winery and on a fabulous yacht, an attempt on our lives and a murder of someone we had met and whose company I had enjoyed, I had made my decision. Peter had often told me he enjoyed a quiet life, yet I had found life with him was never without incident. Still I now knew I really did want to spend the rest of my life with him. It would be up to me how I made that life ... and his.

Walking through the airport terminal my eye was caught be the headlines in a newspaper. 'Drug Bust. Ten kilos of seized drugs linked to luxury yacht.'

I pointed out the headline to Peter. "Ten kilos? I thought Adamson said they seized almost twenty kilos."

"I hope whoever has the rest has more luck than the others involved with that boat."

"What do you mean?"

"Well, Magenta is dead, Markham's dead, the crew are in jail and so are the two thugs from Sydney. The financier of the drugs has lost his money. Possession of those drugs doesn't seem to bring joy to anyone."

"What do you think happened to the diamonds?"

"I expect they are at the bottom of the harbour in Fremantle."

"What! Why?"

"Because that is where I threw them."

"Why?"

"Because they had caused enough trouble. I liked Markham. He may have pushed the legalities but he wasn't a bad man. I felt he needed some memorial. The diamonds seemed appropriate. One day someone may find a small jigsaw puzzle of seven Australian states made of what looks like gravel and small stones encased in a plastic moulding."

I had thought I was beginning to understand Peter, but there was a lot more that I was going to have to learn.

Links:

Many of the locations mentioned in the story exist in reality and are open to the public. They are well worth a visit.

Readers seeking more information may wish to view the following websites.

Ku Ring-Gai Chase National Park
www.nationalparks.nsw.gov.au/visit-a-park/parks/Kuringgai-Chase-National-Park

Mindil Beach Market
www.mindil.com.au

Adelaide River War Cemetery
www.ozatwar.com/adelaideriverwargraves/index.htm

Elsey Cemetery
www.austcemindex.com/cemetery?cemid=685

Travelling in the Kimberley
www.kimberleyaustralia.com

Kimberley School of the Air
www.kimberleyschoolair.com.au

Kimberley Art
www.kimberleyfoundation.org.au

Bradshaw Foundation
www.bradshawfoundation.com

Sun Pictures
www.broomemovies.com.au/history.html

Kimberley Quest Cruises

www.kimberleyquest.com.au

The Dolphins of Monkey Mia
www.parks.dpaw.wa.gov.au/park/monkey-mia

Western Australia Maritime Museum
www.museum.wa.gov.au/museums/maritime

Ship Wreck Galleries
www.museum.wa.gov.au/museums/shipwrecks

The Batavia and Dutch exploration and trade
www.museum.wa.gov.au/research/research-areas/maritime-archaeology/batavia-cape-inscription/batavia

Albany Tourism
www.amazingalbany.com.au/

About the author   *www.valverdemaclean.com*

Interesting books:

For a book on the early days of the pearling industry in Broome find a copy of Ian L Idriess's *Forty Fathoms Deep*.

For readers interested in learning more of the Aboriginal Art of the Kimberley, I recommend *The Lost World of the Kimberley* by Ian Wilson. This is available in print or eBook formats.

Another very interesting book is *Bradshaw Art of the Kimberley* by Graham L Walsh. As it was a limited edition print copies are expensive to acquire. The author also produced a number of other works on the subject.

For anyone looking to visit the Kimberley, *Destination Kimberley* by Birgit Bradtke is a great guide and full of information for those planning on driving in the region. Check out the website at *www.kimberleyaustralia.com* for an eBook version.

"Magenta" is the follow-up to
Valverde Maclean's well-received first novel
"The Disappearance of Merry."

A young woman disappeared. Her brother was killed in a car crash. It's an old mystery but someone still doesn't want questions asked. Suzie and Peter must travel Australia to find the answer. All the while avoiding death as they relive their own pasts.

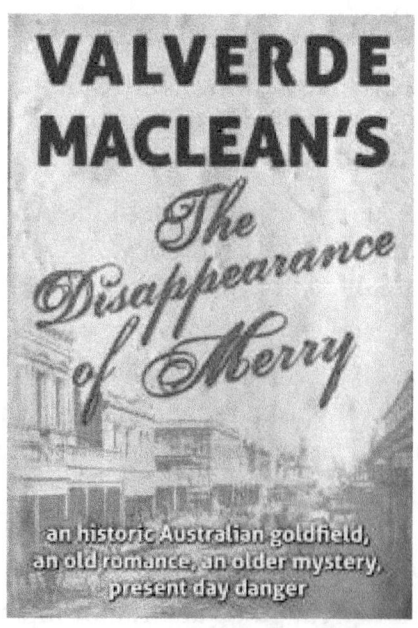

Reader's Comments on *"The Disappearance of Merry."*

"Very interesting read, and I loved the idea of Suzie and Peter reconnecting after so many years. A book that has everything: romance, intrigue, murder and history."

"I finished reading your book this morning. I average one book a week and I always judge an author by how hard it is to put the book down and go and get some jobs done. I can assure you that I found your book very difficult to put down. When can I place my order for the sequel?"

"Lent my book to a friend who read it in two days. She enjoyed it and couldn't believe the ending."

"Love it. I started it last night and can't put it down. Written to really capture your attention."

"I have just finished and thoroughly enjoyed reading *The Disappearance of Merry*. At first I had a little trouble identifying characters but as the story unfolded the characters fell all into place. I enjoyed the author's research on different subjects throughout the book. I recommend this as an easy but intriguing read."

"It was a good read. I read it in one day ... much to the detriment to the rest of my life! I screeched when I came to the end. When is the sequel?"

"Once or twice when I was reading the story I wondered how likely some of the events would be. Then when I remembered some of the coincidences in my life I decided that they were reasonable."

"I got to the end of the story and ... thinking about it, I enjoyed the journey. Especially the references to both present and past times. Next time I am in Melbourne I am going to take a walk to some of the locations, and Ballarat during the Begonia Festival. I still want to know more!"

This page intentionally left blank.

About the author

Valverde Maclean has a passion for Australia.

His first novel *The Disappearance of Merry* was well received by readers who enjoyed the combination of romance and mystery. They also had the pleasure of reading about today's Australia and discovering, or for some rediscovering, an Australia they had heard of, or remembered.

He has travelled widely throughout the country and has lived and worked in both the southern and northern areas of Australia. This experience shows in the way he writes of Australia far from the big cities.

His interest in Australian history, particularly the development of the inland and the ramifications for the economic life of the nation, are a background to his stories.

He is also very interested in the present day changes and challenges to Australian culture.

He now lives near a small village in the beautiful Sunshine Coast Hinterland.

www.ingramcontent.com/pod-product-compliance
Lightning Source LLC
Chambersburg PA
CBHW070446030726
47503CB00004B/913